Jack O' War

by

ROBERT ASTON

**Jack becomes embroiled
in battles for supremacy,
both in our world of Middle Earth,
and with the inhabitants
of Higher and Lower Plains.**

Published by New Generation Publishing in 2016

Copyright © Robert Aston 2016

Cover design by Jacqueline Abromeit

First Edition

The author asserts the moral right under the Copyright, Designs and Patents Act 1988 to be identified as the author of this work.

All Rights reserved. No part of this publication may be reproduced, stored in a retrieval system or transmitted, in any form or by any means without the prior consent of the author, nor be otherwise circulated in any form of binding or cover other than that which it is published and without a similar condition being imposed on the subsequent purchaser.

www.newgeneration-publishing.com

Acknowledgements

As with my previous books, I am indebted to Mr Robert Taylor (former editor of the *Black Country Bugle*) for serialising what has now been made into the third volume in the 'Jack' trilogy.

Among the many sources of information that I have consulted are the histories of Dudley by Mr John Hemingway and *'The Castles and Moated Mansions of Staffordshire and the West Midlands County'* by Mike Salter.

Thanks to the management and staff of Dudley Zoological Gardens who, together with the 'Guild of the Blessed Saint Edmund', have provided the opportunities to explore the castle and its medieval past. Also invaluable have been the guides for the castles of Tutbury and Kenilworth and that for Saint Mary's Priory at Coventry.

And thanks to Saint Edmund's Church in Dudley for agreeing for us to use the Crown and Arrows emblem that is depicted in steel outside the church as inspiration for our front cover.

The staff at Coseley library have continued their help when struggling with recalcitrant computer software, and for obtaining historical articles from distant sources.

My heartfelt thanks to my wife Janet, for putting up with my irritability when disturbed, for shouldering the burden of the household chores, and (most of all) for suggesting improvements to the manuscript.

And a special thank-you to all the folks who've made favourable comments about the preceding two stories, and who've encouraged me to persevere with this one.

I do hope that you like it.

Robert Aston
Coseley in the Black Country, 2014–16

Donjon and Gatehouse
from the north-west

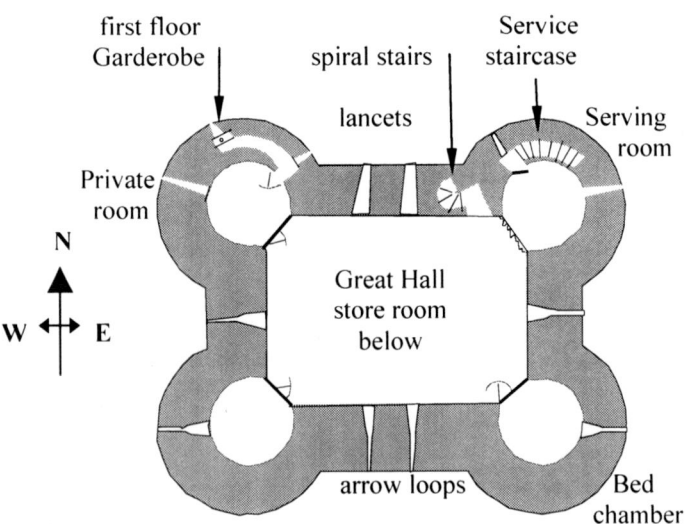

First Floor of the Donjon

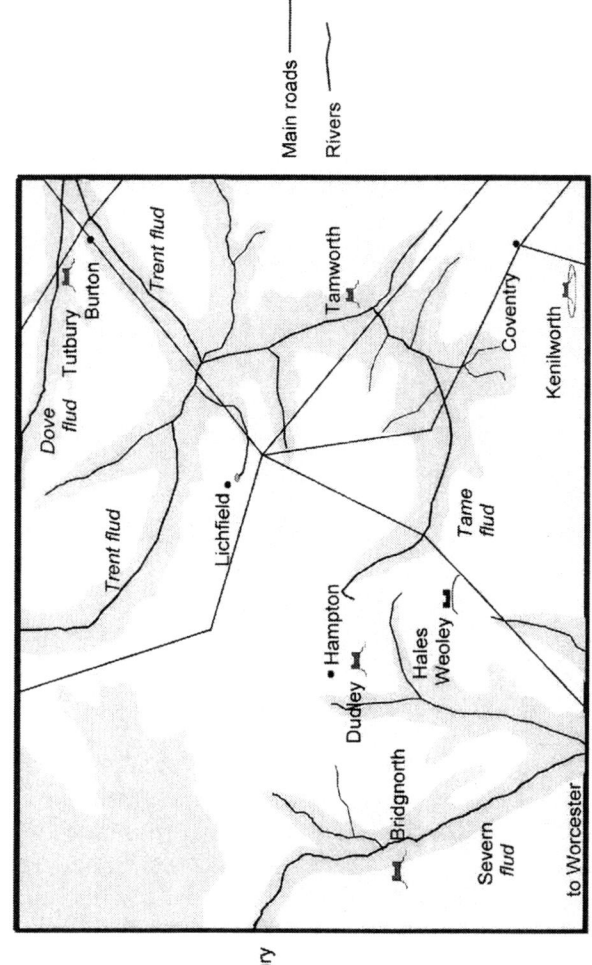

The Field of Battle - circa 1322

Glossary

Ar, arr, arrr	Yes, with varying degrees of emphasis.
Aketon	Jacket padded with layers of cloth for protection.
Aventail	Maile protection for the neck and throat.
Bailey	Enclosed area adjacent to a Motte. Sometimes more than one.
Baxter	Female baker.
Bascinet	Basin-shaped helmet.
Blunts	Blunt headed practice arrows.
Bolt	Short arrow, used with a crossbow.
Buttts	Shooting range for archery practice.
Canstow?	Can you?
Coif	Maile protection for the head.
Coney	Adult rabbit.
Cookney	Cook's assistant.
Crustades	Pastries.
Deosil	Clockwise, as the sun moves across the sky (in the Northern hemisphere).
Destrier	War-horse.
Donjon	Massive stronghold tower. Now known as the Keep.
Fletchings	Feathers or flights of an arrow.
Garderobe	Toilet.
Grimoir	Book of magical lore.
Hauberk	Shirt of maile or overlapping plates to protect the upper body.
Lancet	Tall and narrow wind-eye, usually pointed at the top.
Lant-horn	Lantern.
Lenten	The season now known as spring.
Maile	Interlinked iron rings.

Maul	Heavy wooden mallet. Used for smashing enemy helmets (or the heads of old relatives).
Motte	Mound on which the Donjon stands.
Nock	Hard pieces at the ends of a bow, or at fletched end of an arrow.
The Ordainers	Barons who seek to restrain the King's excesses.
Palfrey	Horse for ordinary riding.
Pavise	Man-sized shield that stands upright on the ground.
Poppet	Doll.
Solar	Apartment reserved for the use of the gentry.
Surcoat	Loose linen garment, worn over armour.
Thurible	Bowl for burning incense.
Undrentide	Midday.
Wind-eye	Window.

Maile Hauberk and Coif

Part One

The Road to War

CHAPTER 1

"Yah," yelled an urchin through the bakehouse doorway. "Who's back at work as a *Cooook-neeeee*?"

Jack turned away from his pastry bench to hurl a ball of dough at the ruffian's retreating figure. "Cheeky pup," he muttered as he limped back to his bench and flung a handful of flour across its surface.

He'd returned to the castle as a hero, and although he was as fit and as strong as ever, the sword-wound that he'd sustained in the Old Park still made him unfit for active soldiering. But at least, they'd put him in charge of the castle's armoury.

He sighed as he scooped up a handful of flour-paste from the trough. Why *did* his grandmother have to sprain her wrist by slipping down the gatehouse steps? That made him the only one able to bake the Baron's favourite crustades. He pummelled the dough into submission. *So, now he was having to work as a Cookney once aGAIN.*"

The wind-eye gave him a clear view out to the archery butts, where a wayward wind was playing havoc with the arrows in their flight. The bowmen's howls of derision increased his sense of outrage.

A blast from a horn rang out across the courtyard. Was it Noontide *already*? The garrison had been ordered to assemble at the gatehouse steps to hear an important announcement.

Untying his (pristine-white) apron, he allowed it to fall and kicked it under the bench. Although exempted from attending the meeting, he slouched to the doorway and peered across the courtyard.

The round-towered Donjon glared down from its mound, its lancet wind-eyes aflame with flickering

1

torches. Below and to its left, the gatehouse portcullis had been lowered to prevent intrusion or escape. For a crowd of restless soldiers surrounded the stairs that led to the door on the upper floor. A second horn-blast echoed around the courtyard – that door crashed open – and the Baron stepped out onto the staircase landing. He was wearing the suit of maile that had come from a London armourer.

When Jack had been a boy and living in Netherton, he'd been made to rivet maile for the local blacksmith. So, as he'd lifted the Baron's new hauberk from its wrappings, he'd marvelled at its lightness and blue-tinged lustre. The matching Coif and Aventail was now protecting the Baron's head and throat. And all of this was shimmering as he glared down at the men who were standing at unease below him.

"YOUR ATTENTION," he roared in a tone of absolute command. A cloud of mist enshrouded his black-bearded visage. Even the wind was holding its breath. "KING EDWARD HAS ISSUED A DECREE FOR ALL TRAINED FIGHTING-MEN TO JOIN HIS ARMY AT COVENTRY. HE IS DETERMINED TO CRUSH HIS ENEMIES, ONCE AND FOR ALL." He stamped a boot and icicles beneath the steps shuddered into shimmering, tinkling cascades. His audience shuffled uneasily. Although the exploits of Kings and Earls were of little personal interest, these had a horrible knack of getting them embroiled in highly dangerous situations.

High above a tower of the Donjon, the flag of the De Somerys' hung limply on its pole.

"Prook," called the castle's resident raven as it soared up on great black wings to alight upon the cap. "Prook," it called again, ruffling the ragged feathers on its throat as it added a white embellishment to the blue and gold of the flag. Cocking its head to one side, the bird peered down at the courtyard as though taking a keen interest in the proceedings.

This was more than could be said of Jack, who was still skulking in the bakehouse doorway. Nearby stood his friend John Blunt – so nicknamed because of the bulbous head of a practice-arrow that protruded from his hat. John squinted up at the besmirched banner. "I hope that's not a bad omen for the future," he muttered quietly.

Jack didn't answer. The Baron had adopted a quieter tone of voice, but his words were as vehement as ever: "So, my reason for calling you here," he growled, still glaring down at his audience, "is to select men to enlist in the King's army."

As the soldiers all fell silent, the raven tutted loudly.

"However," the Baron added, "since my enemies have already made two raids on this castle, I don't want to leave it inadequately defended again." This sent sighs of relief hissing around the courtyard until the Baron raised his hand for it to stop. "The first attack had to be driven-off by the local *peasantry*."

While the soldiers hung their helmeted heads with shame, Jack grinned proudly. He'd recruited those archers himself and led them in the repulse of the hostile war-band.[1] But the Baron's next words brought him back down to Earth with a bump. "Their second raid was only too successful."

"And we all know who helped 'em to do it," John muttered with a smirk.

Jack shrank back into the shadows of the doorway. He'd been the guard on duty when Nicholas de Somery had ridden up to the Outer Gate. He'd waved a signet ring to prove his kinship with the Baron, so there'd been no indication that he was actually an enemy. Two of his three accomplices had been total strangers, but he knew the third by sight. He'd called himself 'Merlin' when he'd sold him those strange beans in Dudley marketplace.[2] On both of

---

[1] 'Jack o' Knaves'
[2] 'Jack o' Beans'

those occasions, the 'Merlin' had known the current password of the day. In the mistaken belief that he was only doing his duty, Jack had allowed the thieves to take two fine palfreys and a bronze-plated chest full of coinage. Horrified at discovering his error, Jack had been keeping a low profile ever-since.

"Why should Englishmen want to fight other Englishmen?" John Blunt murmured, glancing in Jack's direction. Jack didn't answer. In spite of himself, he'd become interested in what the Baron had been saying and was assessing his own situation.

His skill as an archer might be more valued than cooking in a time of war. And a time of war, this undoubtedly was.

The most powerful barons in England had revolted against the King and he was gathering the army to confront them.

England had been suffering from similar conflicts since the time of the Magna Carta, and although none of those present in the courtyard could know it – unless something occurred to alter the future course of history – it would continue to happen for the next three hundred years, until an upstart named Oliver Cromwell would bring his King to the headsman's block and the Donjon to a state of ruin.

However, in this year of Our Lord 1322, the white drum-towers of the Donjon stood solid and majestic against the pale-blue winter sky.

The Baron of Dudley was still bellowing out his message: "THE KING HAS PROMISED TO REWARD EVERY FIGHTING MAN WHO FOLLOWS HIS STANDARD INTO BATTLE. THERE ARE FORTUNES TO BE MADE!"

The whispering in the courtyard had acquired a brighter tone as the Baron peered down at his men: "I shall leave the defence of this castle to a few trusted guards. My new Steward has the authority to requisition provisions from the burgesses of the town and to enlist what bowmen he needs from the surrounding peasantry. The rest of you will accompany me to join the King at Hales's Abbey. He is gathering an army as he marches up from Gloucester. They should arrive in about two weeks' time."

Thoughtfully, Jack stroked his painful wound. 'Fighting-men', the Baron had said. Beneath the thin linen of his tights, the scar tissue was still tender to the touch – a constant reminder of that badly parried sword-blow in the Old-Park. It would probably exempt him from military service. But *did he want it to*?

Life as a married man hadn't turned out to be anything like as rapturous as he'd expected. Initially, he'd worshipped Felicia with a passion. He'd even vowed his devotion in front of the entire garrison when they'd got married at the castle's chapel.

But since that delightful day, she'd been turning his life into a living Hell; spending every daylight hour complaining about how she'd begun married life with high expectations, and how – now that her father was no longer the Steward – her expectations were *not* being achieved. And what was *he* going to do about it?

To add insult to injury, she didn't confine her complaining to their living-quarters. Ignoring the fact that wives are supposed to be subservient to their husbands – at least in public – she'd rebuked him within the hearing of his fellow guards. With the sole exception of John Blunt, they were laughing at him behind his back, saying that he should have put his foot down from the start, and that it was too late now to bring her to heel. *Too late*. What a depressing thought. And every time he'd tried to claim his Marital Rights, she'd begun an argument that immediately quenched his ardour. No wonder his eyes were drawn to Marion, who'd grown ever more attractive with the passing years. She was a member of the Welsh nobility, still held hostage to ensure their peace. But now that she'd grown to self-assured maturity, she was even more voluptuous than ever, especially when the wind blew her dress against her body.

Occasionally, their eyes had met when their paths crossed in the courtyard. But instead of immediately averting her gaze, she'd held his for just a little bit too long. What thoughts lay behind those hooded grey-green eyes? Was she feeling pity or contempt? Or could it be that she liked him. His heart beat faster at the mere idea of it. No. No. *No*! What was he thinking of? He shook his head to dislodge its dangerous thoughts, forcing them back to the present situation. And that included the screaming of his baby son. When he complained about having his sleep disturbed, his protests fell on unsympathetic ears.

"Now you know what *I* had to put up with from *you*," his grandmother always retorted.

Well, bugger *this* for a game of soldiers. All things considered, a period of military service might be just what was required. He might even gain some of the wealth that Felicia craved for.

Encouraged by the prospect, he stepped out to join the others, wincing as a burst of pain shot down his leg. Wouldn't the wound disqualify him from active service? Why should it? It didn't make him any less skilful as an archer. He could hit the disc at the centre of the target more often than the others. Moreover, he wouldn't have to squat to retrieve his errant arrows when he missed it altogether. The wound might even exempt him from hand-to-hand fighting.

Judging by the Baron's rising tone of voice, he was working up to some sort of climax:

"And while I have been away fighting the Scots," he was shouting, "my enemies have been slandering me to the King. Me! John de Somery – who was knighted by *him* and swore my fealty *until death*."

'*Until death* us do part!' Jack recalled the priest's solemn words at the marriage ceremony. Well, if that was to be the way of it...

"I don't have to remind you," the Baron bellowed, "that it was *your* wages that were stolen." He raised a hand to halt the angry murmurs. "But now that the King is on the offensive, we can help him to bring the traitors to account *and get our money back.* ARE YOU *WITH ME?*"

The rising pitch of his voice produced a surge of excitement in his men.

"*YEA!*" they all cried in unison. This included Jack, who had now joined his enthusiastic comrades. If the Baron would accept him, he would enlist this very day.

"RIGHT!" cried John de Somery, smiling grimly down. "We leave in one week's time. Make your arrangements and be READY."

Still perched on the cap of the flagpole, the Raven uttered a guttural 'click' and nodded its head approvingly. And as the soldiers were being lined-up by the Steward, it spread out its great black wings and soared up into the darkening sky.

CHAPTER 2

Left…right…tap…left…right… "Ouch!"

Jack lurched sideways as the heel of his lance skidded on an iced-up puddle. Although his wound had healed quite well, another burst of pain had shot down his leg.

Forced to hurry along in a column of marching soldiers, he retrieved a small bottle from his pouch and took a hasty swig. Tramping resolutely onwards, he waited for his Gran's potion to do its work.

Beneath his feet, the petrified prints of innumerable boots formed a jumbled chaos in the frozen ground – every ridge of it hurtful through the thin leather soles of his own. The lance provided a welcome support, as long as he was careful about where he placed its heel. The flag at its top provided a mobile assembly-point for the Baron's men as they arrived from the widespread sections of his manor. Of the Baron himself, there was no sign. Stretching away in front and behind him, countless other men were marching to the sounds of scrunching boots and scuffing of steel on steel. Here and there, other upright lances displayed banners with colourful heraldry.

Many of the men around him were limping as they marched along – presumably from wounds sustained in battle like himself. Most wore padded Aketons to protect them from enemy arrows and from the biting wind. Jack shivered, for between his surcoat and shirt, he only had a Hauberk of maile. His Gran had grudgingly bought it after failing to dissuade him from enlisting, but he'd had to get it barrelled in grit to remove the blood and rust. He'd replaced its missing rings himself, using skills that he'd learned as a boy while working for the blacksmith in

Netherton. Although it was lighter than his old one, it was sapping the heat from his body. Nevertheless, if he ever let it out of his sight, he'd never see it again. And here he was now in a seemingly endless stream of marching foot soldiers.

Left…right…tap…left…right…tap…

"How long will it take us to get to Coventry?" The questioner was John Blunt – Jack's only friend in all that moving mass of grim-faced warriors. Beyond the bobbing steel helmets, and a mist of condensing breath, the familiar hills of Clent gleamed brightly beneath a coverlet of snow.

"It depends," Jack growled back irritably.

"On what?"

"On the terrain. On the weather. And on whether or not we have to defend ourselves against attack."

They were tramping along a road the Jack had been brought to by the friend that he still called 'The Forester'. It looked very different *now*. Back *then*, there'd been bustling cottages, with the strip fields behind them all green with sprouting crops. But the cottages were all deserted, some with their doors hanging open on broken hinges. Bare patches of earth showed where cottages had gone missing entirely. "What could have happened here?" he wondered out loud.

"It's been like this all the way up from Gloucester!" someone had muttered behind the pair of friends. They'd been joined by a rough-looking stranger whose patched-up jerkin showed the unmistakable signs of recent combat. The newcomer shrugged. "An army as big as this one must scavenge for its food."

"Is that what's in those wagons then?" John was nodding at a column of carts that was rumbling along beside the marching men.

"From the way that them oxen are having to strain," the stranger said casually, "they'm prob'ly full of armour and weapons. By the way, they call me Nutcracker."

John stared at the huge wooden mallet that rested on the newcomer's shoulder. "What use is *that*?"

"This is my chosen weapon for close work. I'm a bit of a specialist, as yer might say."

Jack half-turned round and winced as he tripped on his pole. "Why not use an axe?" he said as soon as he'd recovered.

"I can't stand the sight of blood," said the Maul's possessor, easing its considerable weight to relieve his shoulder. "I've stove-in quite a few helmets, I can tell yer. An' if the poor sods ain't killed outright, they has a hell of a job trying to get their heads out."

Jack's preferred weapon was his bow – six feet of the best Spanish yew. He felt its comforting weight across his back, protected by a tube of well-waxed linen. Beside it hung a quiver of matching arrows.

"What's it like?" he asked.

"What's what like?" said Nutcracker.

"A battle."

"It depends." Nutcracker eyed Jack's bow-case and leather quiver. "As an archer, you'll be sending your arrows at the enemy as fast as you can. You'm lucky. That's killing at a distance." He transferred the Maul to the other shoulder. "But if the arrers don't stop 'em, yer'll have to engage in close combat like the rest on us. Then you stand with your mates and slog it out until either you or your opponents is overcome."

"It sounds dangerous," said John Blunt.

"It is," Nutcracker muttered with a grimace.

"Then why are you here?" John asked.

"I've no choice. When my Lord Warenne says jump, I jumps. Anyway, I like the loot."

"What's 'loot'?"

"Ev'rythin' that yer c'n grab for yourself after we've won a battle or sacked a city."

"You're not from round here, are you?" John said bluntly.

"Nay lad. I live near London."

"Have you seen the King then?" Jack asked. From what he'd been hearing about their monarch, he couldn't wait to lay eyes on him.

"Aye," said Nutcracker. "He's up ahead with Warenne and the other earls. I doubt if we'll see much of *him.*"

*

They had trudged along for hours when Nutcracker stopped suddenly.

"Hold on," he said, drawing himself up to his considerable height and shading his eyes to peer ahead. "Summat's happening up there."

In the distance, a dark smudge lay across their path with the sound of distant roaring coming from it.

As they drew closer, it became clear that the column had stopped. Or at least, the pack animals had. Soldiers were milling around in aimless confusion, while the animals were all lying down on the muddy roadway, oblivious to threats and kicks from their irate drivers. And amidst all of this mayhem, a middle-aged man in a red and golden surcoat was riding up and down on an enormous white horse and screaming with impatient fury.

"You wanted to see the King," Nutcracker bellowed above the uproar. "That's 'im there."

Jack had never seen a monarch before and he was both surprised and disappointed. For although King Edward was a large and imposing man, he wasn't wearing a crown or even a gilded helmet. Instead, a head of light-brown hair swung loose above broad shoulders. And although he was in perfect control of his horse, it was obvious that neither he nor his mule-drivers had any control over their beasts of burden. They still refused to budge.

"Why can't they get them moving?" Jack shouted, never having seen the like of this before.

"They'm mules and they've had enough," Nutcracker announced. "I've seen it many a-time before. They will not budge until they feel like it – no matter what anybody does."

And so it proved to be. With the dusk now fast approaching, the troops were stood down and tents and fire irons distributed among them. And very soon, the sweet scent of cooking suffused the camp as the soldiers settled down for their evening meal.

*

Jack was scraping the last of the stew from the inside of his helmet when the Baron appeared in the firelight. His golden surcoat was badly rumpled and his countenance heavy with concern.

"No need to get up," he barked. "Just listen and obey." After straightening-up the banner that Jack had left leaning against the tent, he opened the tent's flap further and tucked it behind the pole. "Tomorrow," he announced while peering into the interior, "we shall reach the city of Coventry…one of the largest in England. The burghers have allocated us a field on the outskirts of the town where we shall await more of the King's army. There will be plenty of work to keep you occupied during the daylight hours, and you will be free to visit the city in the evenings." He glared around. "BUT DO NOTHING TO UPSET THE CITIZENS. Their goodwill is vital and their allegiance is not certain. In fact, many of them probably sympathise with the Ordainers."

"By your leave, my Lord," Jack's Sergeant said, struggling to his feet, "but who *are* these Ordainers?"

"I thought that it was common knowledge." John de Somery, sounded surprised. "They're barons who've risen against the King. They are furious about him confiscating their lands and handing it to his new *favourites*."

With guffaws of derision coming from the back of the tent, the Baron turned away and stared thoughtfully into the fire. He hadn't meant to reveal so much. If these men knew what was actually going on, they might refuse to go any further – just as the mules had done.

After a while, the Baron turned abruptly back to his instantly-alert soldiery. "When our army is assembled," he bellowed, "we are to capture or kill any rebels that we encounter. The King isn't bothered which."

He stamped his feet on the frozen ground. "God willing," he cried, "the Earl of Lancaster will soon be brought to heel." When next he spoke, his voice was tinged with regret: "But if the King's cousin meets us in battle, it will be a declaration of Civil War. Let us hope that he's got the sense not to do it."

"By your leave, my Lord," Jack's Sergeant piped-up again, "you promised us the spoils of war. If there's no battle fought and no castle plundered, shall we have to go back home empty-handed?"

"No you won't," the Baron cried, gazing around. "Even if Lancaster surrenders without a fight, you'll get the money that I promised you. Aye, and be well-rewarded for your service to your King."

Hearing mingled grumbles of relief and doubt, the Baron changed the subject. "As I said before: the allegiance of the burghers of Coventry is by no means certain. While we are encamped there..." he glared around at his men, "I want no drunkenness. No thieving and no brawling; in fact, no trouble of any kind. Anyone found guilty of these offences will be strung-up in the main square as a warning to others. GET IT?"

They got it – although many were the complaints when he'd marched off into the darkness. Everything that would have made the campaign more endurable was banned.

"Is that right?" someone asked from the back of the tent.

"Is *what* right?" the Sergeant demanded, closing the tent flap securely.

"The bit about them...Ordinaters."

"I think so." Noticing a lump of cheese unattended on a nearby table, he unsheathed his dagger, skewered the morsel and popped this into his mouth. "Although 'tis a pity..." he added indistinctly, "that the nobs can't settle their differences without shedding blood."

"*Our* blood," the enquirer corrected, in the anonymity bestowed by the shadows.

"If they wasn't at each other's throats," the Sergeant countered, "they wouldn't have to pay us for doin' the fightin'. And whether it's amongst themselves or with the Welsh or the Scots or the French, every war provides us with food and ale."

"That may be the sooth," the anonymous someone said. "But as soon as the fightin's over, we shall have to go back to starving while the nobs go back to lording it in their castles."

"Who *are* the King's new *favourites*?" asked a soldier who was looking for his cheese.

"There's two of 'em; the father and the son, an' both named Hugh de Spenser."

"Oh *them*," said the soldier while glaring at his neighbour accusingly. "I heard as the son was exiled, and now he's pirating in the Channel."

"He *was*. But the King has called 'im back to 'elp 'im to raise this army. They'm picking-off the Ordainers one by one."

"Is that what happened to the Mortimers?"

"Arr. They was among the ring-leaders. Their castles were on the Welsh side of the Severn, and they formed an effective barrier in the Marches. But the King forgot about that when he decided to attack 'em. They burnt down all the bridges from Worcester to Shrewsbury – that one being built of stone and not combustible. Not wishing to confront the King with force of arms, they accepted his offer of clemency if they surrendered. He immediately accused 'em of Treason and sent 'em off to the Tower of London for execution."

"It mek's yer wonder if we'm fightin' on the right side," the anonym muttered in the shadows.

"*Who said that?*" The Sergeant drew his sword and marched further into the tent. When nobody owned up, he retreated back to the exit flap. "If I hears any more talk like *that*, I'll cut yer head off meself. Such talk is Treason and you know what the punishment for *that* is. Just be thankful that you'm fightin' for the King."

And with that puzzling thought, they all turned in for the night.

CHAPTER 3

Jack awoke to the sound of muffled voices. He wasn't in his tent. So where the Hell *was* he? The prickling of straw beneath him brought his memory flooding back.

He'd spent a pleasant evening in a Coventry alehouse, winning at Bones and drinking far more than he was used to. Then while making his rollicking way back to the encampment, he'd come across this isolated cottage. With its wind-eye shuttered-up, he'd assumed that the tenants were either absent or asleep. And since the byre next to it was dry and well stocked with straw, he'd lain down until such time as he could walk without falling over. But that had been last night, and the first traces of dawn were visible through the open doorway. He sat up abruptly, the headache that he'd woken up with having vanished. *He was going to miss Parade.* No he wasn't. The sun had not yet risen. There was plenty of time to get back to the encampment. He peered into the gloom. An ancient plough leaned drunkenly against one wall. Farm-tools lay strewn about in casual disorder. There was no sign of recent activity.

Nevertheless, the owners of the voices were still gabbling away on the other side of the partition that separated his refuge from the living space of the cottage. The tenants would be getting ready for work. If they discovered him, they would probably report him to the authorities and he shuddered to think what could happen to him then.

Yet the voices sounded cautious and conspiratorial. Were they hatching some sort of plot against authority? If so, he didn't blame them.

As he got up to leave, Jack noticed a patch of light on the earthen floor. Low down on the partition, a flake of daub had broken away from the wattle. He knelt to place an ear to the jagged hole.

"So you agree to cast the spell?" The speaker was male and he sounded relieved.

"Yea," a second man whispered back, "but it will cost thee plenty. Plotting to kill the King is High Treason and we both know what the penalties for *that* are."

Jack froze, his aches and pains forgotten. The men behind the partition were plotting to kill the King and his slightest movement could alert them to his presence. And if they were prepared to risk death by disembowelling, they'd have no hesitation about sending *him* to meet his maker. He had his dagger with him, but it wouldn't be of much use if *they* had swords. Within reach lay a slashing implement – a billhook blade at the top of a six-foot stave. While imprisoned in the Dudley coal mine, he'd discovered how deadly these could be in hand-to-hand combat. That had prompted him to get some for the castle's armoury, with only slight modifications to their blades. Reassured, he returned his attention to the hole.

"Nay!" the first speaker protested. "How *can* ye be caught? You cast a spell here and the King dies somewhere far away. What could connect us with the deed?"

"You keep saying 'us'. Who are these associates that you keep referring to?"

"'Tis better that you do not know. Let me just say that they are very influential in the city."

"Fair enough! But you also said that there were others that you wanted taken care of as well as the King."

"Yes. We might as well clear out the whole nest of vipers while we're at it."

"How many?"

"Here is the list."

Parchment crackled as it was unfolded

"There are seven names written here," said the spellbinder quietly. "There's the De Spensers, the father and the son. I can understand *that*, but why do you need to hex them when they've been sent into exile?" Without waiting for an answer, he carried on: "I've never heard of these others. I can do it, but it will cost you more. A lot more." A pregnant pause ensued until: "I tell you what: I'll do the lot for ...thirty-five pounds."

A gasp. "*That* much? You don't come cheap, do you?"

"This is dangerous work and even a magician needs his creature comforts."

After a lengthy pause, the customer cleared his throat. "Very well," he said. "Since you are taking such a great risk, I am sure that my associates will agree to that. By the way, how much will it cost us to hex the Prior as well?"

"The Prior of Coventry?" A short sardonic laugh. "I hate *him* myself. I'll throw *him* in for nothing."

"So that's agreed then?" The customer sounded even more relieved than before.

"Agreed," said the magician with audible satisfaction. "When do I get my money?"

"Payment by results seems fair to me."

"That's too late," the magician retorted. "I need to be away from here before your victims start dropping like flies."

"What do *you* suggest then?"

"I suggest a trial run: I shall begin to cast the spell for all of your victims, but I shall only take it to completion with one of them. I trust that one of these men lives locally? I know the Prior does, but I'd rather keep *him* for later."

"The last one on the list lives not far away from here."

"Very well. You will be able to see for yourself how effective my spell is. And when you have paid me my fee – all of it – I shall complete the rest. Agreed?"

"Agreed!"

The sound of spitting came faintly through the hole, followed by that of footsteps plodding away. With no doorway in the partition, Jack was safe — at least for the moment.

"When will you do it?" the customer asked at a greater distance.

"Come back at dusk tomorrow," said the magician to the accompanying click of a latch. "I shall have wax dolls for you to mark, thus identifying your victims to my fiend. On the day after that, you shall have your demonstration."

"You said fiend. Did you not mean *friend*?"

"No! *Fiend* I said, and *fiend* I meant."

"So who did you say your...fiend was?"

"I didn't say. It is better that you do not know."

"Too-shay!"

The draught through the hole increased, and then died away as a distant door banged shut. A key clicked in a lock.

Jack remained kneeling beside the hole, afraid to move until he was certain that the criminals had departed. What should he do now? Go and tell his Sergeant? Or the Baron? No. They would think him either daft or stupid. He couldn't tell John Blunt, having fallen-out with him over his endless criticisms. And if any of the other men learned of this, he would be taunted even worse than he was already. But whatever he decided to do, he was going to come back to the byre on the following evening.

*

So, well before dusk on the following day, Jack eschewed his game of Bones to take up his position in the byre. Actually, this was no great sacrifice. Like the dice that the rectangular plates were derived from,[3] pure chance determined what spots you got and therefore your immediate fortune.

---

[3] There is one at Oxford Museum. The name 'Domino' was applied later.

However, the spot that he was in at present was entirely of his own choosing. So, after making quite sure that the room next door was empty, he enlarged the hole in the partition by prising out twigs of wattle. Then by propping himself up on a bundle of straw, he obtained a clear view of the room – his sharpened sword lying comfortingly by his side.

He didn't have long to wait. Dusk was just darkening the byre when the clicking of the door-latch signalled that someone was about to enter the cottage. But as Jack peered through his spy-hole, the door banged shut and the room was plunged into almost total darkness. Steel struck percussively on flint. To the sound of someone puffing, a glowing scrap of tinder lit up a plump and bearded face. Then the brighter light of a candle-flame revealed that its owner wore a tall pointed hat and a black cloak covered with symbols. Presumably, this was the magician.

In the middle of the room stood a small square table, with the lighted candle and two bowls of unglazed pottery. A tall and slender youth emerged from the shadows. He looked nothing like Jack's impression of the forceful character that had commissioned the spell on behalf of the burghers of Coventry.

While the magician placed more items on the table, his companion filled a bowl with some dark substance. Suddenly, the silence was broken by three sharp raps on the door, whereupon the magician nodded for his assistant to let their visitor in.

After flinching as a wind-blast hit his eye, Jack watched a middle-aged man step quickly over the threshold. A voluminous cloak enshrouded his portly figure, and a wide-brimmed hat concealed his face in shadow.

"I see that you have company," the newcomer rasped as he closed and bolted the door. "Can he be trusted?"

"This is my assistant Robert," the magician said hastily. "There is too much work here for one. See?" He turned back to the table. "I have prepared these poppets for thee."

On the table lay a row of dolls – each about six inches long and an inch in diameter. The magician pointed to one that had a wax crown on its head. "That represents the King," he announced as if it wasn't obvious. "But for the others, I need you to scratch identification-marks on them." Picking up a figurine, he presented it to his customer. "Make a mark on this to identify the person that you have chosen for the trial-run."

The customer produced a dagger and scratched something on the figure with its tip. Taking the poppet back, the magician mumbled something over it before replacing it on the table. Then the other poppets each got similar treatment – four that had little wax shields being the easiest to engrave.

"How long will it take for the spell to work?" the customer demanded when the task was complete.

"It varies. The first will begin to take effect immediately. The De Spensers will take longer. I cannot tell you how *much* longer. My spirit-guides have informed me that the vile pair have petitioned the Pope to protect them against magical attack. But be assured of this: once this spell has been cast, no one can stop it. Not even a Pope. And remember, spells have to work through seemingly-natural causes, and that can take considerable time to accomplish." While the customer considered this in silence, the magician dragged a sheathed sword from underneath the table.

"Have a care," the customer cried, holding his knife by the tip of its blade and drawing it back over his shoulder. "I can pierce your heart before you can get that out of its scabbard."

"Nay! Nay!" the magician cried out. "See?" After slowly withdrawing his sword from its scabbard, he held it out on open palms at arm's length. "It's not sharp. I use it to cast a circle of protection around us."

After examining the blunt implement, the customer shrugged and handed it back.

"You could still do a lot of damage with it. Protection against *what*?"

"You will know soon enough. I assume that you have cleansed yourself as I told you."

When the customer had nodded his affirmation, the magician marched three paces over towards Jack's right. Mumbling something under his breath, he jabbed his sword into the floor and proceeded to scratch a circle in the ground with the table at its centre. Arriving back at the start, he bowed respectfully. Then returning to the table, he re-sheathed the weapon and returned it to its resting-place on the floor. When he eventually straightened up, he was holding a bunch of black candles. After igniting one of them from the first, he carried it over to the starting-point of the circle and placed it on the ground just inside the line. Then standing to attention, he described a five-pointed star in the air with the tip of a finger while mumbling quiet words to whatever might be listening. Three more candles were spaced equidistantly round the circumference – each having a star made over it to the words of a different incantation.

Returning once more to the altar, the magician stared out across the circle to a point further over to Jack's right. With his view restricted by the hole, Jack moved his head to follow the magician's gaze. A triangle had been scratched on the ground – its sides about three feet long and an apex pointing towards the altar.

The magician raised both of his arms imploringly. "Adrasteus," he called in a subdued but urgent voice. After repeating the word nine more times, he added: "I conjure thee to honour us with thy presence upon this earthly plane."

For a time, nothing happened and the customer began to fidget. "Is this going to take all night?" he muttered. "I've got to report back to my associates."

"I must insist that you be quiet. I'm having to concentrate all my energy on this rite." Suddenly, he dropped to his knees and bowed almost to the ground.

"Adrasteus is here," he whispered excitedly. "Can you not feel it?"

The customer shuffled his feet. "All I can feel is the cold."

"That's because Adrasteus is drawing heat from the air around us to give him power. He's prowling around outside the circle now."

Jack shivered, instinctively reaching for the cross that hung from his neck. For good measure, he also touched the hag-stone dangling beside it.

Uttering a strangled cry, the wizard struggled to his feet. "He's trying to break into the circle." Standing stiffly upright, he pointed at the triangle. "I command thee, Adrasteus, to get thee within the Triangle of Art." Almost immediately, he cocked his head as though listening to a reply. But all that Jack could hear was the pulsing of his heart-beat in his ears.

The magician was smiling grimly. "Forgive me, Great Adrasteus, but I am weak and have to take precautions. Nevertheless, I thank thee most respectfully for granting us this audience."

"Why can't I see him?" the customer asked in a low voice.

"Because he is from another realm," the magician answered from the side of his mouth. "He's invisible in ours...but perhaps he'll deign to give you a sign that he is present."

Immediately, the room was filled with dazzling crimson light, scorching Jack's eyes with its brilliant luminescence. As he shrank back in horror, the sudden movement dislodged a sheaf of straw. It slid down onto the ground, rustling loudly as it fell.

"What the Hell was that?" the customer screamed. "There's somebody in the byre. I'm going round to silence him.."

While groping blindly for his sword, Jack heard the sigh of another being slid from its sheath.

CHAPTER 4

Kneeling beside the spy-hole, Jack began to tremble. What could he do, struck blind as he now was? There was no point in trying to hide under the straw; the customer would undoubtedly probe it with his sword. And if he managed to get to the door without falling over, the swordsman would catch him as he stumbled around outside.

Hurried footsteps sounded through the hole, but Jack remained paralysed with uncertainty and fear.

"Do not leave the circle," the magician's voice rang out. "Adrasteus will tear you limb from limb."

"If I don't catch that spy, we are all doomed anyway."

"It was only the rats," the magician screeched. "This place is crawling with 'em." He gave another cry, his terror clearly palpable through the wattle and daub of the partition. "The demon is trying to escape from the triangle. Quick, Robert. Put more incense in the thurible."

The hole glowed with crimson light, but of decreased intensity. Dizzy with relief to find that he hadn't been permanently blinded after all, Jack listened to the magician's quavering voice as he continued: "I adjure thee, demon, to stay within the Triangle." Several rapid heartbeats later, he added with considerably-reduced anxiety: "That's better." Then, and apparently to his customer, he ordered: "Come back and join us at the altar."

So he hadn't left the circle after all.

With his vision and courage returning, Jack applied his eye to the spy-hole once again – the scents of incense and sulphur assailing his nostrils. Just visible in the gloom, three figures stood facing the triangle. There was still nothing there. After bowing his head respectfully, the magician raised it to address its invisible occupant: "Hail to thee, Adrasteus, and welcome. Let there be peace between thee and me."

The crimson light flared up again. And as it died down, the magician continued with audibly-growing confidence: "I have summoned thee here to wreak havoc upon our enemies."

The crimson light flashed twice more – somehow managing to express an eagerness for the task. The onlookers watched in silence as the magician pointed at the table and announced in a fervent but respectful voice: "Those poppets have been marked to identify the persons that we beseech thee to eliminate from this world."

The crimson light flashed again as though in acceptance.

"And in return, we offer *thee* as a sacrifice: the Prior of Coventry, to do with as thou wilt." Again, the crimson glow brightened momentarily before fading back to dimness.

"So here they are for your attention…" The magician held out each of the dolls in turn while gasping out some garbled incantation. Each time, the light flashed once, apparently to demonstrate the demon's understanding. "And this last poppet," the magician announced finally, "is for the *first* of our victims. He lives quite close to here and should be easy to attack."

Following another quick burst of crimson light, the magician spread out his arms and bowed stiffly from the waist. "I trust that you will help us to achieve our purpose."

The light flashed three times, as if confirming that a compact had been made. "I humbly thank thee for deigning to visit us mere mortals on this earthly plane. In the hope for a successful outcome to our petition, may I beseech thee to withdraw quietly. And may you have a pleasant journey back to the regions from whence you came, and may peace exist between us."

After flashing once more, the crimson glow went out, leaving the room lit only by the light of the candles.

Almost immediately, the air flowing through Jack's spy-hole grew noticeably warmer.

"Adrasteus is gone now," the magician announced, turning to his customer and patting him on the back. Ignoring his flinch, he continued: "So that's all that can be accomplished for the present. When I have un-cast the circle, you will be free to leave. Say naught of what you have seen to *anyone*…for if you *do,* Adrasteus will wreak a terrible vengeance."

The magician now reversed his casting of the circle. Moving to each of its candles in turn, he described the invisible star in reverse while chanting unintelligibly into the air. As he blew-out the flames, the room grew steadily darker. By the flickering light of the candle on the table, he placed the others away in a leather satchel. Suddenly, he turned and stared at Jack's hole in the partition. And when he marched determinedly towards him, Jack froze with horror again. This was just as well, for the magician grasped a besom from the wall nearby and used it to sweep the scratches from the floor.

"What happens next?" the customer demanded as the magician leaned the besom against the wall.

"Come back at the same time tomorrow for the next stage."

"What will that entail?"

"I shall initiate the trial-run."

"Until tomorrow night then," the customer growled, and then added in a menacing tone of voice: "Now give me that candle and I'll take a look next door."

But when he got round to the byre there was no one there and the spy-hole was hidden by a bale of straw.

*

On the next evening, Jack was back in the darkened byre with his eye pressed to the spy-hole once again. The circle had been cast already, and the four lighted candles positioned inside its circumference. Illumined by the larger one on the altar, the conspirators were peering down at the wax figurines.

"Which of these is for the trial run?" the magician whispered.

"This," the customer announced. As he picked one up, it glistened as though covered with sweat.

Taking it from him, the magician held it close to the candle flame. "Is this who I think it is?" he murmured with surprise.

"Maybe," said the customer, guardedly.

"But what can *he* have done that you should want him destroyed by a *demon*?"

The customer shrugged. "That is *my* business. Pray proceed with *thine*."

"Have it your own way," the magician said, as he passed the doll to his assistant. "It is of no concern to me." He drew a long shiny pin from his hat and passed this over as well. "While you prick the poppet," he commanded, "say this after me: 'By the power of Adrasteus'."

"By the power of Adrasteus..." the assistant muttered faintly.

"I hereby smite thee..."

"I hereby sm—"

"Not there," the magician interrupted hastily. "Stick it where it won't cause a fatal injury."

"But you said that the purpose of this was to kill him."

"All in good time. First we make him squirm. 'Tis better for business that way."

The assistant shrugged. "What have I got to say again?"

"Hell's teeth," the customer exploded. "I've engaged a couple of idiots to commit High Treason."

"S-sorry, s-sire," the magician stammered. "It's just that Robert's a bit slow on the uptake." And to his sheepish helper, he repeated: "By the power of Adrasteus, I hereby smite thee."

The assistant pronounced the words as he'd been bidden, but ducked as though expecting a bolt of lightning to strike him dead. When this didn't happen, he pierced the poppet's stomach with the point of the pin.

The magician turned to his tight-lipped customer. "That should give your subject something to shout about," he said with a smirk. "By Undrentide tomorrow, this spell will have begun to take effect. I suggest that you go, or send somebody in your stead to the place where he resides. I predict that you ... or your representative ... will be suitably impressed. And this time tomorrow evening, come back here and pay me my fee. Then we shall finish him off and proceed with your other victims."

The customer remained silent as the magician performed his closing-down rite and brushed the circle and triangle out of existence. He remained so as the magical equipment was packed away. And no further word had been uttered when a gust of wind through the spy-hole announced that the door to the cottage had been opened. As it closed with a bang, the room became still.

Jack reached for a bale of straw to cover the spy-hole.

"Master?"

Jack froze. The sorcerers were still there.

"What do you want now!" the magician groaned.

"You told *him* that spells can take a fair bit of time to work."

"What of it?"

"How can that first victim be attacked *tomorrow* then?"

"You spotted *that*, did you?" the magician said more quietly. "So you're not so daft after all. Let us hope that our customer didn't notice it as well. You see, I have a few tricks of my own to hurry things along – at least for the easier subjects."

"What are they, Master?"

"It is better not to know. Then you can't tell anybody – even if they torture you."

"Hell's teeth."

"Nay, lad. It's not Hell's teeth that you should fear. It's the *Church's*."

"But haven't we just summoned up the Devil from Hell?"

"Nay, lad. At least, not the Devil that they preach about in Churches." He crossed himself. "God is the maker of all things, and that includes beings that live on other plains. The Church calls some of these 'Angels', while others are classed as 'Devils'. But to us, they are all 'Daemons'. Most of them are helpful to us if we treat them right. Some of them ignore us, and others take delight in causing misfortune. They all have their own specialities. According to my Grimoir, Adrasteus's is bringing down the powerful at the height of their worldly success."

"Pride before a fall then, Master."

"Exactly."

"And are that man's victims all like what you said?"

"The Despensers certainly are. They've wormed their way round the King to become the most powerful men in the country...second only to the King himself." The magician had lowered his voice almost to a whisper, so that Jack had to put his ear to the hole instead of his eye. "And the King also abuses his power most shamefully. As for the other victims: our customer says that they're *all* cast from the same mould."

"So do these daemons *really* do what you ask?"

"Mostly they do...as long as I perform the rite correctly and treat them with proper respect."

"How can you be sure of that, Master? You told that man that the spells have to work though, er...what did you call 'em...? Seemingly-natural causes?"

"Let me see...Canstow bend a blade of grass just by willing it to do so?"

"No," the assistant admitted, guardedly.

"You *can* if you *blow* on it."

"So?"

"Can you sink a ship by wishing for it to happen?"

"No, Master."

"There *is* a way to do it. If you follow the right ritual, a daemon called Rubiel will gather up all the winds over the Western Sea to conjure up a storm that can sink even the most seaworthy vessel."

"How d'you know that?"

"Well, some Scots once got Rubiel to send them a storm to sink the King of Norway's battle fleet. And when that disaster happened, he abandoned his claim to The Isles."

"I don't understand," the assistant said.

"Neither do I, but it works when you perform the right ritual. That's what the Circle and the Triangle are for: to concentrate your energy and send the daemon out to do your bidding. Like an arrow, it's killing from a distance."

"What will happen to the King and the De Spensers?"

"We'll just have to wait and see."

A draught through the spy-hole foretold the pair's imminent departure.

"I say, Master..." The novice had adopted a wheedling tone of voice, "can you conjure up a daemon to make me attractive to women?"

"I doubt if even the daemon *Gremory* could manage *that*. Anyway, the Secret Arts are *not* to be used for such a trifling matter."

"It's not a trifling matter to *me*." Then after a slight pause: "Will you conjure up a daemon to make my—" The rest was lost as the door banged shut and a key clicked in the lock.

With a sigh of relief, Jack lay back in the straw and pondered on what he'd just seen and heard. And on the fact that he'd seen something like it as a child.

Back in their cottage in Netherton, he'd been woken by the sound of the outside door creaking open. His Gran had crept out into the night, and he'd followed her round to the byre next door. By peeping through a crack in its wall, he'd watched her scratch a circle on the ground. It was smaller than the magician's and had only one candle at its centre. Then she'd taken off all her clothes – the first time that he'd seen a woman naked. Her ritual had also been different: prancing round the circle while beating on a bowl with a wooden spoon. He'd watched her antics with interest and amusement until she'd stepped astride the besom and then...and then he couldn't stand the sight of it any longer.

He'd never plucked up the courage to ask her what she'd been doing. It was obvious to him now that she'd been casting a spell, but he couldn't believe that she ever hated anyone enough to wish them dead. It was true that she was always complaining about how his father had gone off and left her to cope with his unruly offspring. Jack shuddered as he remembered a doll that he'd found in her box of personal belongings. Had *that* been a part of the same magic spell? There weren't any pinpricks in the wax, but it did have a tuft of hair stuck to its head – hair the same dark colour as his own. So, if the doll *had* been intended to represent himself, was the spell intended to harm him or to help him? "Don't be daft," he told himself reproachfully. It could only have been to *help* him. So had it worked? He considered the sequence of his life's events. There had been long periods of agonising boredom separated by short bursts of very great danger. He'd always managed to escape from those – largely as a result of his own efforts. But now that he looked back on it, there *did* seem to have been some pattern to it, as though some guardian angel had been watching over him and keeping him safe. In the hope that this would continue, Jack struggled to his feet – brushed the straw from his tights – and wended his way thoughtfully back to camp.

*

On the following day, the army began preparing to move out. But with his mind completely occupied with magical mysteries, the first Jack heard of it was when John de Somery appeared outside their tent.

"As you may already know," the Baron announced, ducking inside while shaking rain-drops off his cloak, "the Earl of Lancaster is marching south to meet us in open battle." Smiling grimly at his men's sudden silence, he continued: "He will undoubtedly use his castle at Tutbury as a base. The great River Trent lies between us, and the King has commanded us to secure the nearest bridge until his main force arrives." The slurping of soup resumed. "Finish your meal, by all means. But be ready to march at dawn tomorrow."

As he turned away, he seemed to notice Jack for the first time. "That limp of yours is no better," he observed quietly. As Jack blushed with shame, he added: "I've got *just* the right job for you. Tell the man in charge of the horse-pound that John de Somery requires a palfrey that is suitable for the bearer of my banner."

Before Jack could think of an appropriate reply, the Baron squelched off into the drizzle. Although Jack was aware of the glares of the other men, he wasn't much bothered about that. Perhaps he'd been staring too long into the brazier, but the Baron's head had seemed to be surrounded by a crimson halo.

Was John de Somery one of the victims of the spell-casting?

CHAPTER 5

It was evening again, and Jack was back inside the byre – lying in the straw and peering through the spy-hole as before. His eyes confirmed what his ears had already told him: there was nobody present in the room next door. The table had gone, but the circle of protection was scratched on the earthen floor. Suddenly, this glowed with crimson light. Flaring up, it became a ring of leaping flames. Some of these were drawn towards the centre, where they rose to form a column of spark-flecked smoke. Scarcely able to breathe, Jack watched transfixed as something began to take shape amidst the swirling mist. He half-expected the demon called Adrasteus – with wide staring eyes and gaping slavering jaws. But what was actually materialising was…was…the *figure of a naked woman*. Adrasteus was *female*. Silky strands twirled around her body – Will o' the Wisps that did not hide her nudity. Jack rubbed his unbelieving eyes and looked again. She was still there, clearer than before, and raising her arms 'til her wrists met above her head. And as the veils drifted softly to the floor, her body was exposed in all its voluptuous glory, bathed in flickering light from the blazing flame-ring. When Jack eventually transferred his gaze up to her face, he saw with a start that she was watching him intently. Her expression softened as she smiled, seeming to understand both his longing and his fear. Her red lips parted – began to form a word. She was about to speak…

"*The Baron wants you.*"

Startled, Jack sat up in his bed – bitterly resenting the deprivation of his dream.

"What's that?" he demanded, scowling at the boy who'd robbed him of his fantasy.

"The Baron wants you," the lad repeated with unconcealed impatience. "Our scouts have reported that Lancaster's men have been setting the bridges on fire. We shall be heading for a place called Burton. Oh! And the Baron says to get your horse and don't forget the banner."

"Here we go again," Nutcracker groaned from further back in the tent. "We had the same trouble trying to get across the Severn."

"I've got to go," Jack said, reaching for the banner-pole and using it to haul himself onto his feet.

"They brew good ale at Burton," Nutcracker shouted as Jack shrugged on his cloak and stumbled out through the tent-flap. Pulling the woollen cloth around his throat to keep out the rain, he limped across to the horse-pound and chose the most docile-looking animal that he could find. And once she'd been got ready, he scrambled up onto her saddle and rode in search of his master.

*

Although the Baron was surrounded by other mounted nobles, Jack located him immediately. Sitting a full head taller in the saddle than the others, his twin-lioned surcoat glistened in the growing daylight. As Jack rode up behind his Lord's white destrier, the Baron twisted round and glared.

"What kept you?" he demanded.

"I'm sorry, Sire. They had to find something to support this shaft." Jack rocked it back and forth in the socket that hung down from his saddle.

"Well, sit up straight and hold it upright." As the Baron turned back to his associates, Jack heard him mutter: "This headache is killing me."

Jack froze. Could his master be a victim of the magician's spell? If so, should he report what he'd seen in the cottage at Coventry? No! This wasn't the right time. Maybe there never *would* be a right time. No mere archer could ever be on speaking-terms with a noble. Gripping the banner-shaft more firmly, he followed the riders as they spurred their horses into galloping motion – their archers and footsoldiers following behind.

*

Ignoring the well-used roadways, the party headed North – stopping to water the horses at the rivers that they forded.

After riding for the greater part of the second day, a muddy roadway cut across their path. Its wheel-ruts told of frequent use, but the only vehicle in sight was a cart overloaded with barrels. And judging by the cart's unsteady wobbling, they were empty.

As the cart came within earshot, the Baron cupped his gauntlets round his mouth. "Is the town of Burton around here?" he bawled.

"I've just come from there," the carter called back. "Leastwise, I would have done if they hadn't closed the bridge." As he flapped the reins to keep his donkey moving, the Baron wheeled his horse round to block her way.

"Don't you *dare* to drive around *ME!*"

The donkey snorted as her owner yanked the reins. And with the bit digging into her mouth, the cart lurched to a standstill.

"How can I run a tavern with no ale?" the driver whined.

"What is the insolent knave going on about?" the Baron asked the nearest of his companions. This was John de Sutton, his brother-in-law and a frequent visitor to his castle.

De Sutton shrugged: "The monks of Burton brew fine ale and it travels very well. I suppose that the oaf keeps an ale-house somewhere on *this* side of the river."

"Ar!" the carter agreed. "And them sods over there will 'av drunk it all by now."

"Who are *they*?" the Baron demanded, obviously growing ever more affronted by the carter's insolent manner.

"They never said. But one of 'em was holdin' a flag."

"Whose flag was it?"

"How should I know?" Recoiling from the Baron's furious glare, he adopted a servile expression. "It was red, my Lord," he mumbled, "with yeller lions on it."

"Lancaster's flag," the Baron muttered, and then enquired in a commanding tone of voice: "Is he on the bridge in person?"

"I dunnow, my Lord." The carter scratched his scurfy scalp and added: "But I did hear one of 'em say as he was sleepin' in Burton Abbey 'cos he's scared of witchcraft."

At the mention of witchcraft, Jack ceased from shaking raindrops off his cloak. Should he reveal what he knew? No! There were too many people within hearing.

The carter fidgeted with his reins. "I'm sorry, your honour, but I've gotter get back home before it gets too dark to see the way. It's a good many miles from here an'

I've had a wasted journey. Can I go now, er...if you please?"

"Certes," the Baron muttered, tossing a coin down into the cart. "But just one more question: how many men are on the bridge?"

"I only saw a couple, but I'm sure as there was more."

"Very well," the Baron growled as he tossed a second penny into the cart. "You may go on your way. Tell no one that you have seen us here."

Immediately, the carter whipped his donkey into skidding motion. "No, me Lord. Certainly not, me Lord. Thank you, me Lord."

As the cart disappeared round a bend in the road, the Baron turned back to his companions.

"Depending on how many of Lancaster's men are on the bridge, we're probably too late to secure it. But it's built from stone so they can't burn it down like they did to those others. I intend to keep it under observation until the King arrives in force. Follow me."

After crossing the road, they rode on at great speed until the land sloped steeply downwards.

The rain had petered out and even though dusk was fast approaching, they had a clear view over a wide and waterlogged valley. Below them, three branches of the Trent flowed through snow-speckled marshes and beds of battered-down reeds. On high ground beyond that wasteland lay the houses of Burton town, with the squat square tower of its Abbey on their left. Clouds of steam around this showed that the monks were brewing their ale. As Jack licked his lips in hopeful anticipation, his attention was drawn to something moving on the nearest branch of the river. A frame of blackened timber was being carried along on the floodwaters, a relic of a burnt-out bridge from somewhere upstream. It halted, spun slowly round, and then resumed its fitful progress down the river, to crash at last into a narrow, stone-built structure. And what an amazing structure it was.

Brushing his eyelashes free of raindrops, Jack gaped down at it with wonder. So this was the Burton Bridge...a seemingly endless row of arches bestriding the three arms of the river and the wasteland that lay between them.

Not only was this bridge incredibly long, it was curved like a chain that – while secured to both sides of the valley – was dragged sideways by the force of the flowing water. *Could* a bridge be made flexible like a chain? Nah! The impact of the burnt timbers had made no impression at all on its ship-shaped piers. It looked solid enough to last for a thousand years. The men who'd built it were magicians. *Real* magicians, who used stone to create their marvels instead of mumbled words and mystical gestures. But marvellous though it was, it was too narrow for a large army to get across quickly – even if unopposed. And the glinting of steel all along its length showed that Lancaster's soldiers were there in force.

"Look down there!" The Baron had grabbed John de Sutton's arm and was pointing down at the near end of the bridge. Around its battlemented gatehouse, soldiers were digging frantically. One semicircular ditch had already been completed and a second was almost finished.

"We should have got here sooner..." De Sutton was stating the obvious. "We'll *never* prise them out of there now."

"We may not have to," the Baron retorted, twisting round in his saddle in search of the bearer of his banner.

"Come here," he shouted, beckoning his minion over. And as his minion spurred his horse forward, he pointed to a flat-topped boulder that lay on the brink of the hill. "Go to that rock and wave my banner for those below to see."

After lifting it out of its shoe, Jack slid down from his saddle and, using the pole as a prop, he limped across to the indicated slab. At the near end of the bridge, the labourers had finished their digging and were retreating into the gatehouse. Nevertheless, he felt very exposed as he waved the golden flag from side to side. He was beyond the reach of arrows, but he'd heard of machines that could hurl missiles to much greater distances.

"Canstow see any response?" the Baron shouted from further away than before.

"Yes, Sire! They've stopped digging, and they're erecting Pavise shields around the entrance."

"Goddes' Blood!" the Baron cried, turning to his companions. "The King has ordered me to present Lancaster with his offer of peace on the condition that he lays down his arms. But now that his men have dug themselves in like that, I shall probably be killed before I get close enough to deliver it." He shrugged. "But it seems that I have no real alternative but to try."

The other nobles nodded gravely, but chose to make no comment.

Resignedly, the Baron turned to Jack. "Get on your horse and come along with me."

Jack paled. So *this* was the task that he'd been selected for, to ride up to the enemy lines and deliver the King's demands. And if Lancaster's men were as savage as he'd heard, they'd shoot him down before he got anywhere near them.

Now he knew why he'd been chosen.

He was expendable.

CHAPTER 6

Jack remounted his horse and followed his master towards the track that led down into the valley. His knees began to tremble at the thought of being sent to his death. Why had he enlisted when he could still be baking crustades in Dudley Castle?

"Wait," the Baron cried, holding up his hand. "Get a white rag and hang it beside my banner."

Mystified, Jack returned to the others and begged a length of white linen from the chapelain. In answer to his query, the cleric told him that this was one of the ways of requesting a temporary truce. Without something of the sort, any would-be ambassador could expect to be killed on sight.

But no matter how Jack tried to tie the rag to the banner-pole, it kept on sliding down. What should he do now? In desperation, he looked around for assistance.

A dozen yards away, a cart had got bogged down in the mud – weighed down by its cargo of rolls of thin grey metal. That was the lead that Jack had seen being stripped from the roofs of churches all the way up from Coventry.

"Canstow spare these little bits?" Jack asked, reaching into the cart and picking out two strips of lead – each about six inches long and four inches in width. But instead of signifying his agreement or refusal, the Carter stood staring at the Baron's banner. Although it hung dejectedly from its pole, the two blue lions upon it were clearly visible.

"You're one of De Somery's men," he muttered. "I pity thee. They say as he's the worst tyrant in the country and that takes some doing, I can tell yer."

"He's treated me well enough so far," Jack said.

"You'm lucky then." The man scrambled up onto his cart. "Hup," he grunted as he hauled up a roll of lead and rested it against his chest. "Huh," he gasped as he slung it out of the cart. It hit the sodden ground with a 'SQUMP', splashing Jack's legs with mud.

"Thanks," Jack cried, retreating out of range.

"I suppose," the man continued while bending down to pick up another roll, "that...Hup...even the fiercest of lions can be kind to those that are under its command. Talking of lions, have you seen the King's yet?"

"The King's what?"

"The King's pet lion. Adam of Lichfield. Huh. That's the King's lion-keeper (SQUMP), says that he keeps it on a silver chain. That don't seem safe enough to me." The man paused in his efforts and rested his hands on his hips. "He says that the King makes him feed it on the innards of disembowelled Ordainers."

When Jack failed to show a reaction, the man peered down at the strips in Jack's hand. "Is that all you want? Them little bits? Go on then. Take 'em. It won't make no difference to the Trebooshay when it arrives. That's if it ever *does* arrive."

With no time to enquire what a 'Trebooshay' might be, Jack used the strips to fasten the white linen to the pole. It worked; unevenness caused by the carpenter's adze stopped the rag from sliding down. Yelling out his thanks, Jack remounted his horse and made his way back to the Baron.

By the time he reached him, John de Somery was clearly impatient to be gone.

*

"Do *not* come any closer," a defender called from behind the earthen rampart.

On hearing this challenge, the Baron reined-in his horse. Above the distant gatehouse, Lancaster's flag proclaimed that *he* was in possession.

"I AM JOHN DE SOMERY," the Baron cried, motioning for Jack to wave his banner about. "AS YOU CAN SEE, I COME IN PEACE TO PARLAY WITH THE EARL OF LANCASTER.! I HAVE HERE . . ." – He held up a roll of parchment whose dangling seal gleamed like a splash of blood – "I HAVE AN OFFER OF CLEMENCY FROM THE KING . . . PROVIDED THAT THE EARL SURRENDERS HIMSELF TO THE CROWN."

"And the Earl of Lancaster has left word that we should inform you where you can stick it," the defender cried. "Come any closer and you are dead men."

"No surprises there!" the Baron muttered, turning his horse away.

Jack hung his head, convinced that he was about to be sent to deliver the message – even if it killed him.

"Relax, soldier," said the Baron, noting his servant's doleful expression. "Do you think that I want you to deliver this message in person?"

Jack kept silent.

"Nay. One over-zealous archer could bring you down and start a needless war. If either of us is slain, it will be the signal for all-out battle to commence. But on the other hand, if I fail to deliver this document, every soldier's death in the inevitable conflict will be set to my account. I should never be released from Purgatory when I die. Whenever that might be."

Once again, Jack resisted the impulse to report what he'd seen at Coventry. Instead, he blurted out the next thing that came into his head: "I know how to deliver the message."

Immediately, he wished that he'd kept his mouth shut. For one thing, no mere soldier *ever* talked to the Baron like that.

Ignoring the insolence, the Baron wheeled his horse around in a tight circle to draw rein beside his minion's smaller mount. "You think that you can get it over there without getting killed?"

"Yes, Sire." Jack hauled his quiver round to his front and folded back the flap. After inspecting the arrows carefully, he drew one out. It was longer than those that were used for killing and a tuft of wool was tied on behind its head. "This will carry the parchment as easily as burning tow."

The Baron snorted, his eyebrows raised. "Do you think that I am willing to send it tied to a bloody *fire-arrow*?"

Swallowing hard to suppress his fright, Jack had no alternative but to demonstrate what he meant. After unwinding the wire that held the woollen fibres in place, he scraped them off with his knife "You see, Sire," he said as he compared the exposed section of shaft against the palm of his hand. "If the message is folded to a hand's breadth in width, it will fit on quite easily."

"And you think that such an arrow would fly true?"

"Yes, Sire. I am sure of it. I've shot one like it from a wind-eye at Dudley Priory."

The Baron grew silent and thoughtful. Eventually, he shrugged. "Carry on then," he said. "But have a care. That document is priceless."

Jack slid down from his horse and, ignoring the pain in his side, rammed the banner-pole upright into the mud. The Baron handed down the parchment and Jack folded it over repeatedly until it was narrow enough to fit round the end of the shaft. While looking for something to hold it in place, he noticed the strips of lead that secured the white rag to the banner-pole. Since their usefulness was (hopefully) over, he prised one off. Wrapping the parchment round the arrow behind its head, he used the lead to prevent it from unravelling. His bow was slid from its sheath of well-waxed linen and flexed a couple of times to awaken the dormant timber. Then retrieving the string from inside his helmet, he fitted it to the bow and nocked the arrow on. He was worried about the dangling seal, but there could be no turning back now.

"Right," the Baron muttered, bending low in the saddle to seize the banner-pole and raise it up aloft. "YOU OVER THERE," he yelled towards the rampart. "WE ARE ABOUT TO SEND YOU THE KINGS OFFER OF MERCY. SEE TO IT THAT THE EARL OF LANCASTER RECEIVES IT WITHOUT DELAY." To Jack, he murmured: "Go to it, soldier, and do not miss."

Estimating the range as fifty yards, Jack raised the bow and hauled the arrow back until its flights caressed the surcoat on his chest. After taking a deep breath, he let the arrow go.

'Thwack.'

Instead of flying true, the arrow corkscrewed into the air, leaving behind its stripped-off flights to float gently away on the breeze, and the message in its lead tube to fall heavily to the ground. Jack flushed with embarrassment and shame as the defenders of the bridge howled their derision.

"You idiot," the Baron snarled as Jack stooped to retrieve the document. "Why did I let you talk me into such a hare-brained scheme?"

"It w-will w-work," Jack stammered desperately. "It's just that I fer-forgot to close the end of the tube."

"Well if you think that I'm going to risk a second failure, you can forget it. Give me the parchment."

Jack tugged the document from the tube and shamefacedly handed it over. But as he tossed the metal away, he noticed the white cloth still hanging on the banner-pole. With trembling fingers, he took a standard arrow from his quiver and twisted off the twin-barbed iron head. After draping the cloth over the end of the shaft, he forced the head back over it.

Three quick beats of a palpitating heart, and the arrow was nocked and launched into the air. It flew towards the bridge – the corners of the cloth rippling like pennants in a gale.

Jack whooped with joy. "You see, Sire," he exclaimed as the arrow fell behind the rampart. "It *will* work. Let me try again, I beg you, Sire. I will not let you down a second time."

For a while, the Baron sat silently astride his horse, caressing the parchment and staring at the rampart. "Very well," he said at last. "But you will rue the day if it goes amiss."

But Jack was feeling confident.

A second fire-arrow had its wadding replaced by the parchment roll – this time encased in a tube whose leading end was battered well and . . . truly . . . flat. And for the third time that day, Jack fitted an unusual arrow to his bow and drew it back against the tension of its string.

"Wait," the Baron cried, looking askance at the dangling seal. "That will upset the flight. Pass the arrow to me and I'll cut the bloody thing off. I don't want to take more chances than I have to."

Once that had been accomplished, Jack raised his bow once more, hauling the arrow back as he'd done before. His fingers began to tremble. They ached to release the string but did he dare to let it go? They made the decision for him.

'Thwack.'

The missile shot up into the air, carrying its offer of clemency towards the earthen rampart. The defenders fell silent as the arrow flew towards them, gathering speed as it swooped down to the ground.

"So you managed it after all." The Baron was gazing at the spot where the arrow had vanished. After wiping his brow on a corner of his surcoat, he turned to Jack with the semblance of a smile.

Jack tried to grin but his mouth would not quite let him.

Abruptly turning his horse around, the Baron murmured quietly: "There's nothing for us to do now but wait for Lancaster's answer." Shaking the reins, he urged his horse towards the path that led back up the hill to the encampment. "Now is his chance to prove that his quarrel is with the De Spensers and not his King." As his mount broke into a canter, he shouted back over his shoulder: "And if he *does* lay down his arms, let us hope that Edward will be merciful. For all our sakes!"

Jack said nothing. He had not expected or received any thanks or recognition for his efforts. Nevertheless, he had the distinct impression that the Baron's attitude towards him had softened slightly. Or was that just wishful thinking?

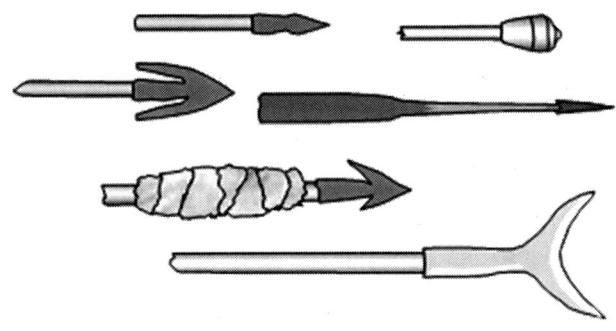

CHAPTER 7

Twenty-four hours had passed since Jack's arrow delivered the King's offer to the rebels on the bridge. And since no reply had been received, a frontal attack was to take place at dawn on the following morning.

Dusk descended slowly on the hilltop encampment. Swords and spears were issued to the warriors, and brandished to exercise the appropriate sinews. The accompanying grunts and curses ceased as their Sergeant began to select men for the first assault. Jack held his breath as he listened to the lengthening roll call, only letting it go when the last man had been chosen. He was not having to go and fight. Not this time anyway.

Instead, Jack was marched across to a position that overlooked the bridge. Other archers were spaced-out along the brow of the hill. What could they be thinking as they crouched in pensive silence? Were their thoughts of wives or sweethearts? Or of the wearisome boredom of waiting around on a cold winter hillside for the order to begin what they'd come for?

As for Jack, he was more concerned with his chances of survival as he limped to his allotted spot at the end of the line. After stringing his bow, he laid it on the frost-encrusted ground. Danger and death lurked in the darkness below him. Why had he volunteered to fight for a cause that he didn't understand, yet alone believe in? The promise of a rich reward seemed far away.

The bridge could just be made out as a dark curved line against the pale shades of river and marsh. Its gatehouse lay below him – and just beyond the range of his trusty bow. However, from experience gained on the battlements of Dudley's Donjon, he knew that his elevated position should give him another forty yards or so. Moreover, with the hill shaped like an upturned bowl, the arrows would hug its lower slope like an eagle after a coney. All things considered, he should be able to reach the gate without a change of bow and suitable arrows.

He lined up his arrows in front of him — thrusting their barbed heads into the ground with the flights within easy reach. And from the rustling and rattling behind him, more were being unloaded for use when he'd sent them on their way.

"They tell me that this is your first battle," murmured a voice on Jack's right. "Are you going to be all right, lad?"

Jack was too amazed by his neighbour's concern to answer right away. Ever since he'd been given a horse to ride, none of the other soldiers would look him in the eyes, let alone speak to him.

"I think so," he replied guardedly. "Thanks. What happens next then?"

"Our job is to keep up a hail of arrows on the defenders of the bridge until our footsoldiers are ready to move in."

"Some of Lancaster's men are relatives of mine," someone announced from further along the line of archers.

"I expect as we've *all* got friends and relations down there," whispered another. "But what can we do?"

Jack had been worrying about Felicia's cousins. Roger and Ted might be down there on the bridge, for their father was a known sympathiser with the Ordainers' cause. And although he'd tried to block Jack's marriage to Felicia, his sons had welcomed him unreservedly into their family. Jack smiled as he recalled their name: De Audley sounded like the town that he had come from. If Felicia's cousins were down there, he should at least try to send them a timely warning.

"We could use Blunts for our first volley," Jack said out loud, risking the renewed antagonism of his comrades. "It might give 'em headaches, but they could take cover before the real shooting starts."

A mumble passed along the line as the idea was passed from one man to the next. Judging by the tone of the mumbling, most of the archers had friends or family on the opposing side.

"Hey, boy," somebody whispered to a passing arrow-boy. "Fetch us some Blunts will yer? We'll have a whip round for yer if you can get 'em to us without nobody seeing."

So the boy brought the men a Blunt arrow apiece and received a penny from each for his trouble.

While waiting for the command to begin shooting, the archers listened to the chinks and clinks of armour as the footsoldiers crept past in the darkness. Yet even had it been lighter, their rust-stained helmets and maile would have made them difficult to see as they made their shuffling way towards the side-vale. And when they had all departed, it was the archers' nerves that were jangling and not the iron rings.

Eventually, since he was the archer standing closest to his Sergeant, Jack received a whispered command to get ready to shoot. While passing this on to his neighbour, he tugged the Blunt arrow from his belt, noting with satisfaction that the others were doing the same. When sufficient time had elapsed to have all the arrows nocked and ready, a simulated owl's cry sent them speeding up into the sky. Jack watched his flights disappear into the darkness. Could the yard long shaft reach the bridge? Would any of them? By way of an answer, tongues of bright flame spread swiftly round a ditch. And when the second had been ignited, the bridge was defended by two demilunes of fire. Smoke and vapour hid the flames as a second owl's hoot sent another shower of arrows down – man-killing Sharps this time.

But as these vanished into the glowing haze, a tiny red spark rose out of it. Soaring up into the winter sky, it grew in size as it skimmed the glowering clouds. Then roaring like a dragon, it crashed to earth behind the crouching archers.

"The traitors have got a Mangonel," somebody shouted. "Thank God they haven't got our range yet."

Feeling safe, at least for the moment, the archers sent another shoal of arrows down onto the redoubt. But they were not safe at all. The fire-pot had burst behind them, causing rivulets of flame to avalanche down the hillside. And as bowmen scrambled for their lives, a second crashed onto the hill beside the first. Then another. And another. Each landing a few yards from the first. Although none of the archers were hurt, they were shepherded off the hillside — whereupon a bellowed command ordered them back to camp.

*

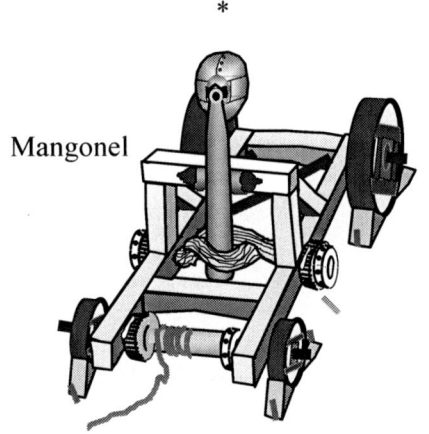

Mangonel

"That Mangonel explains them old scorch-marks on the hill," John Blunt muttered as he and Jack stood warming themselves beside a steaming cauldron. "Them sods have been getting our range."

"In that case," Jack said, bending to ladle bean pottage into his helmet, "why didn't they hit us?"

"How should I know!" John said bluntly. "Perhaps they didn't know exactly where we were."

"Or perhaps they don't want to kill us," somebody growled on the opposite side of the cauldron, "any more than we wants to kill *them*."

Another soldier cleared his throat to speak: "I've heard as Lancaster don't want to give the King an excuse to declare war on 'im."

"Good for *him* then," murmured one of the pair of chess-players who were seated at a table nearby. They'd been playing for some time now and the end seemed not far off. Although the players were focused on the game, the onlookers were growing restive. 'White' had the most pieces on the board and was the favourite to win the coins that were piled up on the table. Nevertheless, Black's Queen stood threateningly beside White's Rook. Picking up his Bishop, White leaped it diagonally over his Pawn to remove the Queen from the board.[4] "Check," he announced loudly.

"Hey John," Jack whispered, watching the game as it moved towards its inevitable conclusion. "These men are talking to me again. Got any idea why?"

"Don't yer know?" Black said as he moved his King to the corner of the board. "We heard how you delivered the King's offer of peace on a fire arrow. Did the Baron tell you to do that, or did you think of it yerself?"

"I thought of it myself," Jack answered, dipping a crust of bread into his pottage and transferring it to his mouth. "At least, the idea popped into my head," he admitted thoughtfully.

Ignoring the crumbs that were splattered across the board, White captured a Pawn that Black was hoping to promote into a replacement Queen. "Well, wherever it come from," he said, "if Lancaster accepts the offer of peace, we shan't have to fight. And when all's said and done, we'm only here for the food and the money."

His opponent grunted: "We might be gettin' fed, but we ain't seen a penny yet."

---

[4] The rules of chess were different in those days.

As the onlookers muttered, White stared across the board at his opponent. "Come on. It's your move."

"I can't," Black said, leaning back and folding his arms across his chest. "I've managed to force a Stalemate." He chuckled. "When I sacrificed my Queen, I thought that you'd spot what I was up to."

"Arrr," growled somebody in the crowd. "Any fool could see that."

"Well, I didn't," White snapped, reddening. "I mistook your Bishop for a Knight. I can't tell the difference between some of these pieces." He glared around at his audience. "Who carved 'em anyway?"

"Well whoever carved 'em…" yelled a voice at the back of the crowd, "they did me a very good turn. Your wagers all belong to me." To shouts of frustration and anger, the bet-taker scurried away from his former clients.

"Come to that," Black muttered as he began to divide the coins on the table into two equal piles. "If *all* of us gets killed, the King won't have to pay-out either."

With that unhappy thought, they all went back to warming themselves by the fire.

*

In the few hours left before dawn, a row of Pavise shields was erected across the hillside. Thankful for this protection, the archers returned to showering the bridge with arrows.

When a horn's blast ordered them to stop, their comrades in the valley ran forward to span the flaming ditches with stolen barn doors. The defenders immediately destroyed these by spraying them with burning oil.

From his hilltop eyrie, Jack watched grimly as men ran screaming from the flames to roll themselves on the wet and icy ground. And after several such attempts had failed, the attackers gave up trying. They failed again the next day. And the day after that. Lancaster had achieved *his* Stalemate.

CHAPTER 8

"He wants to see you right away."

Jack looked up from the arrowhead that he'd been sharpening to meet the eyes of the Baron's messenger. What did their Lord want *now*?

He found the Baron's pavilion without much difficulty. After all, who could miss a great cone of a tent with blue lions all over its golden sides? John de Somery − looking equally splendid in his similarly-decorated tabard − was pacing up and down.

"Go and collect your horse," he ordered while heaving himself up onto his destrier. "Then come along with me."

Made wary by his master's voice, Jack fetched his horse from the pound, and then followed his lord as he rode among the tents. He couldn't help but admire the Baron's bearing as he sat easily in the saddle of his huge white warhorse. And although Jack's horse was smaller, he tried to adopt a similar haughty manner.

Leaving the siege-camp behind, the riders drew ever farther away from the river − always keeping the conical spy-hill on their right. It was almost midday when they arrived at a city of tents and gaudy pavilions. Although a great many soldiers were busily going about their business, an uncanny silence hung about the place.

Ignoring them all, the Baron led the way towards the biggest and most majestic pavilion of all. It stood well apart from the others − the royal flag flying above the apex of its roof. Around its wall of red and gold, armed guards were stationed in order to prevent intrusion. Seeing the two horsemen approaching, the guard beside the entrance-flap swiftly unsheathed his sword.

"Who goes there?" he challenged.

"The Baron of Dudley," replied John de Somery. "Come at the expressed command of King Edward." Without waiting for a response, the Baron rode boldly up to the guard and slid down from the saddle. "I'm going in," he said as he handed over the reins. Nevertheless, raised voices within the tent gave him cause to pause.

"...but, my Lord," an unseen speaker was saying, "there is no need for us to pay the men anything."

"Look, Hugh," said a deep imperious voice. "We had difficulty getting them to enlist. If they don't receive some money soon, they could begin to drift back to their homes. They might even defect to my cousin."

"Have a care, my Lord," the first speaker cried out. "There is somebody lurking about outside. WHO GOES THERE?"

The Baron pushed past the guard who was trying to deny him entry. "John De Somery of Duddeley!"

"Come on in," came the deep imperious voice from within the tent.

Jack peered past his master into the candle-lit interior. Behind a long wooden table sat two impressive men – both middle aged and both of powerful stature. Although the one on the left wasn't wearing a crown, Jack recognised the King immediately. A tabard with his heraldry lay across the back of his chair. And as he turned to speak to the man beside him, his shoulder-length hair brushed a robe of 'Coventry-Blue'.

The King's associate was dressed to impress. He wore a golden surcoat adorned with crimson chevrons. Below a three-plumed hat in the same expensive colour, grey eyes stared at the newcomers with a decidedly hostile glare. Behind this seated couple, two armoured knights stood erect and vigilant, with their hands resting lightly on the pommels of their swords.

"Did you overhear any of that?" the King demanded.

"Any of what, Sire?" the Baron replied, dropping to one knee to make his obeisance.

"What Hugh and I were discussing," snapped the King.

"Nay, My Lord" cried the Baron, springing to his feet. As he shook his head with vigour, the rings of his Aventail hissed as if unhappy with the lie.

"I see that you are still wearing armour," the King remarked casually.

"Yes, Sire," the Baron said, colouring up slightly. "An attempt on my life cost my dear brother *his*. And if I may remind my Lord, a tax collector that I sent on your behalf was waylaid and killed by the rebels. These are dangerous times, my Lord."

"Indeed they are," the King agreed, "but tell me: what is the present situation at Burton Bridge?"

"Lancaster's men are in possession, my Lord. They have erected earthwork defences around the entrance and are guarding the gatehouse strongly."

"With how many men?"

"It is difficult to say, but enough. The bridge is fortified and easy to defend. And they have a Mangonel with them."

"Is there any other way to cross the Trent?"

"None that I know of. The bridge at Rydeware has been broken down and the ford at Walton has been made impassable by the rain. My scouts report that we cannot cross the river – there or anywhere else."

"We knew about those already," the King muttered impatiently. "It seems that we shall have to wait until the floodwater subsides. In the meantime, my cousin will be gathering reinforcements – from Scotland as like as not." He peered past the Baron to the entrance flap. "That soldier behind you; is that the one we've been hearing so much about?"

"I believe that it is, my Lord," the Baron said, beckoning for Jack to join him in the tent. "This is my banner-bearer. His name is...?"

"It's Jack, Sire," Jack whispered as the Baron led him forward into the presence of his monarch.

"Bow before your King," the Baron hissed, grabbing Jack's collar and forcing him down onto his knees. "...is Jack," he said aloud.

Ignoring Jack completely, the monarch waved a bejewelled hand towards his highborn attendants. "You know one another, I presume?"

"Yes, my Lord," the Baron said. He bowed very slightly to the man beside the King. "Hugh de Spenser. My greetings to you."

So *this* was Hugh De Spenser, Jack thought, unable to stop a smirk spreading over his features. This was the man that everyone was talking about. The man whose closeness to the King offended the whole country.

After nodding a cursory acknowledgement, Hugh De Spenser peered down at a chart on the table in front of him. Even from that distance, Jack could see that it was a map. Dotted about on it were tiny heraldic shields – including some gold ones with the De Somery pair of lions. The only other emblem that he recognised was that of the Earl of Lancaster.

Observing Jack's scrutiny, De Spenser stood up suddenly, releasing the chart, which immediately curled up into a roll.

The Baron kicked Jack's foot. "Get back down on your knees," he growled, and then addressed the standing knights: "My Lords Atholl and Warenne, good Undrentide to you both."

As the earls nodded perfunctorily, the King regarded Jack with what seemed to be a smile upon his lips.

"So *you* are the archer who delivered my offer of mercy to my cousin."

"Yes, Sire," Jack mumbled nervously.

"Forgive him, my Lord," said the Baron. "He knows not how to address his betters."

To Jack, he whispered: "Address the King as 'My Lord'."

"Nay, John," laughed King Edward. "Let the lad speak freely. I have no objection to the speech of common men. I sometimes prefer their company to that of courtiers. At least they won't try to overthrow me."

As the pair behind him looked down their Norman noses with disdain, the King turned back to Jack. "Where comest-ow from, Jack?" he asked kindly.

Perceiving that his servant was too afraid to speak, the Baron spoke up on his behalf: "My Lord, he hails from Netherton; a village in my manor."

The King smiled broadly. "And is this the same '*Jack*' that procured those *magic* beans?"

Jack blushed. He'd been trying to live that episode down. Clearly, his reputation had spread far and wide – even reaching the ears of his monarch.

"Hah!" chuckled the King. "I laughed out loud when I heard of it. Good for thee, lad." The anxiety that had formerly clouded the King's eyes had been replaced by a sparkle of merriment. "I could do with some cheering-up in these frightful times." He gripped De Spenser's clenched fist. "How shall we reward him, Hugh?"

De Spenser was staring at Jack with an expression of loathing on his features. "Give him another message for your cousin," he said, "to be delivered in person by Trebooshay."

There was that word again. Jack still didn't know what a Trebooshay was, but he had a strong suspicion that De Spenser's suggestion wasn't intended as a prize.

"Nay, Hugh," chortled the King. "Be not so unkind." He rose from his chair and strode manfully round the table to raise Jack to his feet.

"You came here on a horse?"

"Y-yes, my Lord."

"You can keep it – either for yourself or to sell it on."

"Th-th-thank you," Jack stammered, flushing with delight. If Felicia could see him now: hob-nobbing with *the King*.

But the King was already returning to the table. Scooping up De Spenser's chart-roll, he resumed his seat beside him.

"That's all for now, John," he said with a wave of dismissal.

As the Baron backed respectfully away, Jack stole a last look at the assembled nobility. While the others were studying the map, the King's favourite was staring back at him unnervingly.

Just as the retreating pair arrived at the entrance flap, there was a commotion outside the tent. Almost immediately, the guard that they'd encountered rushed past them and dropped to one knee before the King.

"My Lord," he cried. "Pray forgive the intrusion, but there is a man outside who says that he's just come from Burton. He says that the river-level has dropped so much that it is possible to cross the ford."

"Bring him in," cried the King, unrolling the chart again and using four be-jewelled daggers to nail it to the table.

The man was brought in, leaving a trail of muddy footprints on the purple ground sheet.

"My Lord," he mumbled nervously. "The river has fallen to a level that is now passable. I crossed the ford myself to get here and, if I may make so bold" – he squelched across to the table and pointed a trembling finger at the chart – "it is there...just five miles to the west of here."

"At last." The King beamed round at his companions. "Now we can attack my cousin from the rear."

*

Thoughtfully, Jack mounted his horse and followed the Baron out of the King's encampment. What could he have done to arouse De Spenser's hatred? Was it a disrespectful expression in his eyes, or the smirk that he'd not been able to suppress? Whatever it was, his grandmother always said that you couldn't have too many friends – but that even *one* enemy was one too many. And somehow, he'd aroused the enmity of the second-most powerful man in England.

Part Two

Battle

CHAPTER 9

When Jack got back to the camp above Burton Bridge, the preparations for the assault drove all thoughts of De Spenser from his mind. The Trebooshay had arrived at last: just cartloads of long lengths of timber – some strengthened with iron bands.

With no time to stand and stare, Jack rejoined the archers on the brow of the hill.

After swigging more of his grandmother's potion, he strung his bow and returned to the business in hand:

Accept a sheaf of arrows from the Arrow-boy...
Line them up with their heads shoved into the ground...
Bend over forward to nock an arrow onto the bowstring...
Stand up while plucking the arrow from the ground and drawing it back in one continuous motion...
Aim high towards the bridge and then release...
Bend over to nock another arrow onto the bowstring...
and again...and again...and again...

Although he soon grew bored, at least he was doing what he'd enlisted for. Up until now, his soldiering had consisted of long periods of marching and riding followed by short ones of hanging about and waiting.

But in spite of the cold and the wet and the boredom, he'd gradually grown accustomed to the life; after all, there was no one nagging him by day, and no screaming kid at night. The archery didn't worry him; he couldn't see who was on the receiving end of his arrows.

But when this phase came to an end, he'd have to descend the slope facing enemy arrows, and then fight to the death with other desperate men.

Sword and Buckler

Jack had been trained to a very high standard with the sword and buckler. But the wound in his side became painful when twisting around. In fact, there was very *little chance of him living beyond this day.*

It is not unusual in those foreseeing impending death, to find that their bowels are adding their own brand of discomfort. And so it was with Jack – prompting him to make a frantic dash for the latrines. Well, it was more like a rapid limp, aided by a staff that he hid from critical eyes inside his bow-bag.

He'd previously been thankful that the toilet was a long way up the hill – that being the direction from which the wind was coming. But it looked as though he wasn't going to make it in time, and he cursed that uphill distance with each step.

*

As one of a line of soldiers with their bums hanging over a trench, Jack listened to the claps of expulsions all around him. Had the Bloody Flux broken out again – that deadly feature of the Scottish campaigns? They said that once one soldier caught it, it ran through the camp like a mudslide, or to put it more accurately: a *muck*slide.

After a lengthy stay to be sure of completing his business, Jack began the slow trudge back down to the brow of the hill. The Trebooshay had been erected now, a pair of enormous 'A-frames' with a tapered arm pivoted at their apex. A heavy-looking box hung from the short end, with a rope attached to the long end keeping it level. On a platform halfway up this great contrivance, a man was peering down at a cart below him.

"Hurry up," he shouted and a bucket rose jerkily up towards a pulley. "Belay it now," the man commanded as the bucket halted beside him. After he'd transferred several rolls of lead into the box, he sagged against the A-frame. "That should be enough," he gasped. "We can take a rest now."

A second man emerged from behind the cart. Tugging off his gloves, he rushed over to shake Jack's hand.

"Why, it's that poor bugger of De Somery's," he cried, "Fancy seeing *you* here."

"Thanks for the strips of lead," Jack said. "They came in very handy."

The Carter laughed. "I heard about what yer did with 'em. Very clever that was."

"So *this* is the Trebooshay, is it?" Jack said in order to change the subject. When the Carter nodded his confirmation, Jack gazed up at the wooden framework.

"You could use it for drawing up water from a well, but I can't see one here."

"Nay, lad. This will be used for smashing down the bridge's gatehouse. See that?" The Carter was pointing to the tangle of ropes that was hanging from the long end of the beam. "That's a net for hurling rocks down into the valley. Them's 'em there." He nodded at a heap of them nearby.

Jack's stomach clenched in horror. If Hugh de Spenser had had his way, *he* would have been sent flying down into the valley like a lump of rock. Although relieved that this wasn't likely to happen now, he was still worried in case Felicia's cousins were down there defending the bridge. The fact that his father might be as well didn't concern him in the least.

"Yes," said the Carter peevishly. "They'm too jagged for my liking. If they gets caught up in the net, they'll swing over and smash into the ground. Me cart could be hit by flying bits of stone. That's why we'm supposed to be wearin' helmets," he added quietly.

"Why not use muck?" Jack asked with the stink of it still in his head.

"Muck?" laughed the Carter. "You mean, load it up with muck? Nah! It'd slip out through the mesh."

"Not if we put it into ale-casks."

"That's a good 'un. *Hey, Sarge!*" The Carter waved to a soldier who was supervising the stone-gathering operations. "This lad suggests that we shoot sh-muck at 'em instead of rocks."

After giving his men leave to take a rest, the Sergeant marched across. "Did you say shmuck?"

"Yes," Jack said. "The latrine trench is full of it. It'd be easier to shift than the rocks and it won't destroy the bridge."

"After all," said the Carter, "once we've driven out Lancaster's men, we'll have to drag the Trebooshay's timbers over it. And the more it gets smashed up, the harder that'll be."

The Sergeant stroked his beard. "The King's grandfather tried using it at Kenilworth." He chuckled. "But because of the lakes that surround it, all they did was pollute the water for miles around. And anyway, I don't fancy the stink if we ever get down there."

"It won't be so bad for *us* as it would be for *them*," Jack countered quickly. "After all, it's our own muck."

"Very well," said the Sergeant, returning to the Carter. "Get some empty casks and fill 'em at the latrine."

As the Sergeant stomped away to rejoin the waiting stone-shifters, the Carter drew Jack to one side. "What did you have to go and suggest *that* for? How am I supposed to get turds through them little holes in the ale-casks?"

"Have you seen the latrine trench lately?" Jack couldn't resist a smirk. "All you'll need is a tundish and a ladle. And at least the poor buggers down there on the bridge won't get crushed."

"Just shat on from a great height," the Carter retorted as he turned away in disgust.

*

As Dawn began to light up the hillside, the firepots fell from the sky with greater frequency. Whether by accident or intention, one of them landed on a group of archers who were standing around and discussing Jack's latest idea. Hearing their laughter turn to shrieks of agony, those still active on the brow of the hill cast aside their bows and hurried to help their stricken comrades. Some of the victims escaped almost unscathed by beating out the flames on their clothing. Others tore off their clothes and stood shivering as urine was splashed on their naked bodies. While these were allowed to return to their tents, their less-fortunate mates lay screaming and writhing on the ground.

"Get back to your posts!" screamed the Sergeant. "And keep up the shooting. The monks can take care of this."

Clad in black robes, these arrived with poppy-juice and daggers at the ready, whichever was the more appropriate. And in an amazingly short length of time, the casualties had been born away, the remaining flames extinguished, and the steam and smoke dispersed by a freshening breeze. All that remained was a patch of blackened earth from which protruded the badly charred head of a practice arrow.

John Blunt had been hit.

His stomach churning, Jack hurried to the tent where the monks were now attending the wounded and dying. Along each wrinkled sidewall, men lay still beneath white linen sheeting. One of them tried to sit up, but screamed and fell back to writhe about in agony.

"John?" Jack whispered. "Is that *you*?" The face was a blistered ruin of its former self.

"Arr," it groaned. "Willtow do me aaaaa...c-couple of f-favours?"

"Of course I will. What are they?"

"Will you tell my folks back home that I died honourably?"

"You're not going to die," Jack assured him, although it was obvious that his friend hadn't long to live. "What's the other one?"

"Stab me through the heart."

"I'll do the first but not the second. The monks will soon have you back on your feet again. They have to. You owe me money."

That was a mistake. The figure on the bed attempted a laugh, but cried aloud instead. After one great spasm, it lay still, its bloodshot eyes still focused on Jack's face.

"I'll deal with this now," a monk whispered into Jack's ear. And as he covered John's face with the sheet, he added: "We shall pray for him and the others at Compline."

If that was intended to give him comfort, it didn't work. Less than one hour previously, John had been full of life – a laughing, cursing, infuriating comrade, who often expressed his doubts about the legitimacy of this war. But now he was gone forever, leaving behind just a carcass of badly braised meat.

Jack headed back to his post a changed man – his spirit badly shaken. This war was supposed to bring honour and wealth, not agony and pointless death. But n*ow* it had become *personal. Now,* there were scores to settle.

*

It had been rumoured that a new commander had been appointed to direct the assault. And that Robert Waters was determined to make a name for himself, even if it killed them.

Before Jack could rejoin the archers, Waters arrived on horseback. Instead of dismounting, he stood tall in his stirrups and assessed the situation. He stared down at the bridge. He stared up at the Trebooshay. Then he stared down at the bridge again. After sliding nimbly down from the saddle, he beckoned his men to gather round.

"First," he cried, "I want that bloody Mangonel knocked out."

The Sergeant marched up to him and saluted. "They keep moving it," he said respectfully. "We can't see where it is because of the smoke. We are about to shower the bridge with casks of sh-muck so as not to cause too much obstruction when we've taken it."

"Have you gone *mad*?"

"It was *his* idea," the Sergeant said, staring hard at Jack.

"No!" cried Waters. "Use the rocks. Have you got the range?"

"Not yet," the Sergeant admitted, "but it won't take long."

"I want it done now," Waters screamed. "Our men are in position down there and getting ready to launch a frontal attack. The rest of you, get back to your posts."

But as the other archers went to resume their places on the brow of the hill, Jack held back to see the Trebooshay in action.

To the "click, click, click" of the windlass ratchet, the long end of the arm was hauled down towards the ground. Once there, it was secured with a hook on a length of chain. The net was then laid out along a channelled plank and one of the rocks placed in it.

"Let her go!" screamed the Sergeant.

Released by a tug on the securing-hook's chain, the arm swung up and over – the loaded net flying out in a wider arc from its end. Having passed above the pivot, one of the net's ropes detached itself and the rock was launched out towards the bridge. Jack smiled with recognition as the missile hurtled into the valley. This was just a mechanical version of a sling that he'd used as a boy when driving crows off their neighbour's fields.

Now that the Trebooshay had performed its task, its arm swung wildly back and forth above the pivot – its ropework flailing and lashing the rocking shaft. Jack turned to see where the rock was going to land, but it had vanished into the smoke that enveloped the gatehouse. Nevertheless, he distinctly heard a 'thump' as it hit *soft* ground.

"It's fallen short!" Waters shrieked. "Put more lead into the weight-box." While the operators waited for the arm to stop swinging, the Carter went to fetch his cart from where he'd parked it.

On the right hand side of the gatehouse, a point of scarlet light gleamed through the smoke.

"There's your Mangonel," Waters screamed. "You can see where it is. I want it taken out NOW! Forget about the extra lead, and use the next groove on the left."

"Use that round rock over there," the Sergeant commanded, pointing to one that was markedly heavier than the first.

"And be quick about it," Waters shouted.

With much frantic activity, the arm was hauled down again and the net loaded up with the rock. The restraining hook was pulled, the arm swung up and over, and the rock flew out and down towards the smoke. The point of light flared-up in a blaze of incandescence. The Mangonel was self-cremating with its pot of burning tar.

"Right," Waters shouted above the ecstatic whoops of his men. "Now concentrate on the entrance to the bridge. And *now* you can put more lead into the weight-box." He turned suddenly on Jack. "What are you loafing about here for? Have you no work to do?"

"Yessir," Jack replied hastily. "Just going, Sir."

"Going where, soldier?"

"Back to the archers."

"I'll come with you then."

Together they made their way to the ragged line of archers. The hillside was now peppered with smouldering craters, as though the inside of it was on fire and the smoke was belching out through scores of holes.

"What a bloody mess," Waters roared. "Somebody, go and fetch the ale-cart."

"Beg pardon, Sir," whispered the Sergeant, who'd followed on behind. "But did you say what I thought you said?"

"I did. There's to be a constant supply of small-ale issued to these men."

As soon as the ale-cart arrived, Waters leaped up onto its footboard and called the archers around him. "This beer has been donated by the locals," he shouted. "It might not be as good as monks' ale, but it's the best they have until we get rid of Lancaster's robbers. They say that the sooner we do it, the better they'll like it. Get drinking, men."

The cheering was heard from miles around, so it must have been heard by the guardians of the bridge.

While mugs and tankards were filled from large wooden barrels, Waters called out over his cheerful men: "You know what to do...fill your buckets with piss and use it to douse the fires. Meanwhile, carry on shooting."

Waters' plan worked. The combination of fear and over-distended bladders ensured that the buckets were quickly filled and the fires brought under control.

With a diaper protecting his nose, Waters marched back and forth among his men, urging them to keep up a constant stream of arrows on the bridge below. At length, he stopped pacing, picked up an empty bucket, and banged on its base with the pommel of his sword.

"Attehn...*shun*," he bellowed, gasping at the stench. "I'm going down into the valley to take charge of the assault. (Gasp) Carry on shooting until you hear a blast from our horns. (Gasp) Then advance down the hill, releasing arrows as you go. And I want no loosing-off all over the place. Our footsoldiers will be advancing from the left, so I want only careful aiming. Take your time and pick your man carefully."

"Can we take the Pavise shields to protect us?" an archer asked.

"What? These?" Waters launched a kick at one of the man-sized shields. It hardly moved. "That's quite impracticable. Your Aketons should give you enough protection."

"They say as Robin Hood is down there," someone muttered, but loud enough for Waters to overhear.

"That's just a rumour," Waters shouted, "that's being spread about to frighten you. Ignore it." Taking charge of his horse, he vaulted up into the saddle. "Good luck!" he cried as he rode off towards the path that would take him down into the valley.

Silence fell along the line of archers. Because of their elevation, the enemy arrows always fell short. But this wouldn't be the case when they got lower down on the hill.

Slowed down by his painful wound, Jack was going to be an easy target.

Trebooshay

CHAPTER 10

All too soon, the signal-horns blared out and the archers began to descend the rock-strewn hillside. Below and from the left, Waters' soldiers surged along the riverbank with swords and lances held ready for tasting blood. Although the bridge's defenders tried to repel them with crossbow bolts and arrows, the attackers were not to be deterred. They had scores to settle, vengeances to wreak.

The ditches surrounding the gatehouse formed barriers of fire – until the Trebooshay sent barrels of urine plunging down into them. Among the reeking fumes, barn doors were flung across the embers and to the clashes of contesting swords, the enemy were driven slowly onto the bridge.

As one of the line of archers, Jack targeted his arrows on enemy soldiers as he picked his way downhill among the boulders. Hampered by his hip, he was gradually left behind, but the others joined together to maintain the line. An archer who'd stepped in front of him sagged silently to the ground and Jack immediately experienced a blow in the middle of his chest. Staggering backwards under the impact, he stared in horror at the blood-spattered hole in his surcoat. He'd been hit. But why was he still standing? If he was dead, why did he feel just the same? He probed the painful spot with fearful fingers and gasped with surprise and relief at what he found there. The hauberk was intact beneath the surcoat. The rings there were distorted but still unbroken. He wasn't dead after all. He wasn't even wounded.

"Thank you for the hauberk," he murmured to his absent Gran. "You've stopped that arrow from killing me."

He eyed it as it lay beside his feet. Its head was broad and barbed for killing horses. Thank God it wasn't a Bodkin for piercing maile. The shaft was thicker than any that he'd seen before, so the bow that had propelled it must be powerful, and the archer who'd drawn it, mighty. Could the most famous bowman in England be down there on the bridge? As far as Jack knew, Robin Hood was still residing in Share-wood Forest. Nevertheless, a bow of such great strength could explain his legendary prowess at the butts.

Two of Jack's fellow archers were raising their stricken comrade to a sitting position, blood spurting from a hole in the middle of his back. The arrow had gone right through him before slamming into Jack's chest. If he hadn't got in the way, Jack's hauberk couldn't have stopped it.

When the spurts of blood petered-out, his helpers laid him gently on the ground and hurried to take their places in the line. But as their descent of the hill resumed, Jack hung back with fear and foreboding. Lancaster's archer now had his position and range, but he wasn't nimble enough to take evasive action. He steeled himself for the shock of sudden death. But instead of finding himself blasted into eternity, he felt a frantic tugging on his sleeve. Jack slowly turned his head, expecting to see the Grim Reaper at his side. But it wasn't the Angel of Death that stood beside him; a dishevelled boy peered up with fearful eyes. His message was the usual one: "The Baron wants you." And as he turned to go, he added quietly: "He said for you to get your horse and don't forget his banner."

*

John de Somery sat perched on his great white destrier; his expression as dark and threatening as a thundercloud.

"Where the hell have you been?" he demanded. Eyeing Jack's blood-spattered surcoat, his frown softened slightly. "You've been hit," he said, looking Jack up and down. "But you don't seem badly hurt. How can this be?"

"My grandmother's hauberk saved me."

Wheeling his horse around the Baron called over his shoulder: "Follow me. If we don't get there in time, the battle will be over."

A word of encouragement would have been nice, Jack thought as he spurred his smaller steed in pursuit of his master.

*

When the Baron and his banner-bearer arrived at the river Trent, the crossing of the King's army's had begun. Men with poles were stationed at intervals across the ford, showing its limits and the depth of water flowing over it.

Ignoring the other horsemen, the Baron drove his mount down the muddy bank and into the speeding water. With her strong and sturdy legs, she breasted the current with ease − spray foaming around her chest like a ship under sail. After only a brief pause, Jack's lesser mount followed on behind. Dragged sideways by the current, she managed to struggle across to the Burton side of the river.

With Jack still in his wake, the Baron rode up to a group of mounted knights who had assembled on a nearby hilltop. But by the time he reached them, they'd begun to form a line abreast on either side of the King. Astride his great white charger, the monarch was staring at the rise in the land that hid the town of Burton from his view. A gilded coronet encircled his pointed bascinet and his tabard gleamed with glimmering threads of gold. These made him a prominent target for an enemy archer, but there were no bushes close enough to offer concealment. Nevertheless, any of the knights around him could be a traitor in false heraldry. One quick stab or slash could result in Lancaster gaining the throne. The Baron may have thought so too, for he chose a place in the line not far from the King.

Twisting round to confirm that Jack was still behind him, the Baron roared for his Helm.

"I can't get close enough," Jack shouted back. "Sire," he added out of fear of giving offence. With a manoeuvre that Jack hadn't seen before, the Baron sidestepped his horse towards the one on his immediate right.

"Have a care," its rider bellowed — immediately doing likewise. Jack now had a clear way through to the side of his master. Driving the banner-pole into the ground, he retrieved the helm from his saddlebag and held it out with trembling hands. For although he'd polished it to sparkle with unblemished splendour, tiny spots of rust already besmirched the steel. After noting this with obvious disfavour, the Baron lowered it carefully over his head. He then hauled his shield around onto his left shoulder — its two blue lions seeming eager for enemy throats. "Now hold my banner upright," he demanded.

Jack tugged its pole out of the ground and slipped its heel back into its socket. Then he peered at the distant skyline like all the others. Lancaster's men were nowhere to be seen. On either side, the mounted knights were raring for the forthcoming battle — their heraldic surcoats covering maile and polished sheet armour. The horses' colourful caparisons fluttered like ladies' dresses as the highly-strung beasts attempted to break from the line. A distant murmur grew louder as a single knight rode up along the front of it. Even at a distance, Jack recognised the heraldry on his tabard, now pressed against a hauberk of platelets by the back draught. Hugh de Spenser had come to claim a place beside his King. But instead of doing so – as everyone there expected – he slid down from his horse and flung himself onto the ground.

"MY GRACIOUS LORD," he shouted in the sudden silence. "I BEG THEE NOT TO UNFURL THE ROYAL STANDARD." He raised himself up onto one knee, adopting what he apparently thought to be a striking pose. "That would unleash the scourge of Civil War upon this nation."

The King stared silently down at him.

De Spenser struggled to his feet. "The men who oppose us are not traitors," he continued undeterred. "They're just obeying your cousin's orders and do not merit the penalties for Treason."

"Yes," the Baron murmured, not realising that Jack could overhear him. "If Civil War *does* break out, many castles and manors will be destroyed. That would leave fewer for *you* to get your greedy hands on."

The riders held their breaths and their horses stopped pawing the ground. And in the stillness of that pregnant moment, all eyes were turned towards the King. Instead of answering De Spenser's entreaty, he turned towards his herald and nodded his royal head. And as his (still-furled) Standard was raised aloft, three trumpet-blasts blared out loud and shrill.

Jack had never heard a sound like that before. Nor had his little horse. She bolted, breaking out of the line and heading for the unseen enemy. Leaning back against the reins and with his heels thrusting into the stirrups, Jack struggled in vain to check the animal's headlong flight. With his banner streaming out above his head, they hurtled up the hillside towards the town. Behind them, three more trumpet-blasts sounded, followed by the long drawn-out roar of an army surging forward. With his ears filled with the thunder of pounding hooves, Jack snatched a glance over his shoulder. Stretching away on both sides like a multi-coloured bow-wave, a horde of charging knights galloped behind him. Some bore lances upright and proud; others couched low and deadly. A few swung maces to the peril of themselves and everyone around them. Still others held their swords held out above their horse's plunging necks. And all of them were yelling their heads off. Jack's own little steed seemed to be stimulated by the chase, for her fearful flight became charging like the others. A knight in red-striped heraldry came thundering up on Jack's left side, obviously intent on trying to take the lead. But weighed down by heavy plate armour, his destrier remained in second place to Jack's lighter and fleeter steed. Seeming to enjoy the chance of showing off, she veered to the left and the right to make sure of staying in front.

Jack had no choice but to let her have her head. If she stumbled and fell now, they would both be trampled to death.

Past Burton Abbey they galloped, funnelling into the main street and thundering between the houses without thought for the citizens or their chattels. With no room for overtaking, Jack remained at the head of that galloping host as it raced along the street towards the bridge. He was getting glimpses of this now between the houses, its row of round-headed arches confronting a flood of foaming waters. And as he left the town behind, he could see that it had a large and square-built gatehouse on *this* side of the river. Surely, this was the wrong end to fortify in normal circumstances? But in these *abnormal* times, it could stand firm against a host of charging horsemen.

A stream of well-armed soldiers came rushing from this gatehouse – possibly driven out by Waters' onslaught. With no way of defending himself, Jack kept on hurtling forward, holding his banner up and praying for a miracle.

He got it. As an obvious non-combatant, Lancaster's men had no time to waste on *him*. Ignoring him completely, they lowered their spears and bills to meet the charging riders. The knight on Jack's left screamed horribly as a pole-weapon pierced his breastplate. Thrown bodily from his saddle, he fell heavily to the ground. And while he was set upon with knives and swords, his horse was trampling on anyone in her way.

Spurred on by the clamour around her, Jack's little horse sped onward, cleaving a way through the soldiers like a boat's prow through a reed-bed.

Which is what she ended-up doing – skidding down the riverbank into reeds and icy water. Whinnying with shock and terror, she tried to struggle back towards the shore. But the river had her in its grip – tugging at her legs as she scrabbled to get a purchase on the bottom. The out-pouring from the nearest arch wasn't speeding on down the valley like the others. Separated by a rocky outcrop, it swirled leftwards into a backwater. Circling counter-sunwise, it swept the horse and rider towards their deaths in the foaming rip-runs of the river.

CHAPTER 11

Jack gazed longingly at the shore as it sped past. Could he swim that temptingly short distance to the bank? His hauberk shouldn't sink him; with its tiny flattened rings, it was lighter than the 'Standard Issue'. But no. The current was too strong for him to risk it.

As panic threatened to overwhelm him, Jack got a tighter grip on his nerves and on the banner-pole. Lifting the iron-shod heel of the shaft from out of its shoe, he drove it down through the water and into the riverbed. His horse slammed into the pole, the impact almost forcing the shaft from his grip. Nevertheless, it had halted her sideways slide towards the torrents roaring out from beneath the arches. But he couldn't hold on for long. Just as his freezing fingers were loosening their hold on the slippery pole, the pressure on them slackened slightly. The flow from the nearest arch was now subsiding – as though something was blocking it off on the up-stream side. And as the outpourings from the others increased accordingly, the strength of the swirling whirlpool pool died away. Jack's frantic little horse could now make headway against the current. Her frantic hooves struck bottom and soon she was standing shakily in the shallows. With no desire to push his luck still further, Jack stopped her from clambering up and onto the bank. The battle was still raging there, and he was quite content to watch from comparative safety.

Those mounted knights who had penetrated the thicket of spears were wreaking havoc with their swords. Bending low from their saddles, they hacked furiously at the helmets of their foes. The roar of the initial attack had given way to the clash of steel on steel as the two bodies of men struggled for supremacy. A shout rang out above the din of battle: "Caltrops". Someone had scattered those spiky things on the ground. Horses reared and bucked, neighing with pain and toppling their riders backwards from their saddles. But Lancaster's soldiers were no longer pouncing upon them with swords and daggers. The leather soles of their boots gave little or no protection against the inch-high iron spikes. Men and horses began prancing about as though in some grotesque dance. The sound of battle changed again – the clash of steel replaced by screams of agony. With horses trampling friend and foe alike, men of both sides came leaping into the water. After helping one another to remove Caltrops from their boots, they then stood watching in silence as the battle raged above them.

Three blasts from a horn rang out above the melee. With the defence of the bridge now futile, the Lancastrians broke ranks and ran, falling over one another in their eagerness to escape. The battle for Burton Bridge was lost and won.

Caltrop

*

As soon as it seemed safe to do so, Jack allowed his horse to carry him up onto dry land.

It wasn't dry any more. Corpses lay sprawled in crimson mud, and the reek of blood and ordure hung in the air. Monks had arrived to attend to the wounded and dying. But apart from a few soldiers that were stripping the bodies of armour, the recombined contingents of the King's great army were chasing Lancaster's garrison through the town. Flaming torches were being tossed up onto its rooftops – the smoke and steam from their smouldering thatch concealing the retreat.

With his wet clothes freezing on his body, Jack was content to watch them go. One of the Scavengers noticed him shivering. "There's some dry clothes over there," he said and pointed to a pile of them nearby. "Help yourself."

"Thanks," Jack said as he selected a tunic and tights not drenched with blood. A quick stripping off, a brisk towelling down, a hasty donning of clothes and Jack was beginning to feel more like himself again.

"Right!" John de Somery bellowed as he rode up behind his banner-bearer. "God alone knows what you were playing at back there." He laughed aloud as Jack stared back at him blankly. "Thank God the King didn't get the chance to unfurl his Royal Standard." He thumped his servant mightily on the back. "Jack!" he roared cheerfully. "Do you know what you've just done? You've only prevented a full-blown Civil War!" Spurring his horse into a trot, he added grimly: "Lancaster will be securing his castle at Tutbury. Come along with me, and hold my banner up straight for everyone to see."

*

Feeling that he had earned a place among the King's horsemen, Jack carried the Baron's banner proudly as they rode in pursuit of the enemy. Alongside them ran the footsoldiers – swords at the ready for use at any moment. However, the only traces of Lancaster's army were bodies by the roadside. And no townspeople came out to greet them...no shouts of welcome, and no smiling wenches to delight his eyes and warm his heart. In fact, the only sign of life was the horrified face of a wizened old man who shrank back from an upstairs wind-eye. And soon, the riders were out in open countryside once more.

*

It was late afternoon when they reached the town of Tutbury. It was even bigger than Coventry, but just as deserted as Burton. On leaving the outskirts behind, the towers of Lancaster's castle appeared above them, his colours flying proudly above their battlements. At the base of its hilltop eyrie, the gaping doors of a gatehouse gave access to a gully leading upwards. Although the defile was the obvious place for an ambush, Jack and his companions climbed up without encountering opposition. On either side of the top, a fenced enclosure was crammed with sullen prisoners.

With his comrades surging past him like water round the piers of Burton Bridge, Jack gawped at the stronghold of one of the most powerful men in England.

Fronted by a deep, dry moat, the hill rose even higher – its flat crest crowned with a massive stretch of curtain wall. This was strengthened at intervals by the towers that Jack had seen from below. And from their quivering flagstaffs, Lancaster's flags were being lowered.

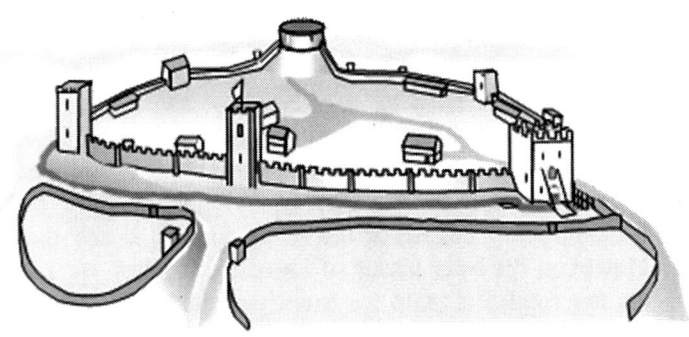

Tutbury Castle

Unlike the castle at Dudley, Tutbury's didn't have a Donjon. But they both had a square-built gatehouse on the right side of its Bailey. Both were three stories tall and equipped with Drawbridge and Portcullis.

Although Jack's fellow soldiers were being herded across that drawbridge, he'd been ordered to stay outside to await the Baron's orders. Sliding down from his weary horse, he tethered her beside the trough that stood beside it. After stowing his helmet away in one of his saddlebags, he thrust his coif back off his head to savour the cooling breeze. It was coming from a stout iron grill that blocked the right end of the moat. From there, the land sloped steeply down to a plain that stretched away to distant hills. It reminded him of the view from Dudley Castle, but with a ribbon of bright water meandering across the middle. A spark of light flashed briefly beside that river, as though a lant-horn flap had been opened and snapped shut.[5]

When it was not repeated, Jack stood gazing at the scene below him and recalling the chain of events that had brought him to that place.

After helping to deliver a cartload of ale to Dudley Castle, he and his Gran had been forced to work in its bakehouse. Then clapped in the Stocks for stealing, they'd been freed by a bunch of knaves who wanted him to teach them how to fight the castle's garrison. When he'd pointed-out their foolishness, they'd threatened to kill them both until Gran had suggested delivering a petition to the Baron. He'd managed to do that for 'em, and then got 'em to rout an attack on that castle. (Awakened by the memory of the combat in the woods, the wound that he'd sustained throbbed with increased vigour.) The Baron had granted him a pardon, and he'd married the Steward's daughter. But with Felicia's constant nagging and the bawling of their son, he'd jumped at the chance of enrolling in the King's army. This had led to him inadvertently leading the charge on Burton Bridge, and thence to Lancaster's stronghold, staring over the darkening landscape and wondering what would happen to

---

[5] Three chests full of Lancaster's coins were lost in the River Dove. They weren't found until 1831.

him next? And if he would meet the challenge of whatever was still to come?

An icy blast came whistling through the grill, reminding him of the Baron's anger if he was found missing from his post.

*

Fortunately, John de Somery hadn't yet arrived at the gatehouse. Just visible through its long and shadowed passageway, a single round tower stood perched on a distant mound. So Tutbury *did* have a Donjon after all. Dark against the glow of the setting sun, its arrow-loop wind-eyes glimmered like fiery crosses. The Baron was probably up there now, enjoying Lancaster's food and wine. A sudden pang of hunger added its discomfort to that of the throbbing in Jack's side. And judging by the sounds of merriment coming up the passage, there was no shortage of either in the courtyard that lay beyond it. Surely he was entitled to some sustenance himself?

Laying his banner-pole on the ground, Jack clomped across the drawbridge and through the portcullised archway of the gatehouse. Unlike the passage at Dudley, this one had a guards' room on the left. After making sure that there was no one in there, he scurried to the inner doorway and peered out. The courtyard was thronged with carousing men, all munching on pies and quaffing from foaming tankards. But as he stepped out to join them, he heard something 'click' behind him. Fearing a crossbow bolt in his back, he took shelter behind the doorjamb. But when nothing further had happened after several heartbeats, he peered into the passage. There was nobody there. And the only sound was of rowdiness in the courtyard. Was the Baron outside on the drawbridge – stamping his boot with impatience? Deciding that his master was the greater of two evils, Jack drew his sword and crept cautiously up the passageway. He hadn't gone far when a square patch of light appeared beside his feet.

A trapdoor had been raised in the flat wooden ceiling. Fearing a downpour of hot oil, Jack flattened himself against the left-hand wall of the passage. But instead of scalding liquid, something solid was being lowered through the murder-hole. It was a chest – about three feet long and channelled along the sides for the use of lifting poles. Suspended on two ropes, it swayed from side to side as it descended...each swing taking slightly longer than the last. At six feet from the floor, it halted – swaying and twisting ponderously on its ropes. Jack shook with the shock of sudden recognition. It looked like the chest that was stolen from Dudley Castle. Could it *really* be the same one? That would be too much of a coincidence. But was it? After all, one of the robbers had called himself Merlin and Jack had heard that the Earl of Lancaster liked to style himself after King Arthur. Merlin and King Arthur? Was there a connection?

This chest was also covered with burnished bronze, now flushed with crimson by the light from the open doorway. And at each rotation, an engraved shield flashed briefly on one end. Two lions 'Passant'. Facing to the left. So it *was* the Baron's chest, and judging by the way that it was swinging, it was still full of his money.

Jack stiffened. If he could get it back, that might atone for him allowing it to be stolen. But as he pondered on how this might be accomplished, an armoured knight strode in from the Inner Bailey. Leading a large black destrier by the reins, he marched over to the chest and halted its swings and roundabouts. After a hurried look behind him, the knight hauled the chest across the horse's withers. Using severed lengths of the slackening ropes, he lashed the chest to the saddlebow.

Jack's blood ran cold. As the man moved quickly and silently about his business, iron platelets gleamed like fish-scales on his chest. Even without his heraldic surcoat, there was no mistaking *Hugh de Spencer*.

Jack sidled along the sidewall until he was opposite the guards' room. If he tried to cross the passage, he'd be seen against the fading light from the open doorway. And if he managed to get to the doors without being seen, he'd be visible crossing the drawbridge. Jumping into the moat was not an option; it was a long way down to its forest of sharpened stakes.

By continuing his crabwise progression along the wall, he came to a shadowed space behind the door. But as he squeezed himself into it, the hinges groaned in protest.

Hugh de Spenser looked up sharply – his helmet *ringed about with a crimson halo*. Could Adrasteus have come to claim him? Or was it merely a cloud lit up by the setting sun?

Jack shrank further into the shadow, hoping that he hadn't been seen. But not only had he been seen – he'd been recognised.

"*You,*" the knight snarled as he vaulted up into his saddle and drew his sword.

Spurring his horse into sudden motion, the knight hurtled down the passage – his sword held high and ready to strike Jack dead.

CHAPTER 12

With the clatter of galloping hooves filling the passageway, De Spenser drove his horse towards his intended victim. After leaning briefly to his right, the knight swung his sword over to slash down on Jack's unprotected head. But with De Spencer being right-handed: it proved to be a difficult blow, especially since Jack was shielded by three inches of English Oak. Instead, the weapon sliced a two-foot long splinter from the edge of the door, and almost wrenched the handgrip from his grasp. Then he was gone. However, both the knight and his mount were experts at manoeuvring in tight places. Halting halfway across the drawbridge, the horse began to reverse back into the gatehouse. But by the time it reached Jack's hiding place, he'd scuttled off down the passage and was lost among the throng of carousing men.

With a scream of frustration and rage, De Spenser thundered back onto the drawbridge, his parting words echoing down the passage: "*I shall get thee yet*!"

"Not if Adrasteus gets you first," Jack muttered from the anonymity of the crowd.

As soon as it seemed safe enough to do so, Jack crept back up the passage and peered out through the archway. Hugh de Spenser was nowhere to be seen. And on learning that he'd ridden off down the defile, Jack returned to his allotted post beside the moat.

*

Jack seemed to have been waiting for ages when the Baron's great horse came clattering across the drawbridge.

"Tomorrow, we ride south," he announced as he drew rein beside his servant. "In the meantime, you can return to camp." As Jack struggled to pull himself together, the Baron added in a calmer tone of voice: "The Earl of Lancaster will be heading for his castle at Pontefract. Pray inform our Trebooshay people that the King wants it taken up there without delay. When you've done that, you can turn in. But be back here by daybreak tomorrow." He laughed mirthlessly. "And don't forget my banner. We've been ordered to capture Kenilworth for the King."

"Yes, Sire," Jack replied, saluting smartly. Should he tell his master about De Spenser and the chest? No. That would call attention to his own part in the theft. In any case, with the prospect of storming another castle, it seemed to be of less importance now.

*

On re-entering Burton town, Jack's sense of pride turned to one of shame. The townsfolk were still in hiding, so no one cried out in protest as belongings were carried away by gleeful soldiers.

While Jack gaped round in dismay, his horse was keeping her head down to avoid the scattered shards of broken pottery.

"Watch where you'm a-going," someone bellowed from in front. They'd blundered into 'Nutcracker' – the now blood-spattered maul lying across his left shoulder – a leg of mutton resting on the other. "Well, I'll be…" he laughed. "If it ain't that archer of De Somery's."

"Where did you get that meat from?" Jack demanded, reining his horse back and turning her to ride alongside.

"Out of one of them cottages." Nutcracker turned his head to bite the stolen meat.

"But these people aren't our enemies," Jack protested.

Nutcracker spat out a gobbet of gristle. "They'm Lancaster's ain't they?" He grinned widely, revealing a mouth full of chewed-up meat. "So go an' 'elp yerself. Yer won't get into trouble. It's only the lawful fruits of war."

Jack felt a sudden chill of horror. "You're leaving the women alone, aren't you?"

"There ain't any. They've all buggered off. Not that I'm all that bothered." He spat out another blob of gristle. "Personally, I would rather have a good stiff meal." After giving Jack's leg a slap, he marched off into the crowd.

*

Even more disheartened and ashamed, Jack rode slowly along the length of Burton Bridge – its stonework shuddering as the floodwaters roared beneath it. Once more he saluted the men who'd designed and built it. Nevertheless, its roadway was too curved to allow the Trebooshay's beams to be hauled along it. Well, that wasn't *his* problem. *His* was just trying to stay alive.

Outside the bridge's entrance, broken arrows lay strewn upon the ground – crushed and splintered by the feet of fighting men. Among them lay loose arrowheads – sundered from their shafts by the shock of sudden impact. Sliding down from his horse, he gathered these into his quiver. He would bore them out and resharpen them before gluing them onto new shafts. Of course, it would be easier to tug unbroken arrows from the corpses that lay nearby, but their ghosts might come and wreak vengeance on him as he slept.

Nearby, a burnt wooden frame was all that remained of the Mangonel that killed his friend and fellow archers. Beside it stood a huge crossbow, mounted on a pedestal and aimed up at the hilltop. The bow was drawn – the Bolt still in its groove. Jack squinted along its length, to a place on the hill *where he'd been hit by a similar arrow*.

"So *that's* the Robin Hood," he murmured, remounting his horse and riding her through the smoke that stank of urine.

On arriving back at the encampment, he patted his weary horse before passing her to the groom who knew her well. And after watching her being attended to, he ensured that she was content among her kind.

*

As dawn broke on the following morning, Jack arrived outside the gatehouse of Tutbury Castle. Together with another knight, the Baron was assembling foot soldiers for the trek to Kenilworth Castle. And because the other knight hadn't got a banner, Jack was ordered to ride behind the two horsemen as they set out at the head of their marching war band. But instead of heading south as Jack expected, they took the road that led to the city of Lichfield. Although this took them well out of their way, it was as straight as an arrow and its surface was free of potholes. And in order to forestall an ambush or a sniper, the ground on either side had been cleared of trees and bushes for a distance greater than a bowshot. So progress was smooth and uneventful ... and soon became monotonously boring.

However, from his position behind the knights, Jack could eavesdrop on their conversations. Thus he learned of their uncertainty about the morality of their mission – and that their oaths of fealty to the King had been pledged in the presence of God and could never be broken.

Another respite from the boredom occurred when the locals gave them a half-hearted cheer as they rode past. Most of the time they were downcast and eloquently silent. Sometimes, a child would run to meet them with a begging bowl held out hopefully. But the nobles pretended not to notice and Jack cursed them under his breath. He'd had to beg like that himself and knew how awful it was. He always tossed a few coins down to the child when he thought that no one was looking – and far enough away to ensure that the soldiers marching behind him could not snatch them.

Although the troop encountered no armed resistance, it took most of the day to reach their destination. After setting up camp on the outskirts of the city, they resharpened the damaged weaponry − partook of their evening meal − and then made sure that the horses were fed and rested.

By daybreak on the following morning, they'd had everything packed away and the soldiers formed into line once more. Jack had been hoping that the plan had been changed and they'd keep on going towards Dudley. But this was not to be. Instead, they took a second straight road that led them roughly southwards. After camping overnight where the road turned sharply left, they headed at last in the general direction of Kenilworth.

*

Bypassing the city of Coventry, they rode through the centre of Kenilworth and then *downhill* with a view of Lancaster's Castle. For unlike those at Tutbury and Dudley, this was in the middle of a lake. The island on which it stood was surrounded with walls of blood-red stone, with a Donjon of similar masonry in the middle. Above that massive edifice, Lancaster's flag hung limply from its pole, a speck of scarlet and gold against the lake's reflected greyness of the sky.

A second Outer Bailey had been constructed on the mainland, with a curtain wall and moat for its protection. Connecting these two great strongholds, a hundred yards long causeway stretched arrow-straight across the lake, its sides protected by battlemented walls and its ends by twin-towered gatehouses. It was said to be impregnable − holding out against the King's grandfather for six whole months. And *he*'d been using Trebooshays and barges. So with much fewer men at the Baron's disposal, he was in no position to mount an all-out assault. All that he could do for the present was to post guards around the lake and wait for the defenders to be starved into submission. But since the castle would be well stocked with food and weaponry, this was likely to be a long and drawn-out siege.

*

Several days passed uneventfully. With no banner-waving duties to perform, Jack was assigned to keeping watch on the causeway, using his bow to harass any traffic that might be travelling along it. In between times, he amused himself by taking pot shots at the ducks.

Nothing much was happening. To his left, the unbroken surface of the lake stretched away to a distant shore. A furlong to the front, the main part of the castle was reflected in the surface of the water. The causeway lay a hundred yards on his right. And although it was bordered with battlemented walls, it reminded him of the one that crossed the lake at Dudley Priory. When he'd gone to beg for Sanctuary there, he'd thought how strong was its location. But when he'd seen it in the daylight, he'd realised that it was built on sloping land – its lake held back by a series of dams and sluices. An attacker had only to break those down and the water would drain away into the valley. Jack scanned the scene before him with heightened interest. Could Kenilworth's lake have a dam somewhere? If so, could it be breached? Probably not, for the King's grandfather would undoubtedly have thought of it. Dismissing the subject from his mind, Jack settled down to keeping his wearisome watch.

Although Lenten was far off, the warmth of the midday sun was lulling him into a state of listless lethargy. *This would not do.* It would be just his luck for the defenders to break out while he was dozing in the windless silence. Even the reeds were motionless. To keep himself awake, he tried to bend one over with his thoughts. But no matter how hard he tried, he could not move it. He'd never thought that he could.

Picking up his bow, he nocked an arrow to the string and sent it soaring across the lake and down behind the battlements of the causeway. He waited for a scream of pain that did not come.

More time dragged by. His thoughts about the lake returned. They all had to have an outlet somewhere, whether by stream or river. There *must* be a way of draining the water out of this one. He'd mention that possibility to the Baron when he got the chance. Jack was still congratulating himself on his cleverness when he saw a horseman riding rapidly along the lakeside. On arriving at Jack's position, the rider stopped.

"I have an important message for John de Somery," he bawled.

Jack pointed at the encampment on the distant hillside. "You see that golden tent? He should be there."

Without a word of thanks, the rider hurtled off. After leaving his horse at the fence that encircled the camp, he sprinted across to the Baron's gaudy pavilion.

Not long after that, the Baron's message-boy arrived with orders for Jack to go to a specified location beside the lake. He was to take the banner with him, and add a white flag of truce as he'd done at Burton.

After retrieving the banner from his tent, Jack tied a white rag to the pole. Then using that as a prop, he hobbled to the designated spot. Uncomfortably close to the smaller stronghold, it was well within the range of defenders' bows. So to give him some protection, a cart had been brought up and tipped onto its side.

John de Somery arrived on horseback – angry and impatient as was his wont. After ordering Jack to wave his flags from side to side, he faced the causeway, cupped his hands around his mouth and bellowed out over the water:

"HAIL, MEN OF KENILWORTH. THE EARL OF LANCASTER HAS BEEN CAPTURED AND EXECUTED. LAY DOWN YOUR ARMS."

After a short pause, a helmeted head appeared above the causeway's battlements.

"We don't believe you!" came the faint reply across the limpid surface of the lake.

"WILL YOU BELIEVE ME IF I SEND YOU PROOF?"

The enemy made no reply.

"I don't trust them," the Baron muttered as he slid down from his horse. "After what happened at Leeds Castle, they'll know what's in store for them if and when they're captured." He reached into his pouch. "Prepare an arrow to take this across to them."

On the Baron's outstretched palm, a gold ring glistened brightly – with a sparkling red jewel set in finely detailed workmanship. There was still dried blood in the grooves. "Slip this onto an arrow and drop it onto the causeway."

Although his Lord's expression forbade protesting, Jack's must have spoken volumes.

"You've done it before," the Baron snapped. "So you can do it again."

Jack propped the banner against the cart. "Yes, Sire," he mumbled, sick with apprehension, "but I haven't got any fire-arrows with me. Shall I go and get some?" He was hoping to find an excuse not to do it.

"There's no time for that. I've been away from Dudley for far too long. What else can you use?"

"I've been using *these* to bring down the wildfowl," Jack tugged a black-flighted arrow from his quiver, "but these crescent-heads are too big to slide the ring on. These others are no good either..." He drew out one with red flights. Although its barbed head was narrower than the crescent, it was still too wide to go inside the ring.

"What about the others?" the Baron demanded.

Jack selected one whose flights were streaked with mud. He'd recovered its head from outside Burton Bridge. "As you see, Sire...a ring will go over the Bodkin head all right, but there's nothing to stop it sliding off over the flights." Jack was certain, now, that the idea of using an arrow would be abandoned. But this was not to be.

"What about those with white flights then?"

"They are no good either."

"Why?"

"They have narrow barbed heads and long and slender shanks."

Jack had worked for the Netherton blacksmith as a boy, and watched him forging arrowheads just like that. They'd been quenched to make them rock-hard at their tips, and the shanks reheated and tempered to render these malleable. "When they go through the rings of a hauberk," the smith had said in answer to Jack's query, "they gets bent over and it stops 'em from droppin' out."

As Jack tugged one of these arrows from his quiver, it got snagged. It was the one with its head bent almost double by striking stonework on the slant. Jack had only kept it in case someday it might be useful – perhaps for carrying a line across a river.

"Although this one is damaged," he said as he wrenched the arrow out, "these are no better than the others." He tipped the remainder onto the ground.

"It's ideal for carrying the ring," the Baron growled, "if you bend the shank still further to trap it in place."

Blushing with shame and resentment, Jack took a pair of pincers from a pouch on the side of his quiver. After slipping the ring onto the U-shaped arrowhead, he bent the shank still further until the tip came into contact with the socket. He had to admit that the ring couldn't fall off now.

"Right!" said the Baron. "Now are you *sure* that you can drop it onto the causeway?"

"I'm not at all sure, Sire."

"Why? I've heard from your instructor that you're the best archer that we've got. And I am reliably informed that you've been dropping arrows onto the causeway all morning."

"I have, Sire," Jack admitted, flattered and appalled, "but I'm not sure how this arrow would fly."

"You managed it at Burton Bridge."

"Yes, Sire. But that was different. I only had to shoot the arrow towards the ramparts. If it had fallen short, or went too far, it wouldn't have made much difference." He squinted again at the causeway. "If I get the range wrong, the ring could end up in the water."

"There's some similar ones down there. Bend one over and use it as a test flight to make sure that you can do it. You will need a ring though." The Baron was staring at Jack's hand. "What's that on your finger? I haven't seen *that* before."

"I got it off somebody at Burton," Jack said, holding it out reluctantly.

"There's an 'F' engraved on it," the Baron pointed out.

"I thought that Felicia would like it."

"So you cut it off a dead man's finger?"

Jack blushed again, unsure if that was a crime. "I don't know if he was dead or not, but if he wasn't, he was in very deep sleep."

"It is of no matter. Proceed with the test."

Jack placed the arrow with Lancaster's ring safely in his quiver and examined the ones that were lying on the ground. To the Baron's great annoyance, he picked up each of these in turn. Eventually, he selected the one whose shaft was nearest in stiffness to the precious one. After slipping his own ring onto its head, he bent the shank to hold it on securely. And as he fitted it to the bowstring and drew back, the Baron turned towards the causeway. Cupping his hands around his mouth again, he bellowed:

"WE ARE SENDING YOU A PRACTICE ARROW FIRST."

'Thwack.'

Aiming high, Jack sent the arrow arcing over the water. It fell neatly behind the battlements of the causeway. This time there *was* a cry from the defenders: "This is my brother's ring. *YOU BLOODY MURDERERS CAN ALL GO TO HELL.*"

Jack blushed a third time. This time with horror.

"Never mind that," the Baron commanded. "Send them Lancaster's ring and be quick about it."

"I shall do my very b-best, Sire." Jack couldn't control the trembling in his voice. Doubting his ability to achieve what was required of him, he retrieved the precious arrow from the quiver. He fitted it carefully to the bowstring. He drew it back until the flights brushed against his chest. Aiming high towards the causeway, he adopted the same stance as before and: 'Thwack.'

His fingers released the bowstring without waiting for his command. The arrow soared into the air, its head sparkling with crimson as it followed the same trajectory as its predecessor. It curved over at its highest point, right on course to drop behind the battlements of the causeway.

Well it *was* on course, until a sudden gust of wind ruffled the surface of the lake.

Blown sideways in its descent, the arrow plopped into the water just short of the causeway.

Jack stared in horror at the ripples where it had vanished.

What the *hell* was he going to do *now*?

CHAPTER 13

Jack quailed as the significance of what had happened struck home. He'd just shot Lancaster's priceless ring into the lake. The outcome would be dire for him, and probably for the Baron as well.

"Don't worry, my Lord," Jack whispered, trying hard to convince himself that what he was about to say was true: "That arrow has a very stout shaft. It will float. It's got to. Yes, my Lord. I'm sure that it will float."

The Baron stood staring at the spot where the arrow had vanished – his fists clenched and his face now ashen with fury.

For the arrow showed no sign of floating to the surface.

He turned upon his minion.

"Do you know what you have done?" he hissed between clenched teeth. "Not only have you robbed the King of a most prized jewel, but you've also removed any chance of achieving a quick victory here. You are going to rue this day. That I promise you."

Jack said nothing, trying to avoid the Baron's glare. This wasn't easy, with his face close to his own and the stench of his spicy breath stinging his nostrils. "I shall have you flayed alive for this. Or worse."

Before Jack could stutter out more apologies, the Baron remounted his horse and was gone. Jack just stood there, staring hopefully across the lake in a turmoil of fear and uncertainty. He couldn't be blamed for a sudden gust of wind, could he? Of course he could. 'He should have allowed for that,' they would say. But the air had been quite still until the arrow began its descent. And wouldn't you know it? The wind had dropped now. In fact, the water lay as still and flat as it had been just moments before. So even from a distance, he could see that the arrow hadn't floated to the surface. As Jack wiped beads of sweat from his clammy forehead, the words of the magician came bursting into his mind: "*My spells use seemingly-natural causes.*"

Jack froze. What could be more natural than a gust of wind?

As Jack turned to pick up the banner-pole, a man's cry carried faintly across the lake.

Although indistinct in the distance, Jack recognised two words: "white flights…"

Heart pounding, Jack stared hopefully at the causeway. A guard was leaning over the battlements and pointing down to where the arrow had disappeared.

A door in the wall opened and a second guard emerged. After hurrying along the bank while stripping off his jerkin, he stepped gingerly down the slope and into the water. When about waist-deep, he dove – reappearing almost immediately with the arrow held triumphantly over his head. A spark of red flashed briefly. The ring was still in place. Thank Goodes' the arrow hadn't been deflected into the stonework. If the head had been snapped off by the force of the impact, the ring might never have been found.

By now, the diver had scrambled up the bank and was hurrying towards the doorway with the arrow carefully held against his chest.

Overjoyed but shameful, Jack hurried to the Baron's pavilion.

Fearful of entering, he stood beside the entrance flap and shouted: "Sire! Lancaster's men have recovered the arrow. They have the ring."

The flap was thrown back and the Baron's head protruded.

"What was that?"

"One of Lancaster's men dove down and got it. It was close to the bank and the water there was shallow."

For a moment, the Baron regarded him with doubtful eyes. Then his expression turned to one of relief. "You are *sure of this*?"

"Yes, Sire. I saw him carry the arrow up onto the causeway."

"And the *ring*?"

"Yes, Sire. I saw it glinting."

"Thank the Fates for that," the Baron mumbled. "Now get back to your post!"

*

Back beside the lake, Jack watched as Lancaster's colours were lowered from the Donjon's flagstaff. Not long after, he learned that the gates of the castle had been thrown open and the keys delivered into the Baron's eager grasp. Kenilworth Castle was in Royalist hands once more. However, this did not meet with everyone's approval. Because the defenders had surrendered without a fight, looting and raping were prohibited. And the men still hadn't been paid.

*

A few days later, Jack was summoned to the Great Hall of Kenilworth's Donjon.

The great block of blood-red stone towered above him as he climbed a staircase to a doorway in the wall. If the Great Hall lay beyond it, why was it dark in there? Taking an extra-deep breath, he stepped briskly over the threshold and marched into the shadows, sending a bucket clattering noisily over the flagstones.

"Who goes there?" somebody barked behind him.

Jack turned abruptly, reaching for his sword.

A guard in the same livery as himself had appeared as if from nowhere and was looking him up and down by the light of a flaming torch. "What d'yer want?" he demanded.

"I've been summoned to see Baron de Somery,"

"Oh him!" said the guard unconcernedly. "He's up on the first floor."

"I thought that this *was* the first floor," Jack said. "I've climbed up a flight of steps in order to get here."

"The hall's upstairs," the guard retorted.

"What is *this* then?" Jack said. "The basement?"

"That's right!" said the guard, and raised his torch aloft. "What d'yer think them are?"

Together with the usual barrels and foodstuffs, sheaves of bolts and arrows cluttered the floor, with racks of bows and pole-arms fixed to the walls. "If you must know," the guard continued, "you are standing on top of the old Motte." Seeing Jack's disbelief, he grinned. "I've been told that when they made this Donjon bigger, they enclosed the mound with thick stone walls and then carried on building upwards. Is there anything else that yer'd like ter know?"

"Yes," Jack replied, still looking round. "How am I supposed to get to the 'First' floor? I don't see any way up."

"See that door?" The guard was pointing his torch at an opening in the opposite wall. "The staircase is in there. The one on the right is where the well is."

As Jack began to thread his way among the provisions, the guard called after him: "Yow look as if yer could do with a drink." He nodded towards a doorway on the right side of the entrance that Jack had come in by. "I've got a barrel o' Lancaster's wine in there. Fancy a drop?"

"I could do with *something*," Jack admitted as he followed the guard into a room in the thickness of the wall.

"Sit yerself down," the guard ordered, and as Jack eased himself carefully onto a stool he nodded. "Did yer get that wound fightin' Lancaster's men?"

"No," Jack admitted. "Not exactly. But I did have to fight two soldiers who were trying to kill me."

The guard picked up an earthenware cup and filled it from a barrel.

"What happened?" he asked as he handed the vessel over.

"I knocked 'em out with my sword."

"What, both of em?"

"Arr."

"Good for you. Drink up now. There's plenty of wine and I can't drink it all meself." He raised a goblet that was already full. "Your very Good Health!"

"And *the same to* you!" Jack took a tentative sip from his cup and grinned. "This is very good," he said. "I've never tasted anything like it. What is it?"

"It's wine from Gascony."

"Well, wherever it's from…" Jack drained the cup in one continuous gulp and held it out at arm's length. "I'll partake of some more of that if you please."

"Certes," said the guard as he took the cup and carried it back to the barrel.

While the esteemed wine flowed slowly from the tap, Jack risked asking a question that had been troubling him for ages. "Can you tell me what this war is *really* all about? Everybody that I've asked just gives me a wink and a nod."

The guard shrugged. "It began when one of the Ordainers left his missus in charge of his castle while he was away. For reasons known only to herself, she refused to let the Queen in. Then urged on by his ownwife's fit of pique, the King fought his way inside and executed its defenders for High Treason."

"Was that *all it was*?" Jack spluttered, aghast at how one woman's lack of judgement could spark off a full-blown war.

"More or less," the guard said sadly. "Encouraged by his success, the King is attacking the other Ordainers one by one." He spat onto the ground. "To Hell with the lot of 'em, I say. They'm all as bad as one another. Drink up while there's still some wine left in the barrel."

*

Jack groped his way unsteadily up the staircase in Kenilworth's Donjon, enclosed in dark red stone that dampened his spirits. However, it may have been an effect of the wine, but his guilt about the wayward arrow had subsided. Instead, he now felt bitter about having to deliver Lancaster's ring in such a hazardous manner. And that heartfelt cry of *'murderers'* had shaken him badly...together with the revelation that all the killing and looting had been caused by one silly woman flouting another who wielded more power. With these weighing heavily on his mind, he arrived at last at a door of polished oak. His tentative knock sounded feeble, even in the close confines of the narrow staircase.

"Who's there?" The Baron's unmistakable voice had penetrated the heavy timber.

"It's Jack, Sire. Your banner-bearer. They said that you wanted to see me."

"Enter."

Jack entered the biggest and most palatial room that he had ever seen. Colourful tapestries adorned the rose-red stonework – made even more merry by fires that blazed in the walls.

John De Somery was scowling back at him from a carved and gilded throne. To his left, an iron stand supported his mud-stained banner. On a table beneath his right elbow, a large round pie lay steaming on a silver plate. "What kept you?" he roared – his usual manner of greeting.

"I came as soon as I got your command," Jack said, blushing at the lie.

"Don't stand there dithering."

Jack stepped hesitantly forward, taking care not to trip up on the threshold. As he approached the table, the Baron fixed him with his most hawk-like stare. "I put a lot of trust in you," he barked, "and you let me down badly. If Lancaster's men hadn't retrieved your arrow, I shudder to think what would have happened. What have you to say for yourself?"

"It wasn't my fault, Sire."

The Baron snorted. "Not *his* fault!" He drummed on the table with his fingers. "Well, whose fault was it then?!"

"A demon's," Jack blurted out. Because it was taking all of his self-control just to keep from wetting himself, his mouth felt free to say what it liked — heedless of the consequences.

"A *demon*?" roared the Baron, his face growing purple with rage.

"Yes, Sire."

"Give me strength. I'm surrounded by fools. And what sort of *demon* was it then? A wind-spirit?"

"No, Sire! A demon that I saw being summoned up at Coventry." He had no choice now but to continue: "I was...er...taking shelter in a byre next to one of the cottages."

"And is that the best excuse that *you* can summon up?" The Baron's face had twisted with contempt. "A demon pushed your arm as you shot the arrow. Is that it?"

"No, Sire! No *thing* pushed my arm. But there wasn't even a breath of wind when I released the arrow. If you remember, Sire, the lake was so still that the castle was clearly mirrored in its surface."

The Baron scratched his bearded chin and frowned. "Now that you mention it. I *do* remember that this was as you say. Lancaster's flag seemed to be hanging upside down on its pole."

"I could have allowed for a steady wind," Jack continued hastily, "or even a blustery one. But not a sudden gust that sprang from nowhere."

"I cannot deny that either. I have missed many a flying bird in similar circumstances. But what is this tale of demons that you are spinning me?"

"It is no tale, Sire. I *did* see a magician conjure up a demon from Hell. Well, I didn't actually *see* it. It was invisible. But I saw the magician send it out to kill the King and Hugh De Spenser...and also several others."

At the mention of his monarch, De Somery's expression hardened – his eyes alert and glistening. He nodded towards a three-legged stool that stood roasting beside a fire. "Bring that over here and sit down."

Encouraged by his master's interest, Jack fetched the stool and lowered himself onto the soothing warmth of its seat.

"Now tell me everything that you know." The Baron was obviously incredulous but now seemed slightly less reproachful.

"Can I speak freely, my Lord?"

"For Goodes' sake yes! I'm fed up with everybody pussy-footing around me as if I'm some sort of ogre."

Not daring to comment about *that*, Jack described the ceremony that he'd witnessed at Coventry – finishing with the assertion that apart from the King, the two De Spensers and the Prior of Coventry, he had no idea who the other intended victims might be.

The Baron listened in silence, waiting until Jack had finished before demanding: "Why didn't you report this at the time?"

So much had happened since then, that Jack wasn't sure why he *had* kept it to himself. "It wasn't my place to tell such tales to the Lord of the Manor," he said truthfully.

"Why didn't you tell your commanding officer?"

"With respect, my Lord, whilst I have been carrying that..." Jack nodded towards the banner. "I've had no commander but your illustrious self."

"Here we go again," John De Somery muttered with a sigh. "Spare me the flattery, soldier."

Suddenly, Jack remembered another reason why he hadn't reported the incident: "I'd been away from camp all night," he confessed. "Without permission," he added shamefacedly.

"That's more like it," declared the Baron. "An overnight's absence *would* get you into serious trouble." The

Baron eased himself in his throne and leaned against its over-painted backrest. "I have to admit that your story might...might provide an explanation for that infernal arrow. But tell me more about this spell."

"I don't know if I should say this but..."

"Spit it out, soldier."

"Something about one of the poppets gave me the distinct feeling that it was meant to represent *you*."

Instead of the expected roar of incredulity, the Baron fell into a thoughtful silence. Eventually: "Why should anyone in Coventry want *me* dead?" Another period of silence was followed by: "If I fell out of the King's favour, all of my possessions could be confiscated." A growl rumbled in his throat. "That cannot be allowed to happen. We must return to Coventry and confront those evildoers. You *will* be able to identify them, of course."

Jack wasn't sure about that. For a long time after the incident, the image of the magician's features had been clearly fixed in his memory. But by *now,* it had faded almost completely away. And he doubted if he would be walking the streets in his conical hat and talismanic robe. As for the person who'd commissioned the spell: *he* had made very sure of his anonymity. Jack hadn't taken much notice of the magician's assistant. "I'm not sure, my Lord," he admitted.

"Well the burghers of Coventry aren't likely to admit that they commissioned the evil deed," the Baron muttered bitterly. "Are you sure that they hexed their Prior? I wonder how *he* is faring." He winced again as he shifted on his throne. "As you've probably noticed," he said ruefully, "I'm in so much pain that I haven't got much patience. In fact, I only decided to use your message-arrow to avoid getting bogged-down in lengthy negotiations with Lancaster's henchmen." He either grinned or grimaced. "That leads me to my other reason for summoning you here."

After a lengthy pause – during which Jack was holding his breath – he continued brightly: "The King has sent word that he's delighted by the speed of Kenilworth's surrender. It has released our men to join him in the north of the country. Therefore, he has suggested that I arrange some sort of reward for your efforts on his behalf. How would you like to be the Steward of the castle?"

"*Kenilworth*, my Lord?" Jack whispered — his mind's-eye suddenly dazzled by a vision of Felicia strutting around the Great Hall.

"Nay," said the Baron quickly, but with the hint of a chuckle enlivening his voice. "*That* office is not mine to bestow. I meant my own castle at Dudley."

"But, my Lord, I know nothing about stewardship."

"That is no great drawback. Since your father-in-law went off to join up with Lancaster, the present incumbent has been filling the post temporarily. He will be only too happy to show you what it entails. Not only that, that wife of yours will doubtless be of great help to you. After all, when her father was the Steward, she was always poking her nose in where it wasn't wanted."

"Thank you, Sire," Jack said, wondering what an 'incumbent' might be. "I shall try to serve you well."

"I am sure that you will. But you don't look very happy about it, I must say."

"No, my Lord." Jack looked hesitantly down at the floor.

"Look at me, soldier. What's troubling you *this* time?"

"I'd rather not say, Sire."

"Hell's teeth. And why *not*?"

"It concerns the war."

"What about it?"

"I've heard that it was started by one powerful woman's fit of pique when offended by another."

"And you believe *that*, do you?"

Jack felt the blood rush to his face. "I don't know *what* to think." He suddenly remembered to add a respectful: "Sire."

"That is a lie that's being spread by our enemies." The Baron squirmed in his throne with barely-suppressed fury.

"Queen Isabella wasn't just refused entry to Baldesmere's Castle; his wife ordered her archers to shower the Queen's soldiers with arrows. Six of them were killed outright. Many others were badly wounded."

The Baron scowled as he scrutinised Jack's face. "And I suppose that you believe that the Mortimers surrendered at Shrewsbury because they didn't want to fight their King."

When Jack nodded almost imperceptibly, the Baron snorted with exasperation. "So you haven't heard what they did at Bridgnorth?"

Jack tried to stop his face betraying his scepticism. He knew that the Mortimers had burnt down the bridge in order to avoid conflict with the King.

"Don't look so stupid," the Baron exclaimed, apparently misinterpreting Jack's expression for one of confusion. "A contingent of the King's army managed to cross the Severn before the Mortimers arrived. Being heavily outnumbered, they had to take shelter within the town until our main force arrived to reinforce them. But the Mortimers battered down the gates and drove what was left of our task force back across the river. Then they burned down the bridge and destroyed the town as well.

"The next bridge upriver was Shrewsbury's — built of stone and couldn't be set on fire. Instead, the Mortimers launched a frontal attack on King Edward's army, relying on Lancaster to do the same at its rear. But Lancaster let them down, and the Welsh seized the opportunity to attack them from *their* rear. So the Mortimers were caught in a pincer movement that was the opposite of what they had intended. Do you doubt my word?"

"N-n-no, Sire. I was just thinking about what you said." In fact, he had been worrying about Marion, who was still being held as a hostage at Dudley Castle.

"But the most damning thing of all," the Baron continued "was the fact that Lancaster had been making secret pacts with the Scots." He gave one of his mirthless laughs. "So don't waste your sympathy on *them*. They had it coming."

Jack had picked up a Scottish coin in Tutbury Castle; that proved that his master was telling the sooth.

The Baron stared deeply into Jack's eyes. "I see from your expression that you believe me now. Is your precious conscience assuaged?"

"Y-yes, Sire," Jack muttered, thinking of all the dead and wounded soldiers that hadn't *had it coming*.

"And my enemies claim..." John de Somery muttered as he twisted round in his throne to tug on a rope that was hanging beside it, "... that *I* am the worst of barons."

Not waiting for a denial, he waved Jack up from the stool and announced in a louder tone of voice: "The King has appointed a Steward for *this* castle so there's nothing to keep us at Kenilworth any longer."

The door crashed open and the guard from downstairs rushed in. Ignoring Jack completely, he dropped to one knee before the throne and asked for his master's instructions.

"I leave for Coventry on the morrow," the Baron snapped. "Make preparations for our departure."

CHAPTER 14

On arriving outside Coventry, the Baron discharged his surviving men and sent them back under guard to Dudley. Then he commanded Jack to take him to the cottage where the magic had taken place. Jack located it immediately, its shutters closed and its door secured with a padlock. Unsheathing his sword, the Baron hacked his way in through the wattle and daub of the wall.

Apart from a slight stench of sulphur, there was nothing to confirm that magic had taken place there.

And of *course*, none of the neighbours had seen anything unusual. Well, that depended on what you regarded as *unusual*, Jack thought as he struggled to remount his steed. The next port of call was the Priory. And if the Prior wasn't dead already, he should still be there.

*

Allowed through Coventry's defences without dismounting, the Baron and his anxious minion entered a maze of deserted streets. By following the directions of the sentry that they'd met at the gatehouse, they came at last to one that was thronged with shoppers. Above their heads, the houses leaned together like gossiping women, their walls resounding with the squeals of slaughtered livestock. At the far end of this hellhole, the facets of a great glazed wind-eye gleamed with reflected sunlight.

Yelling at the townsfolk to get out of his way, the Baron galloped is horse among them and out into open air. And as the riders paused to savour the cool freshness of the morning, a gate in the Priory's boundary wall crashed open. Three black-robed monks scuttled out – two to take charge of the horses as the riders dismounted. The third monk ascertained the purpose of their visit, and then led them across the precinct to the finely carved stone entrance of the priory. Now that Jack came to think of it, when he'd visited that alehouse outside the city he'd noticed a pointed spire somewhere around here. If that was part of this priory, it was hidden behind its ribbed and towered frontage.

A latch clicked loudly. The monk swung a heavy door open on ornate hinges, then smilingly bade the visitors to go inside. And when they'd descended a flight of half-round steps, he closed the door behind them with a softer 'click'. While the Baron knelt down (on one knee) to pray, Jack stared at the nave of the church with open-mouthed wonder. Here was another example of the stonemasons' skill and art. A row of fluted archways paraded down each side – their columns continuing upwards to curve over and meet at a dizzying height above his head. Gilded bosses at their intersections glistened in beams of sunlight that came streaming in from wind-eyes just below them. Although the vaulted space was enormous, each side was further widened with an aisle – hence the need to support the roof with arches.

The monk now led the way through the nearest arch on the left. And as they headed across the aisle towards a doorway in the sidewall, the stonework echoed in protest at the clashes of the Baron's boots on the polished floor tiles. Apparently unperturbed by the sacrilegious clatter, the monk opened the door and ushered his visitors out. Jack stared again – this time with recognition. Although the cloister now revealed was bigger than Dudley Priory's, both were situated on the north side of the nave. The priories could have been built to a pre-ordained pattern. If so: was it decreed by God in the Holy Bible? He didn't get the chance to ask, for the monk was hurrying down the passage that lay ahead. Turning right when he reached its end, he stopped at a doorway halfway along the next one. After knocking three times, he pushed the door wide open and stepped aside for the visitors to enter.

Beyond it lay a long and narrow room with benches and tables arranged along the sides. Here sat rows of black-robed monks whose faces were turning expectantly towards the newcomers, and then away again because their food had not arrived. From a pulpit halfway up in the opposite wall, another resumed reciting monotoned Latin.

Slumped in a high backed chair at the far end of the refectory, the Prior surveyed his flock with drooping eyelids. He'd a pie and a silver goblet within reach on the table in front of him.

"I must see you right away," the Baron bellowed, marching down the middle of the room and motioning for Jack to follow him.

The litany stopped abruptly and the Prior jerked upright in his throne. Putting a finger to his lips, he struggled unsteadily to his feet and shepherded his visitors back out into the cloister.

"Pleashe," he hissed, resting a hand on the grey stone wall. "I musht inshisht that you reshpect our lawsh. We are all bound to shilensh here."

"Shilence my arsh," the Baron mimicked, pointing at the banner that Jack had left leaning against the wall. "Don't you know who I *am*?"

"Of courshe, I know thee." He glanced disapprovingly at Jack, who was pretending to examine a carving in the ceiling of the cloister. "Thou art John De Shumery, the Shinful Baron of Dudley. How can I be of shervish to thee?"

The Baron seemed taken aback by this description. "Did you know," he said quickly, "that some of the citizens of this city have invoked the powers of darkness and sent them to destroy you?"

"That does not surprise me." Although the Prior seemed unperturbed, his voice had lost the slur of drunkenness. "You see," he added bitterly, "the merchants have taken over the manufacture of the fine woollen cloth that was formerly produced in this priory. And now they wax fat and wealthy on their ill-gotten gains. Perhaps you saw their fine houses on the way here? No? Well. That's not the only evil thing they do; they pay their workers pittances while burdening them with crippling rents." Jack risked a quick glance at the Baron, who showed no sign of recognising his own treatment of his tenants.

Noticing that Jack had been listening, the Prior drew John de Somery further along the cloister. Nevertheless, the barrelled vault above their heads reflected their whispered voices. Jack could still hear what was being said, even above the sighing of the wind in the central garden.

"So, every Sunday," the Prior announced, drawing himself up to his full stature, which brought the top of his head almost level with the Baron's shoulder, "I denounce them from the pulpit and call down the wrath of God upon their heads."

"I don't blame you," the Baron muttered grimly. "Selfishness is everywhere. However, I have more urgent things to discuss." Moving closer to the priest, he acquainted him with Jack's account of the spell-casting.

The priest still didn't appear to be worried. "We have the protection of our Blessed Lady and all the Saints," he proclaimed while stretching out his arms. "Even Satan himself cannot penetrate these walls."

"Perhaps I should stay in the Priory with *you* then," the Baron muttered, "and have that protection for myself."

"That will *not* be possible. As a major combatant in the wars, thy presence here would not be conducive to the maintenance of peace and tranquillity within this establishment."

"Tell that to Bishops Orleton and Stapeldon," snapped the Baron. "They have been major players in the war against the Ordainers. And I have to tell you that *their* meddling has *not* been conducive to the peace and tranquillity of this *realm*."

"Be that as it may," the Prior retorted, "but before you leave these premises, perhaps I can interest you in purchasing some personal protection for thyself? I just happen to have here..." He groped in his leather pouch. Not finding what he sought, he shrugged and grinned conspiratorially. "Well, I just happen to have *somewhere*...a cross that is made from the nails that transfixed our beloved Saviour to the cross."

"How much?" the Baron demanded.

"In *your* case, I will let it go for, let me see...three hundred marks."

"I'll think about it," said the Baron.

"Two hundred then," the Prior said, quickly.

"But what about the King?" Jack interjected, "and Hugh De Spenser and the others?"

Both the Baron and the Prior looked round with eyebrows raised. Minions weren't allowed to listen to the conversations of their betters, let alone express opinions of their own.

"He's right though," the Baron said, turning his back on his impudent servant and moving away. "I can understand why the burghers of Coventry might want *you* put out of the way, but why would they want to have the King and the De Spensers killed as well?"

"The King keeps increasing their levies," said the Prior, "and the De Spensers make certain that they pay up promptly."

"By the way," the Baron said, "I noticed that you have brought the pie with you."

"Yes," the priest confessed, withdrawing it from his pouch. "If I'd left it behind in the Refectory, it would be temptation for the brethren."

Jack suppressed a smirk. In spite of what the Prior had claimed about that holy place being inviolate, the Tempter could still get in.

"We get these from Leicestershire," the Prior continued, holding the pie up to his mouth and preparing to take a bite. "That's what the 'L' stands for."

Jack had already noticed that two strips of pastry had been applied to the upper crust before baking.

"But this is unusual," the Prior added, squinting down. "Look at this." He held the pie out for the Baron's inspection.

Even from where Jack was standing, he could see that someone had made an incision between the two converging strips of pastry, thus converting the 'L' into an 'A'. It came to him in a flash: The 'A' could stand for Adrasteus.

The same thought had occurred to the Baron. "Jack claims that the demon's name began with 'A'."

"What name was it?"

"How should I know? I can't remember every little detail." He turned in search of his minion. "Jack! What was the demon's name?"

"Adrasteus, Sire, or something like it."

"Adrasteus eh?" The Prior pursed his lips. "When I was at Oxford University, their library had a list of every known demon. I seem to recall one called 'Adrasteus'."

Jack felt the elation of having his story confirmed.

"And if I remember correctly," the Prior continued quietly, "Adrasteus specialises in destroying the rich and powerful at the time of their greatest triumph." He beamed at the Baron with an air of self-satisfaction. "Well, that lets *me* out. I have no reason to feel triumphant about anything."

"Well I have," the Baron exclaimed. "I have been having considerable military success of late." He was looking quite worried now. "That might qualify *me* for Adrasteus's attention." He gave a short laugh. "That's if he *does* exist, of course. It seems more likely that Jack's magician is nothing but a fraud who uses earthly means as well as spells to fulfil his contracts." He took the Prior's pie from him and examined it closely. "*I* was given one like this at Kenilworth," he said, "but I only took one bite. It tasted so horrible that I spat it out before I'd swallowed any. Thank God (sorry Prior) that you haven't eaten any of this one. Hey, Jack! You used to be a baker. Come over here and give us your expert opinion about this pie."

Jack had been gazing at another stone boss in the ceiling of the cloister. This one was carved in the shape of a man's face with leaves sprouting out of his mouth. He'd seen similar faces in other religious houses – and on an inn-sign in Dudley market place – and on talismans that some of the townspeople hung about their necks. He'd been told that it represented the spirit of the forest – a god from a time before the Nobs and their monks took over. And apparently: it was being worshipped here!

Startled out of his deliberations, Jack took the pie, closed his eyes, and sniffed at the slit in its crust.

"There is pork in here, of course," he said, trying desperately to prevent a dewdrop dripping from his nose. "And oats...and pepper. And (sniff) there's something else as well. But it's such a strange smell that I have no idea what it is."

The Baron snatched the pie from Jack's hand and turned back to the Prior: "Is there any way of testing this?"

Jack blanched. They wouldn't expect *him* to eat it, *would they*? He wouldn't put it past them!

"There's a sty at the back of the Chapter House," the priest said quietly. "We could try feeding it to one of our pigs."

So the trio made their way further around the cloister and out into the yard – arriving at last at the pigsty. It was bigger than Jack had expected, with a partition to separate the sow from her half-grown piglets.

"They say that pigs are the nearest thing to men," said the Prior as he fed the pie to the most enthusiastic piglet of the litter.

Speak for yourself, Jack thought, staring secretly at the priest's ample paunch.

For a while, the animal ran round the sty, wagging its little tail to indicate its pleasure. But then it began to scrape its belly on the ground while squealing as though its throat was being cut. And by the time that the Vespers bell had finished chiming, the poor animal lay dead.

"That could have been *me*," the Prior groaned, ashen-faced, "but for that lad of yours." He nodded towards Jack, who was beginning to wonder if he was in the middle of a horrible nightmare.

"The spell was also directed at the King," Jack reminded them, "and the De Spensers and some others."

"Aye and one of those others might be *me*," roared the Baron, turning back to the Prior. "By the way: have you heard of any strange deaths in Coventry lately?"

"There are *always* strange deaths in Coventry," the Prior said with a smirk. "But there was a *very* unusual case a few weeks ago. One of the ale-husbands suddenly developed a pain in his stomach, and after writhing about in agony, he dropped dead with an expression of terror on his face. His relatives feared that a plague had come amongst them, but when nobody else caught it, they put it down to food poisoning. That was closer to the truth, I think."

"I must return to Dudley without delay," the Baron announced quickly. "My sister has sent word that De Spenser has accused her husband of High Treason. So, Prior, if you will take steps to trace the baker of that pie, I shall send a warning message to the King, along with my refutation of that ridiculous charge against my brother-in-law."

So saying, the Baron turned to Jack: "Come," he said. "We have been absent from Dudley for far too long."

Part Three

Cometh The Demon

CHAPTER 15

Jack's return to the castle had been met with mixed reactions.

Felicia now seemed distant, almost as if he was a stranger. Nevertheless, she couldn't hide her delight when he'd told her of his promotion to Steward of the castle. But although she'd no longer any cause to nag him about his lack of prospects, she resisted his attempts at intimate relations.

Jack's grandmother had been pensive.

"Do yer think that you can handle it?" she'd whispered as she brushed down his tunic of office (much to his annoyance).

"I'll give it my best shot," he'd answered hurriedly. "After all, I *was* Felicia's father's assistant for a while."

"That is the sooth," she'd admitted as she straightened his belt. "And you've changed a lot in the months that you've been away. More grown-up like."

His reception by the other members of the Baron's household had differed widely. Many seemed almost pleased – as one of their number whose ability had been recognised at last.

Others regarded him with barely-suppressed hostility. "Look at 'im," one of them whispered. "From the way as he swaggers about, he thinks he's one of the nobs."

Fortunately, his predecessor in the post of Steward had been friendly.

"You'm welcome to it," the old man had said. "The Baron made me take it on until someb'dy more suitable could be found."

Jack hadn't been sure about his own *suitability*. "Is there anything that I should know right away?" he'd asked.

"You mean: how to maintain your authority over the Household?" He'd laughed as Jack felt his face flushing with doubt about his own capability. "Don't worry, lad. If *I* can do it, a man with *your* build and reputation should have no trouble at all. There's nothing to it if you start off right. Everybody knows what they'm expected to do. Arr, and what'll happen if they disobey orders."

"Whose orders?"

"Yours, my friend. And if they don't obey 'em, the Baron will take it as an insult to himself and make you get rid of 'em." He'd looked around, then patted Jack on the back. "One way or another."

"Even so, I'd rather have their co-operation than their resentment."

"If you'll be advised by me, keep apart from 'em, at least at the start." He'd paused as if in thought, then added: "If yer wants ter win 'em over without 'em noticing it, make this year's Yuletide celebration one to remember."

*

And that is what he'd done. At least, he hoped that he had. Yet even as he strode across the courtyard to the lower hall, the reassuring sounds of the Yuletide merriment floated to him on the frosty air. He'd left his tabard of office behind to hide his identity. He also wore one of the masks that he'd 'bought' for the occasion. Fashioned to look like a stag's head, it completely enveloped his face. Although the antlers were heavy and cumbersome, to keep them balanced on his head he had to walk erect in a stately manner.

But in spite of this disguise, the guard at the doorway turned his back without saluting. He'd been one of his father-in-law's henchmen; the one who'd reported him for stealing. Not only that, while Jack had been risking life and limb in the King's Great Army, he'd stayed safely in the castle, and *sniffing around Felicia.*

Gran always told him never to upset "them what's been put in charge of you. They can make your life a misery". Well, now that *he* had been put in charge, he was going to be the living proof of *that*!

He'd begun with this insolent guard — making him stand outside in the cold while the Saint Thomas's Eve festivities raged in the hall. And he'd ordered the other henchmen to patrol the wind-swept battlements. They'd all be getting the worst jobs in the castle from now on.

He poked the guard sharply in the back. "You've got *two* choices," he growled into his ear. "Either you pay me the proper respect, or you'll get thrown out of the castle. Which is it to *be*?"

The guard turned around with narrowing eyes, but grudgingly made the salute.

"I'm *watching* you," Jack whispered as he swept past him into the hall. But the guard's display of insolence had unsettled him, and he paused behind the partition that formed a windbreak. Soon encouraged by the sounds of hilarity, he took several deep breaths and marched round it into the hall. Normally, this was a cold and comfortless barn where the mundane affairs of the Manor were conducted. But now it had been transformed according to his instructions.

In the middle of the flag-stoned floor, a boar was turning slowly on a spit — donated by the Baron who'd been injured during the hunt. His wife, the Lady Lucy, had been sent word about the accident, but she hadn't yet returned from Weoley Castle.

Gran was baking Wheat Cakes for presenting to the poor on the following morning. And Felicia was in their quarters, taking care of their baby son.

Beneath the roasting pig, bright flames and glowing embers sent spark-flecked smoke swirling up to the shadowed roof space. The stout oak crucks were bedecked with holly and mistletoe — the sprigs tied on with scarlet ribbons that fluttered gaily in the updraught. Between those timber arches, the cold stone walls had been hung with glittering tapestries, while along one side stretched a table with food and ale, constantly being replenished by scuttling cookneys. At one end slumped a boozer who'd drunk too much.

Drummers began a rhythmical beating: '*Thrum*, ba-bubba-bum...*thrum*, ba bubba-bum...'

Other antler-headed men and cat-masked women linked hands alternately to form a living ring around the fire. Then came the low-pitched notes of the bagpipes' drones, followed by the shrill strident strains of the chanters as they piped a gladdening tune. The dancers began to circle, swaying and twisting to the throbbing of the drums and casting wavering shadows onto the tapestries. Jack surveyed the scene with satisfaction as laughter and licentious singing joined the aromas in the air. Surely, there'd never been a festive occasion as good as *this* one.

In one way, he regretted that Marion wasn't here to see it. He'd have jumped at the chance to spin her round by the waist during one of the paired-couple dances.

Nobody knew how she'd escaped from the castle but Jack had a strong suspicion. She'd been the most beautiful woman there and Felicia had seen him kiss her goodbye before going off to the war. And the key to the Postern Gate was no longer where his wife had hidden it.

Perhaps it was just as well that Marion had gone. She was one of the Welsh nobility, being held hostage to ensure that they kept to the truce. But now that her kinfolk had marched into England, her life could be in danger. On the other hand, the arrival of the Welsh army at Shrewsbury had enabled the King to capture the Mortimers.

He sighed. "Ah well. Perhaps it's all turned out for the best after all."

On the opposite side of the circle, two attractive women were dancing with no man in between them. But as Jack elbowed his way through the onlookers to claim that vacant place, he felt tugging on his sleeve.

"Steward?" Clad in the Baron's golden livery, a boy was peering up with sparkling eyes.

Jack grinned behind his mask. Since the lad had seen through his disguise, the revellers would have done so too. So they'd know who'd arranged this Party for their enjoyment.

"Yes?" he barked as the cherished vacant spot in the ring grew closer.

The lad hesitated for a moment, then muttered almost inaudibly: "The Baron wants to see you." After taking a deep breath, he gasped out quickly: "Right away."

Jack peered across the revellers to the staircase that led up to the Baron's private rooms.

"He's not *there*," the boy said quickly. "He's been moved into the Donjon and he don't look very happy."

The page shrank beneath the stare of Jack's deer-headed mask. "*Sire!*" he added sheepishly.

With a regretful glance at the voluptuous pair who were dancing nearby in the ring, Jack discarded the mask as redundant and turned to go.

*

Jack emerged from the spiral staircase onto the first floor of the Donjon. His Lord and master was nowhere to be seen. The lancet and arrow-loop wind-eyes were open to the wind, stirring the banners that hung from the raftered ceiling. Jack had carried one into battle, but that now seemed far away in place and time.

"Is that you, Jack?" Although the voice was John de Somery's, it had lost its power of command. Jack hurried across the hall to the tower-room at the south-east corner of the Donjon. Twelve feet in diameter, the room was about the same in height, and in spite of the wind streaming in through its arrow loop wind-eye, the stink of sweat and vomit filled the air.

The Baron looked up from his bed with red-rimmed eyes. "Come over here and sit down," he ordered wearily. Shocked by his master's haggard appearance, Jack dragged a stool across and sat down beside the bed.

"What's that infernal noise?" the Baron asked grumpily. "I've been trying to get some sleep up here."

"It's the Saint Thomas's Eve Celebrations, Sire."

"Why? It should have stopped by now."

"They're having such a good time down there that it'll probably go on all night."

"Saints preserve us."

"By your leave, Sire, I'll close the Lancets' shutters to keep the noise out."

As he did so, the hall grew steadily quieter until the only sound was that of heavy breathing.

"I'm relying on you . . . to make sure . . . that everything is as it should be." The Baron had spoken while gasping for his breath.

Jack nodded, flattered by the trust that was being placed in him.

The Baron winced as he gave up trying to sit up. "I have heard that you are settling in as my Steward."

"Yes, Sire," Jack replied. "The weapons and supplies have been replenished and guards are ever-watchful on the battlements."

"Good," said the Baron, almost smiling. "I *knew* that you could do it. Do not let me down."

"No, my Lord."

"And how is that meddlesome wife of yours?"

"Felicia is in fine fettle, my Lord, and glorying in the status that my new position has brought her. She sends her best wishes for your speedy recovery. As do all of your household and the burghers of the town."

"That's rich," the Baron retorted, the corners of his mouth twitching slightly. "The burghers call me the 'Cruel Baron of Dudley'."

"It was the Prior of Coventry who dared to call you that!" In risking the contradiction, Jack had relied on a degree of familiarity that seemed to have developed during their shared experiences. "And the burghers have good reason to fear for the future if you lose control of the Manor." (If only because a new master would undoubtedly increase their rents.)

"Tell them not to worry. I know that Hugh de Spenser has hopes of adding it to his holdings, but my standing with the King will prevent him. In any case, I've won too many battles to be defeated by a festering wound."

"If *that* is only what it *is*, my Lord." Jack studied his master's features. "It could be the magician's spell."

"Nay, Jack. That was all a sham. After all..." A fit of coughing wracked his heaving chest. "After all," he repeated, still gasping for breath, "both the King and the De Spensers are still going strong."

Jack was not convinced. Adrasteus could be biding his time. It was rumoured that in spite of his great influence on the King, Hugh de Spenser was heading for a fall. And as for the King himself, the soothsayers had forecast that he'd one day be eaten by a She-wolf.

"I still think that there was evil in that cottage," Jack protested. "That crimson light was not of this world. I am certain of that."

"Don't be so sure." In spite of his shortness of breath, the Baron managed a smile as he beckoned Jack closer. "A new type of powder has been discovered, and they say that when it burns, it gives off light that's brighter than the sun. Some even claim that its vapour can propel an arrow faster than a Springald can, although I can't see how a powder could do *that*."

"I can think of one way of doing it," Jack said, recalling the noisy outbursts in the privy at Burton Bridge. "The vapour from eating beans can propel turds with great force."

"I know what you mean," the Baron said with a wry grin. "But they say that *sulphur* is used in the making of this powder. Do you remember the smell of burnt sulphur in that cottage near to Coventry?"

Jack nodded. At the time, he'd thought that the stench was brought from Hell.

"Well..." The Baron pulled the bedsheet up over his chest. "What happened there had more to do with *powder* than with power."

"But the magician was nowhere near the crimson light."

The Baron made as if to shake his head, but stopped abruptly. "He could have got his assistant to drop some powder into the Thurible. While you were concentrating on that triangle you wouldn't have noticed it, especially since the evildoers were dressed in black."

A little colour had returned to the Baron's cheeks as he argued his case. Now he lay back – beads of sweat glistening on his forehead like droplets of water on waxed linen.

"If I'm about to meet my maker," he muttered weakly, "see to it that you serve my wife...and my sister ...as well as you have...served me."

"I will of course," Jack said, "but it will not come to that. I know someone who might be able to help." Overcome with compassion for his ailing Lord, Jack had spoken without considering the consequences.

"Oh? And who pray is that?"

"My grandmother."

"That old crone who bakes my crustades?"

"That's her, my Lord. I once saw her cast a spell. She should be able to un-cast one as well."

"Is she a *witch*, then?" The Baron made the sign of the cross on his spit-spattered nightshirt.

Jack tried to think fast. Wise-women were not *always* appreciated. When people were sick, or on the point of giving birth, they would seek out anyone who might help them in their hour of need. But once that hour of need had passed, woe betide their helper when they needed someone to blame – whether for turning milk sour, for the failing of their crops, or for fevers and sudden death.

"She's not a witch, my Lord," Jack said quickly. "But she'll do *anything* to protect me from great danger."

The Baron's eyes glazed over. "I must admit," he said eventually. "You *do* seem to have been leading a charmed life. Bring her to me then. I'll try anything to get rid of this infernal fever."

Jack rushed down the spiral staircase, returning some time later with his ashen-faced grandmother in tow. "She says that she doesn't know what I'm talking about," he said as he dragged her towards the bed, trailing the wholesome scent of baking in her wake.

"Help me to sit up," the Baron commanded. And as Jack and his grandmother struggled to do so, he whispered into to her ear: "*Are* you a *witch*, old woman?"

"I am *not*, my Lord," Gran protested emphatically. "But if *I* may make so bold?" She looked him in the eyes to ascertain if it was all right to speak openly. At a nod from her employer, she continued: "When I was living in Netherton, I was their midwife and their herbalist, as was my mother and grandmother before *her*. One of the things as they taught me was how to dress wounds. Pray can I take a look at yours…er, Sire?"

"That will *not* be necessary. My surgeon has seen to *that*, and he's stipulated that the dressing should not be taken off as long as the wound is not painful."

Gran wrinkled up her nose. "If I may say so, my Lord, you also seem to have caught some sort of dis-ease. Perhaps you'll let me try to treat *that*?" She paused, staring at the floor as though unsure how to continue. Then her eyes widened momentarily. "This is Saint Thomas's Day," she said. "It's the best time for driving out demons." Observing her master's incredulous expression, she added: "Like what Jesus done."

"This is *Blasphemy*!" the Baron cried, crossing himself again.

"I dain't mean no disrespect," Gran protested fearfully. "A Friar told me as we should *all* try to live like Jesus."

The Baron gave her a long hard stare. "All right, old woman. Name your price."

Gran took a step back from the bedside, her eyes wide open with shock. "I don't want nothin' for myself." She looked anxiously across at her grandson. "I just want what is best for my Jack."

"Well, in that case, you might as well get on with it. If you succeed, you may rest assured that you'll both be well provided for."

"What if I can't?"

"You'll just continue working in the bakehouse."

Jack had a nasty thought. "You're not going to take your clothes off, are you Gran?"

She glanced up sharply. "Why do you say that?"

"It's just something that I heard of."

"My Lord," Gran said, turning quickly back to the Baron. "If you will allow me to say so, I shall need your full co-operation."

Jack took a quick look at their master, expecting him to be affronted by Gran's insolence.

Instead of that, he shrugged. "Very well. You have it. What have I got to lose?"

Gran perked up visibly, seeming more relaxed – sprightly even – more like the woman that Jack remembered from his childhood.

"If what Jack says is the sooth," she said with obvious concern, "there is evil at work here."

"Get on with it then. I'll do anything you say." The Baron lay back and closed his eyes. "Within reason…"

Gran opened a bag that was hanging from her shoulder and pulled out an earthenware bottle.

"If I may suggest, my Lord," she said, staring hard at her grandson to elicit his support, "I have a little something here that should soothe away the pain."

"That is the sooth, Sire," Jack cried enthusiastically. "If it's the stuff that I've been taking, it works wonders."

"It *is* the same potion," Gran affirmed, "and I've always had good results with it. In any case, I shall need your full attention to break a spell, and pain would make that impossible." With that, she took a horn cup from her bag, poured a little of the liquid into it, and offered it to her Lord.

"How do I know that you're not trying to poison me?" the Baron muttered, while shoving the cup away.

"My Lord," Gran said. "You've eaten enough of my crustades to know better than *that*." She smiled grimly. "And Jack's good fortune depends on your patronage and well-being."

She passed the cup to her grandson. "Here, you drink it."

With a shrug, Jack gulped it down.

"Now confirm to the Baron that it's your usual potion."

"Yes, my Lord. It is."

"And has it helped to soothe that wound of yours?"

"Yes, Gran. It's got a lot better already."

"Now you, my Lord," Gran said as she refilled the cup.

"You expect me to drink after *him*?"

"Wouldestow rather take a nip straight from the bottle then, my Lord?"

"Give it here. How much am I supposed to take?"

"One sip should suffice, my Lord. Two at the most."

The Baron grabbed the bottle and took a swig.

"Very good," Gran said, taking it back. After replacing its stopper, she inserted it into her bag. When she withdrew her hand, it was holding a short length of stick – criss-crossed round and round with bright blue ribbons. "You see this?" she cried, waving it around. "Well this is what I call a wand. I shall use it to cast a circle of fire around us."

"You will do no such thing." The Baron struggled to get out of bed. "You'll burn the bloody place down."

"No I won't," Gran said quickly. "It's not your normal sort of fire. It is not of this world."

"What good is it in *this* one then?"

"Possibly no good at all. But my mother used to put a lot of faith in it."

"Carry on then. But I warn you: one hint of real fire and I shall summon the guard." He nodded at a bell-rope that hung at the side of his bed.

"Can *I* do anything?" Jack asked nervously.

"I need you both to give me your full attention," Gran said. "And to keep up your concentration until the work is finished."

Jack risked another glance at the Baron to see if he was prepared to co-operate. With a sigh, the Baron nodded his acceptance. "Just don't burn the place down."

Holding her stick theatrically between her forefinger and thumb, she stalked to the centre of the room. "I want you both to imagine a spark of blue light on the end of this wand," she said gravely. "Can you manage that?"

Jack screwed up his face with concentration. 'Blue light', she had said. Using the colour of the ribbon and the brightness of the Dog Star as inspiration, he pictured a tiny blue light on the end of the stick. "Done that!" he said.

Gran pointed her wand down at the floor to the right of the open doorway. "Now I want you to imagine a ray of blue light, streaming out of the end of this wand like sunlight through a moth-hole in a wind-eye blind. Only blue." Somehow, her description enabled him to picture it: a narrow blue ray that sliced down through the haze to the spot that she was pointing at.

"Done that? Now where the beam hits the floor, I want you to imagine blue flames, leaping six inches up the wall."

"Don't you need some candles?" Jack asked, remembering the ceremony at Coventry.

"Oh ar," Gran said, looking around. A many-branched candelabrum stood nearby in the hall. She walked stiffly across to it and tugged a lighted candle from its holder. "Where's the north?" she said abruptly.

"I thought you knew that," Jack whispered. "The Donjon faces due north and south."

"Which way is north then?"

Jack nodded towards the wall with the lancet wind-eyes.

"Right then," she said and placed the candle on the floor – a foot inside the curving wall of the tower and in the northerly direction. She then brought in three more and placed them at the remaining Cardinal Points – grumbling under her breath as she straightened up.

"Let's try it again," Gran said, pointing the wand down at the side of the threshold but obviously feeling ruffled. "Got the blue light?"

"Yes," Jack muttered.

"And you, my Lord?"

The Baron sighed. "Likewise," he said shortly.

"And now can you visualise the blue ray again?"

"Yes," the other two groaned in unison.

"And the bright blue flames where it hits the floor?"

Once again, Jack imagined what she had described: a flickering blue flame that contrasted brightly against the shadowed surface of the wall.

"Are you doing this, my Lord?" Gran cried. "Please try. It's very important."

"Very well," the Baron muttered. "I am imagining it."

Immediately, the flames flared up before Jack's mental-eye, doubling in height and vigour. Could this *really* be happening? he wondered, and not just a combination of Gran's potion and her renowned skill at story telling?

"And now," the old woman announced, "I am going to create the circle of protection around us. When I move my arm round to the right, I want you to imagine those flames spreading round inside the wall of this turret. Notice that I'm moving in the same direction that the Sun does across the sky. It's called Deosil. That's 'Deos' meaning God. So you see, I'll be working with the angels, not the Devil. And when I get back to the starting-point, I shall seal the circle and ask them to protect us. After that, we must remain inside it at all times, although we shall still be able to see out into the hall."

Turning back towards the bed, she curtseyed – the first time that Jack had ever seen her do anything so respectful. "My Lord," she said, "is there anything that you require before we begin?"

Wearily shaking his head, the Baron waved her to continue.

"I need a pee," Jack murmured quietly.

"Well you'd better go out and have one," snapped his grandmother. "You'll need all of your attention for what's to come." She turned back to the Baron. "Is it all right if he uses your garderobe, my Lord?"

"If he must," the Baron muttered. "Try not to piddle on the seat."

"And with your permission, my Lord," Gran said, "he can bolt all the outer doors while he's out there. We don't want interruptions."

So after Jack had relieved himself in the garderobe of the opposite turret, he secured the entrances to the hall and hurried back.

"Have you said a prayer?" Jack asked. "The magician said a prayer or somethin'."

"I said it in me head," Gran muttered irritably. "Look. Whose doin' this: me or yow?"

"*When you've finished squabbling,*" the Baron interjected, "can we get on with it?"

"Yes, my Lord," Gran said, picking up the wand again.

As before, she got the Baron and her grandson to imagine the blue flame beside the doorway. "Don't look at one another," she cried shrilly. "Sorry, my Lord, but I must implore you both to concentrate on creating a ring of fire." She began to direct her wand around the edge of the circular floor while mumbling to herself as she did so. "Are you doing it?" she shrilled. "Keep your minds on making strong blue flames. Our lives could depend on it. Our immortal souls an' all, most likely." She continued the movement around the floor…behind the north-facing candle…beneath the arrow-loop wind-eye…behind the Baron's bed (where she exhorted Jack to double his mental efforts)...behind the chair with the Baron's sword and tunic, round to the timber threshold and back to the starting-point. With a flourish of her wand and a mumbled incantation, she announced that the circle of protection was complete.

"Are you both still imagining the ring?" she asked.

To Jack's surprise, he *could* visualise a ring of flames: bright blue in colour and leaping twelve inches up the wall. And there was not a single break in it, not even at the doorway.

"Yes, Gran. I *am* imagining it," he said.

"What about you, my Lord."

"Likewise," the Baron said gruffly, "for all the good that it's likely to do. *Is this going to take all night?*"

"From now on," Gran said, daring to ignore the question. "I must urge you both to keep the ring of fire burning clearly in your minds. No matter what happens." As Jack resolved to do as she'd commanded, she added quietly: "That's if anything *does* happen. You never know with these things."

"So you've done this kind of thing before," the Baron observed.

"By your leave, my Lord, I must crave silence whilst I'm working." She turned towards the doorway and pointed her wand out into the hall. Dimly visible at its centre, the Baron's high chair looked dark and forbidding, as though waiting for someone or something to take a seat. "I summon thee, Adrasteus," Gran announced in a commanding tone of voice. "Or whatever you likes to call yourself," she added quietly. "Come hither and make obeisance before the powers of light and goodness."

Light and goodness? Jack thought. *Never in a thousand years would I have described my grandmother as that.*

"Are you concentrating?" Gran cried.

Of course he hadn't been. And the weakness of the flames in his imagined circle showed that he hadn't been. As he resolved to do much better, the flames recovered their vigour.

For a while, nothing happened. But just as Jack was getting bored with the whole performance, he noticed a tiny point of crimson light. It was hovering about a foot above the seat of the Baron's throne. Suddenly, it shot off round the hall, flashing across the doorway as it rebounded back and forth off the plastered walls.

As they watched it, Jack tugged on his grandmother's sleeve. "You should have trapped it in a Triangle of Art."

Gran pulled her arm away. "What the Hell's a Triangle of Art?" she shrieked, anxious and affronted.

But before Jack managed to answer, the red spot came to a halt outside the doorway. And somehow, he knew that it was looking in at them. Whatever it was.

CHAPTER 16

"Dostow see what I see?" the Baron whispered, staring in horror at the thing that hovered outside the turret doorway.

"A crimson light?" Jack murmured, unable to tear his eyes away from it. "Hovering six feet above the floor?"

"Then you *do* see what I see," said the Baron, his sickness now almost forgotten.

"Maintain the circle," Gran cried. But she needn't have worried. Now that something unnatural was actually happening, the imaginary blue-flames that ringed the turret floor were leaping higher and brighter than ever.

The point of crimson light began to expand. When about a foot across, it simultaneously extended itself down to the floor and up towards the high raftered ceiling. Within that spindle-shaped aura of crimson light, arms and legs began to form. *Female* arms and legs! Jack's half-remembered dream-woman was taking shape before his eyes. Initially, her arms had been raised above her head. Now they were held imploringly out towards him while her shapely hips swayed seductively to the pulse-beat in his ears. Aware that the Baron's laboured breathing had acquired a rhythmical urgency, Jack stared transfixed at the naked figure.

Although he loved Felicia dearly, he was being seduced by what he knew to be an illusion. But this was no time for rational thought. There was Great Magic at work here. An ancient magic – welling-up from somewhere deep within him – taking over both his wilful mind and body.

"Keep the circle burning!" Gran screamed as Jack's rational and irrational minds battled for supremacy. "And you can stop that right now," she muttered as the siren beckoned for the men to join her in the dance. "I ain't impressed, even if these two are."

In an instant, the woman evaporated into a cloud of swirling smoke, to re-form as a nude male figure. Muscles rippled beneath marble-white skin as he struck a provocative pose.

"Nor by you neither!" laughed Gran. "I'm past all that!"

After throwing back its head with a silent laugh, the figure dissolved into a cluster of scarlet filaments. They quickly reformed themselves into a lion – not unlike those on the Baron's banner – but tawny-brown in colour instead of blue. Its tail swished angrily as it prowled about the hall, pausing occasionally outside the doorway to glower in at the fearful occupants of the turret-room.

"Keep the circle going," Gran cried as the flames protecting the threshold began to waver. The beast turned its head to look over its shoulder as if something had caught its attention. The curtain of the servants' room was swept back. There stood a woman in a robe of Coventry Blue. Jack stared in horror at his wife. And as Felicia gazed back at him, her robe fell open to reveal that she was holding their baby son against her breast. The beast was crouching now – shuffling its hind legs as it prepared to spring. It leaped towards the hapless pair.

"Ignore it," Gran shrieked as Jack tried to make a dash towards the doorway. But in spite of his fear and anguish, his feet were rooted to the spot. "You locked and barred that door yourself," Gran screamed in desperation. "That's *not* Felicia. It's a phantom. Maintain the ring. Maintain the ring."

Seeing that that the circle of fire had all but died away, the lion changed direction in mid-air and came hurtling across towards the doorway. But as the flames of protection flared up again, it vanished in a cloud of crimson smoke. Of Felicia and the child there was now no trace. "I told you so," Gran said quietly. "They'll try anything to get in at us. But as long as we maintain the ring, they can't break through."

"What will happen next?" Jack whispered. "We're trapped in here."

"We shall just have to wait and see." Gran wiped her brow on a sleeve. "But whatever it is, make sure that you keep that ring intact. Hang on, what's happening out there now?"

The tiny crimson light had reappeared – hovering above the Baron's throne as it had before. It exploded in a puff of smoke. The red mist cleared to reveal that someone was sitting there. Someone wearing a hauberk of overlapping platelets. Hugh de Spenser sat leering at them through the open doorway.

"Let me get at him," the Baron cried, struggling to get out of bed. But just as Jack had found previously, he couldn't move a muscle.

"Don't let the flames go out," Gran screamed, for they had shrunk to their lowest ebb yet. The flames recovered their vigour, flickering brightly against the shadowed wall of the turret as her two companions renewed their mental efforts.

"Help!" all three screamed as the wall crumbled down around them. But they did not fall. They were supported in the air. And although the floor was no longer visible beneath their feet, the circle of blue flames outlined its former limits. Beyond them they could see the hills of Clent, while thirty feet below them lay the flagstones of the basement.

"It's just another trick!" Gran screamed. "You can still feel the floorboards can't you?"

It was true. They yielded slightly as Jack shifted his weight from one foot to the other. The Baron couldn't though. His bedstead was hovering in the air like some improbable flying machine. He stared around at the remnants of his stronghold.

"What's happened to my beautiful Donjon," he wailed.

Like the tower that Jack had been standing in, its twin on the south side of the Donjon had vanished completely. The northern pair were still there, but only as empty half-cylinders – stripped of their plaster down to the weatherworn stonework.

In the wall that still connected these hollow shells, its lancet wind-eyes stared back with a shocked expression that matched the Baron's gape of shock and horror.

"Keep the ring going," Gran shrieked as giddiness impaired her companions' concentration.

But as they strove to restore the wavering flames, the darkening land exploded with fiery fountains. Showers of sparks shot up into the air. A blood-red river wound round the base of the hill. Processions of men pushed cartloads of glowing embers. This scene from Hell stretched as far as their eyes could see – that's if it *was* their eyes that were doing the seeing.

Jack struggled to keep at least one part of his mind focused on stoking up the flames. He must have managed it, for the ring of blue fire revived.

The vision changed abruptly. The fires of Hell had vanished. Not a single light shone out on all the darkened landscape – not even from Dudley town. Silhouetted against a moonlit sky, a strange black cross was moving among the clouds. Suddenly, the land below it exploded in a silent burst of flame. In that one brief flash of venomous energy, a steeple like the one at Coventry raised a finger of defiance to its attacker. And in the direction of that city, the clouds glowed darkly red with sullen anger.

"It's just an illusion," Jack told himself. "Maintain the ring. Maintain the ring."

And still the circle held.

The scene transformed again. It was still night time, but the land was now peppered with tiny points of light. Pairs of red or white spots crept slowly along on a spider's web of orange-coloured pathways.

By now, both men were finding it almost impossible to keep the flame-ring burning, while trying to ignore the changing scenes around them, and the fact that they were still supported on nothing but thin air.

Suddenly, they were back inside the turret room. The floorboards were beneath their feet again – and still ringed about with bright blue flames. Beyond the open doorway, tapestries, banners and the vacant throne were all back in place.

"Is it over?" Jack asked in a hopeful tone of voice.

"I don't think so," his grandmother whispered. "We shall just have to wait and see."

"Wait for how long?" the Baron demanded.

"God alone knows that," she answered quietly.

For a long time, nothing happened. Nothing moved. The only sound was of heavy breathing as Jack and his companions struggled to regain their composure, while still maintaining the ring of flames around them.

Suddenly, the crimson spark was back inside the hall, this time hovering just above the floor. It swelled into a ball, which then extended out to one side, tapering at the end like a giant fox turd. As the thing continued to grow, six paired swellings erupted along its sides. Forelegs...hind legs...two bat-like wings. The trio watched in horror as a *dragon* was taking shape before their eyes. The ball had now become a monstrous head, which turned towards them and snapped its slavering jaws.

With one beat of its leathery wings, the beast was at the doorway. Ramming a nostril against the opening, it breathed in deeply, drawing the flames out over the timber threshold. There was now a very great danger of them going out.

"Keep them flames burning," Gran screamed.

"I can't keep this up," Jack yelled as he struggled to rejuvenate the flames. "It's winning."

And so it was – or would have done if the arrow-loop in the tower wall hadn't glowed with crimson light. The dawning sun had risen clear of the clouds that had hitherto hidden its rising.

"It can't be morning yet," cried the Baron. "How can this night have passed so quickly?"

But although the night *had* past, a *knight* was about to arrive.

The sun's rays projected a bright red cross on the white linen cloth of the bedsheet. Tossing this aside, John de Somery swung his legs out of bed and stood as erect and as purposeful as formerly. The beads of sweat on his forehead expanded – flowing together like quicksilver until they encased his head in a helm of shining steel. The process continued, flowing down over his body to form a suit of bright plate armour. In one swift movement the Baron gathered up his bedsheet and flung it across his shoulder. The cross had become imprinted on the cloth, but with the roundels missing from its arms. Ignoring the warning shrieks of his two companions, he drew his sword from its sheath and turned to face the doorway. Now keen of eye and fearless in aspect, he strode forth to meet the dragon. In one swift movement, he plunged his sword up to the hilt in the still-inhaling nostril. There was a flash of blinding light, an all-mighty BANG, and then complete silence. The dragon had vanished from the hall, the great room bathed in the glow of the morning sun. Prostrate on the floorboards, the Baron lay unmoving. Armour had he none. Nor was there any life left in him.

* * *

Jack was making his way across the courtyard, wondering how best to report the Baron's death to his widow's private secretary. Sensing that someone was watching him, he turned sharply round. There was nobody there. Just the Donjon staring down from its mound with an even-more contemptuous expression than was usual. Its stonework looked strong enough to last for a thousand years. So, what was he to make of that vision of it reduced to a ruin? And those other images. They had seemed so real that he could still remember every little detail. Were they glimpses of the future? But if that was the case, events that were yet to happen must be as fixed as those in the past. So what was the point of trying to better yourself if your fate was already decided? He shrugged and carried on walking. The visions were just waking-dreams, created by a demon called Adrasteus.

*

Back safely in her bakehouse, Gran regretted that she wasn't able to save the Baron. But she was even more worried that she and Jack could now be charged with murder. They'd got the Baron into bed, replaced the candles in the candelabra, resheathed the sword and hung it back on the chair. She was almost sure that all trace of their magical struggle had been removed. And because the lancet's shutters had both been closed, no one should have heard that loud explosion. Nevertheless, there was a strong possibility that she'd have to prove her innocence by carrying a bar of red-hot iron. So with that in mind, she was soaking her hands in urine.

*

Jack had stopped in his tracks again. If the dragon had been an illusion, *what* had killed the Baron? Had an Angel *really* taken possession of his body? Whatever it was, the shock of defeating the demon had been fatal. Jack almost smiled. The Baron was such a powerful character that he couldn't have been snuffed out completely. Nor could his life's achievements have been swept away down the river of time like the flotsam at Burton Bridge. But what was going to happen to the castle now? As far as Jack was aware, he'd left no son to inherit his lands and possessions. Of course, the most favourable heir would be the Baron's wife, Lady Lucy, but she'd never taken an interest in the running of it. Alternatively, the Baron's elder sister might inherit. Jack had seen her strutting across the courtyard during visits to the Castle. And the handmaids that had served the Lady Margaret had reported that she found fault with everyone around her. However, her husband might be more amenable. Jack had encountered John de Sutton on several occasions during the war against the Ordainers, and knew him to see both sides in most situations. But he wouldn't have seen the other side of De Spenser accusing him of Treason. The Baron had sent a message to the King, pointing out that De Sutton had fought bravely against the Ordainers. But what if the King had ignored this? De Spenser might still able to make the accusation stick, and then the Dudley Manor could be ripe for his picking.

Jack recalled the vision of him leering back at him from the Baron's throne. As far as he knew, the King's favourite had never been to Dudley in person. But the whole country was in uproar because he was forcing the wives and widows of his opponents to sign away their rights and inheritances. So, whichever way the succession went, he could still gain control of the Manor. A mental image of the knight flashed into Jack's mind, riding out through the gatehouse of Tutbury Castle, lashing out with his sword and screaming: "*I shall get thee yet!*"

"Hurry up Adrasteus," Jack whispered as he returned the salute of a guard who was marching past.

CHAPTER 17

"What have you done with my dead brother's body?"

There could be no mistaking that voice, although the silhouette in the doorway did little to confirm the identity of its owner. The silhouette held up its skirts and stamped snow off its wooden pattens before stepping over the threshold of his office. Clomping across to Jack's desk, it thrust an angry female face into the candlelight.

"Good morning, Lady Margaret," Jack said hastily, his chair scraping on the flagstones as he hauled himself to his feet. "Welcome back to Dudley Castle."

The Baron's sister was staring at him in a very hostile manner. Could she have learned how the Baron had died? No! That was not possible. Apart from his grandmother and himself, there had been no witnesses. The demon 'Adrasteus' had been there of course, but he, or she, or it, wouldn't have revealed their last desperate conflict in the Donjon. Well, he assumed that it wouldn't.

"What have you done with my brother?" the lady repeated, her owl-like glare demanding his full attention. Being so much below her in status, he knew that he should look respectfully away. But then he would look guilty – like a hound accused of some misdemeanour. So he continued to stare back at her in the hope that she would see innocence rather than insolence.

"Spit it out!" the lady demanded. "What have you done with him?"

Jack lowered his gaze before answering. "Lady Lucy told me to have him taken to the Priory." He struggled to control the quavering in his voice. "And to make the initial arrangements for his funeral."

While he'd been down at that holy place, a monk had told him that Lady Lucy – John de Somery's widow – was legally his successor. However, it was being rumoured that Margaret – the Baron's oldest sister – was making a rival claim for the Barony.

"He's receiving the full honours due to him," Jack said. "Prayers are being said by day and by night and I have ordered a coffin of the very best Gornal stone." Observing her incredulous expression, he hastened to explain: "The sculptors and masons are still working in the Priory, so I've also asked them to carve an effigy for his tomb, and to make a suitably grand canopy to go over it."

The Lady Margaret snorted while turning to leave. "And God alone knows what kind of mess they'd make of it. I shall soon put a stop to *that*."

As she reached the doorway, her sleeve snagged on its jamb – rasped to splintery roughness by hurrying men in maile.

"Goddes' Blood," she screamed as she came back into the room. "This place *really* does need sorting out." By shrugging with vexation, her shoulders raised the coils of hair that were wound about her ears. These doffed her fur cap very slightly as she moved towards the doorway once again.

Suppressing a perilous smirk, Jack hurried past her to smooth the offending timber with his hand – wincing as the splinters punctured his skin. "Can I arrange for an escort to the Priory, my Lady?"

"I know the way well enough," she snapped.

"But, my Lady, these are dangerous times. Our enemies could attack thee on the way there."

"So you are still harping-on about that wound of yours are you? Well note this, soldier . . . or Steward . . . or whatever you like to call yourself...my brother might have been tolerant of your dis-ability. But I am *not*."

She stepped out into the courtyard, keeping her elbows close to her sides and pressing her skirts against her thighs.

"Carry on with whatever you were doing," she called over her shoulder. "But as soon as I have seen to Sir John's funeral arrangements, I shall return to sort you out."

Jack watched her squelching stiff-leggedly across to the Gatehouse. Above and to the right of it, the drum-towered Donjon squatted haughtily on its mound. As usual, its lancet wind-eyes glowered down with contemptuous disdain. He glared back at them. How dare they? He was responsible for their upkeep now. But despite all that he'd achieved since arriving at the castle, he felt more out of place there than ever.

Returning to his desk, he picked up the in-voys that he'd previously been studying. It was for the repair of five coats of maile and the supply of five new ones. News had arrived of renewed hostility against the De Spensers and the King. Jack smiled grimly as he grabbed his quill and plunged its freshly trimmed nib into the inkhorn. He must send the order to the blacksmith down there in Netherton while he still had the power to help him. His pen scratched on the parchment, leaving in its wake the elaborate scrawl that he always employed as a signature. Once he'd obtained Lady Lucy's approval of the order, he'd make discrete enquiries about how he should behave towards her sisters-in-law. Snuffing his candle out between his finger and thumb, he plunged the room into darkness that was deeper than expected. The bulky figure of a guard now blocked the doorway. It was not one of his own men.

"My master commands you to go to him at once," the soldier announced while peering round the little room. "He's up in the Donjon."

Jack prickled with indignation. "And who might *Your Master* be, may I ask?"

"John de Sutton o' course."

Now that Jack's eyes had adjusted themselves to the gloom, the fork-tailed lion on the soldier's surcoat confirmed that the command came from Lady Margaret's husband.

"Tell him that I shall come up as soon as I've consulted the Lady Lucy."

"I advise you not to delay," the visitor said in an urgent tone of voice. "*Jump when De Sutton says jump.* That's what I always say." After looking quickly over his shoulder, he added in a whisper: "As long as he gets what he wants . . . when he wants . . ., I'm left to my own devices for the rest of the time."

"When I want your advice, I shall ask for it!" Jack snapped, causing his visitor to shrug and stamp off in affronted silence. Nevertheless, as soon as he was out of sight, Jack quickly donned his own surcoat – with the De Somery's two blue lions – and marched purposefully out through the doorway and across the trampled snow towards the Solar.

*

Having failed to gain an audience with the Baron's widow, Jack walked slowly across the courtyard towards the Donjon. Last evening's sounds of hilarity had been replaced with a brooding silence. Was this because the household were grieving for their former master – or concerned about their own uncertain futures – or just nursing splitting headaches or guilty consciences?

After entering the Donjon via its red-lipped archway, he climbed the spiral staircase to the hall. Finding its door to be closed against him, his first impulse was to march right in and bellow his resentment of the discourteous summons.

However, that might not be the best policy in such uncertain times. Needing to gather his thoughts, he climbed the couple of steps that took him up to the tiny landing. Here, the staircase reversed the direction of its twist – a record of rebuilding. With events at the castle also changing direction, what was *his* situation now? Until told otherwise, he was still the acting Steward of this castle. And whatever people might think, he had reached that position by loyal service to the Baron and the King. If he didn't assert himself now, he might never get the chance again. On the other hand, it might provoke De Sutton into dismissing him.

Two steps down and Jack was back at the door. After yanking on the leather thong to raise the latch on the other side, he threw himself against the studded timber. But instead of its usual resistance, the door swung freely inwards and slammed against its embrasure. Jack stumbled forward, clinging to the stonework for support, and as the echo of his entrance faded away, another door banged shut somewhere nearby.

"Goddes' blood!" an imperious voice boomed over to his right. "What the devil was that?"

"It's me," Jack yelled back. "The Steward."

"Come over here then!" the imperious voice commanded.

Jack ignored that for the moment – more concerned about who'd slammed that other door. The tower room where the Baron had fought the dragon lay in line with the slanting embrasure in which he stood. Its door hung open, showing that it was empty. The nearest other door was in the servants' room to his left. Sweeping its curtain-screen aside, Jack peered into the cluttered interior. There was no one there, but a couple of yards along the curving wall, the staircase door was still rebounding from its slamming. And through the widening gap came the sounds of shuffling feet and furtive sniggering. Those stairs led down within the thickness of the wall to the storeroom directly below. By dashing down the spiral staircase, Jack could intercept the sniggering man before he could get away.

"Where the blazes are you?" the imperious voice bellowed again.

Angered by the aggression in that command, and resentful at having to let the sniggering man escape, Jack turned back into the hall. It was even more dismal than usual. The arrow-loops never let in much light and the lancets both faced north – the nearest partly blocked by the raised portcullis.

Jack flushed with outrage and indignation. The table where he sat to issue his commands had been moved to the middle of the room without asking his permission. Behind it sat John de Sutton. No longer in his heraldic surcoat, a cloak of 'Coventry Blue' protected him from the cold. With no torches lit and no fire in the brazier, this was obviously a time of increased austerity.

Alongside De Sutton sat the Prior of St James, black-robed and hooded as befitted his occupation. Jack hadn't seen him since he'd been allowed to claim Sanctuary in the Priory. But gone was his air of slightly ruffled holiness. Within the deeper shadow of his hood, the Prior's eyes glared back at him accusingly.

De Sutton waved Jack forward. "A fine entrance that was," he said without looking up.

"Somebody's oiled the door's hinges." Jack had mumbled his reply – too rattled to think of anything better to say.

"Well it's about time *somebody* did." No seat was proffered and none was brought. "You're the one that they call 'Jack o' Beans', art thow not?"

"Some call me by that name," Jack said, "though I would appreciate it if you didn't address me so in public. As the Steward of this castle, I have been trying to live that childhood incident down."

"Be that as it may," snapped John de Sutton, red-faced and self-important, "I am investigating the circumstances of my brother-in-law's death. You were with him at the end, I believe."

Ever since the magical attack, Jack had known that explanations would be demanded. But he hadn't expected them to be demanded quite so soon. What could he say that wouldn't get him and his Gran into serious trouble?

CHAPTER 18

Angry and resentful, Jack wondered how best to answer.

"Well?" barked John de Sutton, staring at him coldly. "Are you too afraid to speak?"

Jack fleetingly thought of complaining about the usurping of his cherished table, but decided that this was probably not the right time to do so.

"Forgive my having to point this out," he said quietly but firmly, "but now that the Baron is dead, I am answerable only to his widow, the Lady Lucy."

De Sutton choked – his face going even redder. The hall resounded with his gasps for breath. Taking advantage of the brief respite, Jack considered the alternative consequences of telling the truth, the half-truth, or nothing like the truth. Any mention of the demon was too dangerous, so he'd stick to his Gran's idea of saying that the Baron had died from a fever.

"As your superior officer," De Sutton screamed, having recovered his breath but not from his loss of temper, "you will take your orders directly from me!"

Startled out of his contemplation, Jack sprang to attention and saluted.

"If my Lady Lucy orders me to," he muttered.

"She's just a woman!" De Sutton waved a hand dismissively. "I am in charge here now!" With his narrowed eyes and his lips curled back, his appearance suggested some wolves' blood in his ancestry. "I command you to tell me everything that you know about the Baron's death."

Now that the time had come for Jack to relate his highly modified account of what had happened, it didn't seem at all convincing. Inwardly, he quailed before the hostile stares of his inquisitors.

"Well?" snarled John De Sutton. "Tell us exactly what happened or I'll have you clapped in irons."

"Yes, Sire! While the Christmas party was going on, the Baron sent for me. He'd had a bed made up in *that* room over there…"

De Sutton and the Prior turned to follow the direction of Jack's pointing finger. The south-eastern tower room was now devoid of furniture. "He'd got bad pains in his stomach and I thought at first that something that he'd drunk or eaten had gone bad."

"Go on."

"I went and got my Gran…er…my grandmother to bring him something to soothe his stomach. She gave him some of her special potion."

"A *po*tion did you say? Or was it *poi*son?"

"No, my Lord. My Gran only makes *potions*. She uses 'em to *cure* folks, not to kill 'em."

"They say that *all* potions are poisons if the dosage is too great!" De Sutton announced icily.

"The dose was *not* too much. I take the same amount myself."

"Why?"

"For the pain that I get in this sword-wound." Jack stroked his tender scar through the thin linen that covered it. "I always carry a bottle of it and it works for me."

"The Baron trusted her enough to drink it?"

"Well, he did after I'd drunk some first. And as you can see, I'm still here to tell the tale."

"So you admit that you are telling us a *tale*?" De Sutton snorted.

"N-no, my Lord. That was just a fer-figure of speech."

"Perhaps it was," De Sutton muttered, glancing again at the monk beside him.

Jack stared hard at his examiners, hoping that this line of questioning had ended. "Anyway," he said, in order to change the subject, "it wasn't very long before he began to feel much better. In fact, he ordered my grandmother to bring him some of his favourite crustades. Opple and Blockberry they were."

"The contents of the pies are of no interest to me," De Sutton muttered. "Or perhaps they *are*," he added, his countenance darkening.

"What do you m-mean, my Lord?" Jack said, his fear growing ever more acute.

"We have only your word that you didn't poison him."

"Why should we do that? He was very good to us."

"Then why did you bolt all the doors?"

"Bolt?" Jack said, pretending to be mystified. "Oh yes! We *did* bolt the doors." Jack paused again as if in further thought. "The Baron's pain came back worser than before," he said as though remembering it. "So because the potion wasn't working, my Gran wanted to try-out something that she'd bought from a wandering preacher." Observing the dubious expressions of his audience, he added quickly: "He told her that the toe-bone of Saint Chad could cure almost anything."

"I will not ask you again," De Sutton snarled. "Why did you bolt the doors?"

"The preacher told her that there has to be complete silence for the relic to have any chance of working. The slightest sound would prevent it."

"The *slightest* sound, did you say? Yet I have been reliably informed that a loud banging noise was heard. Is that not so?"

"Yes it is, my Lord. When the Baron began shivering with cold, we dragged the brazier over to his bed. It got caught on one of the floorboards and toppled over."

De Sutton leaned forward. "So the Baron was still alive at this juncture?"

"Yes he was, my Lord. It was later that he died. He groaned once, and then he died. But he didn't suffer at the end – thanks to Saint Chad. We tried to bring him back. Of course we did. But it was no use. He was past all help.

And when I went to send for the Chapelain to perform the Last Rites, that's when I unbolted the doors."

Silence filled the hall. Above the inquisitors' heads, the De Somery banners wafted gently in the cross draught. Wistfully, Jack remembered how proudly he'd carried the latest addition at the battle for Burton Bridge. But apparently, that was of no importance now.

"Is there any thing else that we should know?" De Sutton snapped.

"What?"

"Do not *what* me. I repeat: Is there any thing else that we should know?"

"No, my Lord. I d-don't think so."

De Sutton twisted in his chair to address his silent attendant. "Do you have any questions, Prior Robert?"

"None at the moment," the monk answered in a whisper.

"Very well." De Sutton returned to Jack. "You are dismissed for the present, but do not leave the castle." As Jack turned to leave, he added: "Send your grandmother up. And tell her to bring that potion...and the relic."

*

Jack scuttled down the spiral staircase in a turmoil of uncertainty. Had they believed his account of what had happened? Why shouldn't they? It wasn't very far from the truth. And his Gran would confirm every word. So why were alarm bells ringing in his head? '*None at the moment*,' the Prior had said, threatening more searching questions to follow. They were not safe yet. Not by a long chalk.

*

In a corner of the bakehouse, Jack and his grandmother compared their interrogations. Hemmed in by the oven – the birthplace of her crustades – and two thick walls of whitewashed limestone, they couldn't be overheard. Jack had made quite sure that no one was lurking about outside, and left the door open to forewarn of anyone approaching.

Shooing the cat away from the warm stone ledge of the oven, Jack flopped down on the spot that it vacated.

And after establishing that his Gran's account had matched his own, he asked the question that he dared not voice before: "D'you think that they believed us?"

"They seem to have," Gran muttered, pulling up a stool and sitting down beside him. "Leastwise, they never actually *said* that they didn't."

Jack shuffled away from her, resentment contorting his features. "Why did yer have to start all that magic stuff in the first place?"

"You fetched me," she replied, affronted. "Remember?" She hotched up close again on her stool. "And as soon as I got into the hall, I knew that there was something very nasty there. Didestow not sense it?"

"No, Gran. The only nastiness that I sensed was the stench of the Baron's illness."

His Gran moved up closer still.

"And when we entered that tower-room," she whispered, "I felt that something evil was watching us. Didestow not sense that neither?"

"No, Gran."

"Well you're only a *man*," she said dismissively. "Men are not as sensitive as women."

Jack let the statement go unchallenged.

"It grew so strong…" Gran continued in an excited tone of voice, "that I knew for certain that we were in great danger. I couldn't see anything to explain it, so I decided to cast that circle of protection around us. If I hadn't, neither of us would still be alive – and who knows where our souls would have ended up then."

Jack had to admit that the subsequent events supported what she said. With an extended forefinger, he idly drew a circle in the ashes at his side. "It's just a pity that the Baron wasn't protected as well."

"Perhaps nothing on Earth could have saved him," Gran said sorrowfully. "From what you told me about the spell-casting in Coventry, one of Hell's demons had come to claim him. We were very lucky to escape with our own lives."

"So far we have," Jack muttered. "Canstow cast another circle to protect us from the Baron's kinfolk?"

"I don't think that it would be wise. Do you?"

"No," Jack admitted. "But there must be some sort of charm that you can...*what was that?*"

They both looked up, having heard something scraping on the roof.

"It's only the raven," Gran said, wiping sweat from her furrowed brow. "He comes down looking for scraps."

"It didn't sound like a raven to me," Jack muttered, leaping to his feet. His opinion was confirmed when something rattled down over the roof tiles. And then by the clattering descent of a heavy object. Lime dust settled on their heads, adding a further scurfy whiteness to Gran's already snowy locks.

As the unknown object crashed down outside, Jack dashed out through the doorway. He returned a few minutes later, dishevelled and downcast.

"Well, who*ever* that *was*," he said dispiritedly, "he got away before I got round there."

"He couldn't have heard what we were saying," Gran declared, but then wrung her hands in anguish. "Oh yes he could! I never thought to fit the draw-plate. The oven is still warm. Our voices could have been carried up the chimney by the draught."

"What are we going to do now?" Jack moaned, pacing up and down. "If he heard what we were saying, it'll be all over the castle by now."

CHAPTER 19

"Shall we try to escape?" Jack whispered, peering out through the bakehouse wind-eye.

"No!" said his Gran regretfully. "My running days am long since gone. You go by yourself."

"Mine are too," Jack said, rubbing his painful wound. "But the gatehouse seems to be deserted. We might get out unseen. After all, I chose the password."

But before they could do anything, De Sutton's man was framed in the doorway.

"He wants to see the two of you right away. Come along with me, if you please."

*

The hall was even darker now, for the winter's dismal daylight was fading fast. So were the spirits of Jack and his Gran as they stood before the table on the first floor of the Donjon. As before, John de Sutton occupied the Baron's high chair. But instead of the Prior, Lady Margaret was sitting at his side. Both of them looked angry.

"You have *not* been telling us the sooth," Lady Margaret blurted out before her husband had a chance to speak.

"But we *have* told the truth," Jack protested, realising that it didn't sound as convincing as he'd intended. "We told it just as it happened."

"Then explain to me the scorch marks on my brother's body," Lady Margaret said menacingly.

"What scorch marks?" the accused pair asked in unison.

"The soles of my brother's feet are both burnt black. The Prior showed them to me."

"I dunno," Jack mumbled, thinking fast, "unless he stepped on some embers when we knocked the brazier over."

John de Sutton stared at each of them in turn. "I thought you said that the Baron was confined to his bed."

"And so he was," Gran answered, "for most of the time. But he did have to visit the garderobe. He must have trod on the embers while we were helping him across there."

The De Suttons glanced at one another. "And what about the footprints?" they demanded.

"What footprints?" chorused the interrogatees.

"Those over there." John de Sutton nodded towards the spot where the Baron had fallen. "Those two scorched on the floorboards on this side of the doorway."

"They must have been caused by the embers as well," Gran announced after only the briefest of pauses.

"Leaving the clear impressions of two naked feet?" John de Sutton scoffed. "And both of them facing away from the door?"

Gran shrugged. "The Baron must have trodden some embers into the floor. But do not worry, my Lord, he would not have felt no pain with my potion in 'im." She forced a grin to imply that this explained everything.

"Those two denials cancel each another out. The cleaners say that the ashes in the brazier were stone cold when they got here on the next morning."

"No wonder," Gran countered. "It's freezing up here in the summer. In the middle of winter, it gets as cold as a grave, especially when the shutters are open, as they were on that night. Why, the water in the safety-bucket was froze solid when we left."

"By which time," De Sutton roared, "my brother-in-law was dead."

"Yes, my Lord. We'd got him back into bed and he passed peacefully away in his sleep."

De Sutton leaned back in his chair, observing the pair before him with narrowed eyes. "How do you explain the smell then?"

"What smell?" the pair replied with genuine expressions of surprise on their faces.

"The smell of sulphur."

"I threw some of it on the fire to fumigate the room," Gran lied emphatically.

Lady Margaret stood up and pointed at Gran's throat. "I notice that you keep fingering a thing that's hanging round your neck. That proves that you're not telling us the sooth."

"It's just a good luck charm," Gran said, releasing the 'Man o' Leaves' talisman so that it dropped out of sight down the front of her smock. "Yower looks am enough to kill."

"Like you did to my brother," Lady Margaret muttered.

"How many more times do I have ter tell yer? I dain't kill 'im."

Sighing with exasperation, De Sutton produced a pouch and pulled out something small and brownish. "From what you have told us," he announced, "rather than relying on that charm, you seem to have put greater store on this toe-bone of Saint Chad."

"Yes, my Lord," Gran said, screwing up her eyes to see it better. "If that's the same one, it does seem to have had some effect."

De Sutton put the bone back into his pouch. "From the number of these that are being peddled, it makes one wonder how many toes *did* the Saint possess? However," he added as Jack tried to stifle a chuckle, "the custodian of his bones has confirmed that some are missing from his skelet—"

"There you are then," Gran interrupted.

De Sutton thumped on the table with his fist. "As I was a*bout* to say, our butcher says that *your* bone looks more like a pig's." With his eyes fixed on Gran's now-reddening face, he reached for his wife's hand and caressed it with his fingertips. "Leave us to consider what you have told us. But don't try to leave the castle."

As the guard unbolted the door to the spiral staircase, the couple heard De Sutton mutter to his wife: "They are lying. I am sure of that!"

Gran turned, shrugging off the guard's grip on her shoulder. "We have told you the sooth!" she screamed.

"Get them out of here!" yelled John De Sutton.

*

For several days, nothing further happened and Jack and Gran had begun to hope that they were in the clear, until they were ordered back to the Donjon for further questioning.

De Sutton occupied the late Baron's throne once more, but now wearing his yellow surcoat with its lion rampant. Lady Margaret sat on his right, along with her sister Joan. On his left sat Lady Lucy, the Baron's widow. The women were clad in mourning-black – their hair hidden beneath clouts of similar colour.

At a table nearby sat the Prior of Saint James's. That priest had once been kind enough to grant Jack Sanctuary there (under certain conditions). But he'd fled with a pair of shoes and a monk's old habit. Now hunched like an eagle about to swoop on its prey, the priest stared at Jack with eyes aflame with loathing.

Beside him at the same table sat the Priory's Scrivener, his quill pen poised above a sheet of parchment. And next to him, the Chapelain of the castle seethed with expectation – possibly because Jack had once had the effrontery to question the truth of the Holy Scriptures.

These three godly souls wore the black hooded robes of their calling. But as Gran pointed out with a whisper: "From the nasty way that they'm glowerin' at us, it seems to me that *they'm* the most evil ones here."

Jack snorted. "An' they're always tellin' *us* to *love one another*!"

John de Sutton rose to his feet and coughed to clear his throat.

"We have made our enquiries," he announced, staring fixedly at a point halfway between Jack and his Gran, "and some of the facts that we have uncovered *do* support your story."

As the defendants relaxed slightly, he continued in a louder voice: "But others prove to us that you are lying!"

Jack and his Gran both strove to control their expressions – their minds in turmoil – their heartbeats racing. What had they overlooked?

"There is the little matter of the *garderobe*." De Sutton pointed at the tower-room at the north-west corner of the hall. "You claim that the Baron paid a visit to that latrine."

"Y-yes, my Lord," Jack said, recalling that it was himself who'd been caught short.

"To do what, exactly?" the lord asked.

"How do you mean?"

"Solid or liquid?"

"How should I know?" Jack spluttered.

"Must I remind you who you are talking to?" bellowed John de Sutton. "Show proper respect for your betters or your insubordination will be added to your other offences."

"I am sorry, my Lord. I forgot myself. But you said *offences?* Are we being accused of any crime?"

"That is what we are here to determine. I repeat: do you know the purpose of the Baron's visit to the garderobe?"

"No, my Lord. That's not something that one asks one's lord and master."

Ignoring the sharp intakes of breath around him, De Sutton stared Jack in the eyes. "On the morning after the night in question, the Gong Farmer found no night-soil in the garderobe."

As Jack cursed himself for ordering daily muck-outs, De Sutton continued: "Only some frozen piddle on the stonework."

"Well there you are then," Gran cried. "What are you asking *us* for?"

"Because," said De Sutton, "it was on the *outer* wall of the shaft."

Unable to think of anything threatening in these disclosures, Jack's attention was caught by a movement behind the Service Room curtain. It couldn't be Felicia because she'd gone to visit a dying relative. That was confirmed when a procession of servants emerged from behind the curtain. They lined themselves up in front of it – eyes agog with anticipation.

"The point that I'm making is *THIS* . . . . .." De Sutton's shout catapulted Jack back to the subject of the latrine. "The Gong Farmer says that it must have been a powerful...er...flow to have reached so far. And as we all know, the garderobe is...er...was reserved for the exclusive use of the Baron and his lady."

As Lady Lucy blushed, the hall rang out with the sound of servants' titters. De Sutton glared around angrily. "Guard," he cried. "Get them out of here. No! Let them stay. They might have something to contribute to this investigation." Turning back, he continued in lowered tones: "I happen to know that John de Somery had a very feeble flow of late."

Jack was about to confess that it was he who'd visited the garderobe, and thus reveal that he'd lied, when his Gran beat him to it.

"I can explain that," she cried, her words almost drowned by more tittering from the servants. "Another property of that potion of mine is that it increases male...er...vigour."

Suddenly, the hall was so quiet that you could have heard a nose drip.

"Particularly down *there*," she added, lowering her gaze to emphasise her meaning.

Silence filled the hall as her audience considered this new piece of information.

De Sutton seemed to have acquired a heightened interest, for his eyes lit up and his face reddened. This didn't go unnoticed by his wife, who scowled down at her suddenly-clenching fists.

"I have to admit," De Sutton said quickly, "that the garderobe *does* have an aroma like that of your bottle of potion."

"Well that proves it then, don't it?" Gran stared around in defiance, her hands on her hips, her lower jaw working furiously.

Suddenly, a man broke from the crowd of servants and rushed forward to the table.

"Them two are both *witches*," he screamed. "I heard 'em talkin' about it in the bakehouse."

CHAPTER 20

Both Jack and his Gran knew their accuser well and liked him not at all. Jack always called him '*The* Cookney'– as the one who'd envied them from their first day at the castle. He was still a cook's assistant and bitterly resentful of it.

"So it was *you* who was clambering about on my roof," Gran cried. "You've always had it in for us." She turned back to face the nobles. "It's a wonder to me that you let 'im stay on as a *Cookney*. He picks his nose and licks his fingers when he's cuttin' up' your meat."

"Everybody picks their noses," the Cookney screeched, turning his reddening face away to hide it from the gentry, who were looking at one another with disgust.

"*We* don't do it," Gran announced with a smirk of self-satisfaction. "And we always wash our 'onds after we've been to the garderobe. Dun yow?"

It was clear from the Cookney's expression that he did not. Nor did the gentry by the look of 'em.

Resentment returned to the Cookney's face. "What I said is the sooth," he bawled. "Them two cast a spell on the Baron and I can prove it!"

"How can you prove it?" Gran taunted, "when we did no such thing?"

"I heard 'em say how they'd made a magic ring around the Baron. And how he got out of his bed and smote a dragon with his sword."

As laughter filled the hall, De Sutton rounded angrily on his servant. "Keep your fairy tales for little children. Do not presume to tell them here."

"It's not a tale," the Cookney protested, now red-faced with anger. "From what I heard, the dragon was trying to swallow the Baron but he shoved his sword up its nostril." In spite of the screams of hilarity, the Cookney continued: "It's *true* I tell you. There was a big flash and the Baron fell dead."

In the stunned silence of the hall, the Prior's voice could be heard quite clearly:

"That explains those scorch marks – and those on the Baron's sword-hand too."

De Sutton looked surprised and sceptical. But after his wife had confirmed that the Baron's palm was indeed scorched, he beckoned the guard over from the doorway: "Is the Baron's sword available for our inspection?"

"It is, my Lord. We took it to Lady Lucy's apartments."

"My Lady, does he have your leave to fetch it?" When she nodded her agreement, the guard immediately left…reappearing some time later with the sword still in its scabbard. De Sutton seized the weapon and examined the leather handgrip.

"This *is* badly scorched," he said, his eyebrows raised. Taking hold of both the handle and the scabbard, he drew the blade out. Instead of the expected sheen of polished steel, it was patterned with purple whorls. Without a word, De Sutton produced his dagger and scraped it along the sword blade. A sliver of steel adhered to the edge of the knife. "This sword's been in a fire," he said, turning his gaze on Gran. "Can you explain this?"

"No, my Lord. It could have fallen into the brazier, but I can't remember it."

With the sword's handle in his left hand, De Sutton gripped the tip of the blade with the other. Without appearing to exert much effort, he bent the blade until the two came almost together.

"This degree of softening was not done in a brazier," he announced, holding up the hoop for all to see. "It would take prolonged and widespread heating to draw the temper from this steel. It seems that the cookney has spoken the sooth."

"I told yer so," crowed the Cookney, smiling broadly.

With the audience apparently struck dumb, the ministers of the church stared at Gran with hatred in their eyes. The Prior of Saint James's was the first to find his voice: "By your leave, my Lord, I demand that these two witnesses be made to swear upon the Bible that their account of the Baron's death is true."

All eyes turned towards Gran, whose face had grown even paler.

"I shall swear on anything you like," she muttered, trying to pull herself together. "Books all look the same to me. I never learned to read."

"You do not recognise the Holy *Bible*?" the Prior cried.

"I just said so, dain't I?"

"She condemns herself out of her own mouth." The priest turned to address the crowd. "Not only is this woman a witch – she's a heretic as well."

As the servants crossed themselves in awe and fear, Gran wrung her withered hands.

"I bain't no witch. I just help folks when they'm poorly. It's true that I make potions for sick people, but these are mostly to sooth away their pain."

"And you utter no incantations?" the Prior asked with a sneer. "I am reliably told that you DO."

"Folks expects a bit of mumbling whilst I'm giving 'em their potion. They likes it, an' it helps to do 'em good."

"She admits to using incantations!" the Prior cried triumphantly.

"You'm a fine one to talk." Gran shrugged off her grandson's warning grip. "I've seen you lot chanting strange words and swinging a bowl of burning incense. If that ain't magic, I should like to know what *is*?"

"She insults the Holy Benison," the Prior screamed. "You have all heard her blasphemy. *Burn the witch to ashes.*"

"Why d'yer keep saying as I'm a witch?" Gran cried, "when I've told yer as I bain't no such thing? I'm just an old woman that some folks come to when their bodies want healing, just like they come to you lot when their souls need it. We'm more alike than yer care ter admit. Now I come ter think of it, we'm two sides of the same coin."

"What are you trying to do, Gran?" Jack whispered. "Convert him? Look at him. He don't want ter know."

The Prior, while keeping his hate-filled gaze fixed on the old woman, pointed towards the servants who stood in shocked amazement at the far end of the hall.

"Unlike those poor sinners," he cried, "who've been carrying Adam's burden of sin from the day of their birth. *You*," – he pointed at Gran, eyeing her along his forefinger as though it was a crossbow bolt – "have wilfully chosen to follow the path of evil."

"I ain't chosen to follow no path," Gran screeched, her dander well and truly up. "And anyway, what's all this about babbies bein' born with the burden of sin already on their little shoulders? Let me tell you, I've had enough babbies die in me arms ter know as it weren't their fault."

Endorsing murmurs came from the jostling servants.

The Prior seemed about to explode with rage. "She must die before she can infect anyone else with her lies." He turned to John de Sutton for his approval.

But before that lord could reply, Gran started up again, her eyes flashing with contempt: "You lot mek me sick. Tellin' us how we must behave, while carryin' on like yer do behind locked doors."

Appalled by the way that his grandmother's temper was getting them into ever-increasing danger, Jack looked to the Baron's widow for support. But her eyes were cold and unsympathetic. He could expect no help from her. And he quailed before Lady Margaret's venomous scowl.

Her husband rose to his feet and held up a hand to silence the murmuring crowd.

"In view of what we have just heard," he said. "I have no alternative but to clap the old baxter in irons. Guard! As soon as we have finished here, take her down to the Chapel Undercroft and chain her to the wall. And once we have extracted a full confession from her, I shall consult the Prior as to the most appropriate method of execution – hanging or burning."

"It must be both, my Lord," the Prior insisted.

"But I understood that burning is only for *heretics*."

"You have heard the woman's blasphemy for yourself. Only flames can drive the demons from her body and thus redeem her immortal soul."

The hall fell silent as the import of these words sank in. Jack's grandmother was to be hanged and burned at the stake as both witch and heretic. As if to emphasise the latter, the smoke that had hitherto been rising straight up from the brazier began to drift across the hall and out through the lancet wind-eyes.

"But first," the Prior cried eagerly, "she must endure the Ordeal by Fire to demonstrate her guilt." He pointed to the brazier. "There's enough of a fire *there*, and a poker lying ready on the ash tray. We can do it right away."

The Scrivener left his seat to whisper in the Prior's ear. Nevertheless, it was now so quiet that everyone there could hear him: "But your Holiness, Trial by Ordeal has been forbidden by the Pope. He's proclaimed that it presumes to involve the Lord Our God in mere local disputes."

The Prior turned upon him a look to strike him dead. "I knew that," he snarled, "but that applies only to the *Priesthood*. John de Sutton is presiding over this enquiry."

John de Sutton shook his head. "And *I* will have *none* of it," he proclaimed. "These floorboards have been scorched enough already. And anyway, the stink of burning flesh would put me off my dinner. Take her away."

Stunned by what was happening, Jack had hitherto remained silent.

"I demand the right to Trial by Combat," he heard somebody shout. He turned around to find out who it was. Everybody was looking at *him*. He was even more stunned now.

"You fool," Gran moaned. "If you lose the fight, both of us will die."

CHAPTER 21

John de Sutton mopped his brow and gazed up at the smoke-hazed rafters. When at last he spoke, it was with a thoughtful tone of voice: "I've been present at Trials by Combat. After the war against the Ordainers, some of Lancaster's followers applied for what they called 'Judicial Duels' to prove their innocence of Treason against the Crown. But I can't say that I've heard of it being used anywhere else."

"It used to be a popular way of settling disputes," the Chapelain mumbled, loud enough for everyone there to hear.

"Especially for big men with long weapons," called one of the servants from the safe anonymity of the crowd.

"That's not much use to *yow* then, Jack," shrilled a female voice to peals of raucous laughter.

Jack blushed, thankful that his wife wasn't there to hear.

"I must have silence!" roared De Sutton. "This is a serious matter and I will not tolerate hilarity in this hall."

"I object to such a trial," the Prior screamed, his face a mask of loathing and repulsion. "It's an unreliable way of proving the witch's guilt. She's a self-confessed heretic and so must burn at the stake."

Flaring with indignation, Jack shook his fist at the Prior. "You were keen enough to use Single Combat yourself. *Yes*," he added as he turned to the silent crowd. "He wanted *me* to fight so that he could seize land from the peasant farmers." He turned back to the reddening Prior. "Slipped your mind, has it? How convenient!"

For once, the priest seemed lost for words.

In the ensuing silence, De Sutton turned to the Chapelain. "Is 'Trial by Duel' legal for cases like this?"

The Chapelain paused to consider.

"I'm not sure," he said eventually. "It seems to have been replaced by Trial by Jury."

"Which is *what*, exactly?" Lady Margaret demanded.

The Chapelain bowed his head respectfully. "First, the accused must swear on oath that he or she is innocent. Then a dozen reputable men must testify that they know this to be the case." He slumped back in his seat. "But as far as I know, Trial by Single Combat is not ill-legal."

The Prior laughed a short and hostile laugh.

"Well we know that the woman's oath is worthless."

Jack stared at him with scorn. "Of course my Gran will swear that she is innocent. And that's because she *is*. As for finding a Jury like what you said...there'll be no lack of folks who'll back her up."

"That will take too long," De Sutton said, mopping his brow again. "Single Combat it shall be then."

Gran tugged frantically at Jack's sleeve.

"Yer mustn't do it," she whispered. "You'll get yourself killed and all for nothing."

Jack put his arm around her shoulders to give her a reassuring hug. For once, she didn't shrug him off and now he realised why she'd always resisted. There was only skin and bones beneath her several layers of clothing. "Just give me some o' that potion," he said gently, "and I will fight the whole of the King's army for you if need be. Anyway, the need to prove your innocence will give me added strength."

"Silence!" De Sutton cried again. "Guard! Take them both away. Chain the Baxter up as I commanded before. And lock the Steward in his office – though I doubt if we shall find anyone to oppose him."

"I'll do it," the Cookney cried eagerly, "if I can have his job when I defeat him."

"Do you think that you have sufficient prowess?" John de Sutton looked doubtful.

"Yes, my Lord. I have been taking lessons. And anyway, the angels will surely protect me from the Devil's accomplices."

"But not from the evil within thyself," Gran shouted.

De Sutton turned to Jack. "What would be your chosen weapon?"

"Sword and Buckler."

"That's two, but never mind."

"I object," the Prior cried, back on his feet and fuming. "Those weapons will give the ex-soldier an unfair advantage."

"There is some sooth in that," De Sutton admitted, "but what is the alternative?"

"In our Priory," the Prior said, choking back his rage with difficulty, "we have a floor tile that depicts Judicial Combat. If I remember rightly, both combatants have short picks."

"Just like you, Jack," yelled the same woman from the crowd.

Jack flushed with shame as laughter filled the air.

"I shall not tell you again!" De Sutton roared, glaring round at his uproarious domestics. "Any more of that, and I shall order you from the hall." He turned back to Jack. "Do we have any weapons like that in the armoury?"

"None, my Lord," Jack said, in the belief that his own choice of arms would now prevail.

De Sutton twisted in his seat. "Prior. What can you tell us about these picks?"

"Long handles. Short prongs," the priest replied without interest.

"Our miners have some like that," a male voice cried out from among the servants.

"Get me some," De Sutton commanded. "And what about their armour, Prior?"

"What about it?" said the Prior without deviating his gaze from Jack's face.

"What armour are the combatants on the tile wearing?"

"I don't know," the Prior said, still glaring. "How should *I* know?"

"And I suppose you don't know if they are carrying shields, either," said De Sutton with the air of someone whose patience was being strained to the limit.

"Square ones with small round bosses," said the priest.

De Sutton turned to Jack. "Do we have any shields like that then?"

"None, my Lord. But we do have Pavises to protect the whole body, and Bucklers to cover the fist. But all we have in between is a shoulder-shield of the Baron's."

"Only the one?" De Sutton asked sceptically.

"Yes, my Lord. His others got smashed at Burton Bridge."

"Then I shall just have to provide one from my own armoury."

"I object," the Prior cried again, rising from his seat. "That one-time soldier will still have a great advantage."

"There's not much that I can do about that," De Sutton said wearily.

The Cookney now spoke up again: "By your leave, my Lord, let me be the only one armed and armoured."

The hall fell silent at this effrontery.

"No," snapped De Sutton. "That would give *you* too much of an advantage. Yet the odds do need to be made more even. However, since picks are evidently the prescribed weapons for Judicial Combat, I declare that a wide range of these implements shall be provided – and that *you*," he glared at the cookney, "shall have the first choice."

He arose from his seat and turned towards the doorway that led out to the spiral staircase. "Guard! See that you lock these two up right away. And by daybreak tomorrow, I want a suitable enclosure erected in the courtyard. Assemble the picks...as many and as varied as you can find, and a pair of shields of similar size and soundness. Any questions?"

"Yes, my Lord," the guard cried, snapping to attention. "These shields...do they have to be round or square, and large or small?"

"I couldn't care less," De Sutton replied, "as long as they're the same."

"Very well, my Lord. It shall be done as you command."

"Good!" cried De Sutton, thumping on the table with the pommel of his dagger.

"And may God protect the right!"

*

"Time to get up!"

Jack opened his eyes with a start, glad to be free of a nightmare of Witchcraft and Combat. While wondering where such horrible dreams kept coming from, he realised that he'd been sleeping in his office. Why was that?

"It's time to get up and fight!" a male voice boomed through the door.

It all came flooding back. It had been no nightmare. He was having to fight 'The Cookney' to the death.

The previous night had been plagued with fear and doubt. He'd tried to pray to Jesus Christ – but the few words of Latin that he knew seemed inadequate.

"You can't stay sulking in there!" the voice shouted.

"All right!" Jack called back, tossing aside the rug that had been serving as a coverlet. As he struggled to his feet, he clung to the fading memory of the dream, convinced that it contained something of great importance. That was it: his grandmother's potion. He'd almost forgotten that he'd got some stowed away. Throwing back the lid of his personal chest, he scrabbled amongst the jumble. "Just give me time to get ready!" he shouted as his fingers located the bottle. At least he could face the forthcoming ordeal with something approaching confidence. How much of the potion should he take? All of it? No. Potions could be poisons if too much was drunk. Better stick to the usual dose, he decided and raised the bottle to his lips. The thick sticky liquid flowed down his throat – filling his mouth and nostrils with its pungency. A comforting glow spread throughout his belly, and soothed the nagging of the wound in his left hand side. He took another sip to make doubly sure. His nerves somewhat abated, he donned his leather boots and hauled his hauberk up above his head. He shivered as the mesh of iron rings engulfed his body. Then he covered it with his golden tunic. "I'll try to do you proud," he whispered to De Somery's pair of lions as he fastened his belt and scabbard round his waist. With his helmet tucked into the crook of his arm, he strode manfully to the door and thumped it with a leather-covered fist.

"I am ready!" he bellowed through the planks of cold damp timber.

After some grumbling from his guard, who had evidently spent the night out in the rain, an iron bolt shot back. The door swung open and out Jack marched into a courtyard thronged with people.

But despite his striking appearance, no one took any notice of him...he who was about to fight for his life, and for their entertainment too.

He recalled his visions on that terrible night in the Donjon. They *had* seemed to show what was going to happen in the future. So even if he *was* about to die, all these scurrying people would be following him ere long.

Somewhat comforted by that thought, he breathed in deeply, enlivened by the ice-cold air flowing into his lungs. Now chilled inside and out, he gazed around the courtyard – possibly, the last time he would do so.

The Donjon loomed dark and sinister above him – its drum-towers edged with crimson by the rising sun. Torchlight twinkled in its lancet wind-eyes, as though happy to see him get his come-upp'nce at last. "Don't laugh too soon," he murmured, partly to himself. "I am not beaten yet."

He looked around for his Gran.

There she was, slumped against a gibbet with a loop of chain around her neck and faggots piled up against her legs. Close to that intended pyre, a smouldering brazier waited − with long-poled torches to convey its sanctified flames.

"I will not let that happen," Jack shouted, waving her his encouragement. But lost in either prayer or private misery, she neither saw nor heard him.

On the opposite side of the courtyard was the reason for that banging in the night. Posts with sagging chains enclosed a square of muddy turf. A raised platform further on had been furnished with green and golden awnings, with pennons of similar colours flaunting De Sutton's forked-tail lion. And all of this proclaimed that *he* was now in charge.

That lord appeared on the dais and after acknowledging the crowd, he seated himself on a high chair at the front. After him came his wife, then her sister Joan, and finally Lady Lucy, the Baron's widow. Anxious servants brought furs to protect them from the cold, while black-robed monks stood shivering behind them − their heads thrust out like ravens watching slaughter.

Plagued with sudden uncertainty, Jack walked slowly across to the 'Ring', where a pair of coffins lay waiting. As he grimaced at the fact that both of them might soon be filled, he noticed a row of picks laid out on the grass nearby. De Sutton had ordered a selection to be provided and the guard had certainly done so. The ash stales ranged between two and five feet in length − their heads between one and four feet from tine to tine. The largest ones were too heavy − perfect for hewing rock but not for mortal combat.

He grabbed the shortest stave and tested the head for balance. Not so very different from his throwing-axe, it would allow him to kill the Cookney from a distance. But it could be deflected with a shield, and then he'd be at a very grave disadvantage. He swapped it for a three-foot stale, with a fifteen-inch span of head. With the spikes cratered to sharpness by corrosion, they could penetrate riveted maile to a lethal depth. He tried a few experimental swings − the head describing a sidewise figure eight around him.

"I shall have this one," he announced to the official who was evidently in charge of the proceedings. "What comes next?"

"Well, you can't wear *this* for a start," the official said, picking up the hem of Jack's hauberk and examining it closely. "Take it off. According to that black-robed bugger up there…" he nodded towards the Prior, who was also seated on the dais and fidgeting as though impatient to get it all over with. "It's to be thin linen tunics for you two. No helmets neither," he added, grabbing Jack's head-case and sniffing its interior. "I'll make an offer for these if you lose."

Following an ignominious withdrawal from his precious hauberk, Jack was made to disrobe down to his (snow-white) breeches. "Thanks, Gran," he muttered, for the Cookney's were stained with yellow at the crotch.

A shirt of wrinkled linen was slipped over Jack's head and then belted around his waist. In partial compensation for the inadequate protection, the Baron's tapered shield was brought − thirty inches in height and twenty in width. De Somery's blue lions adorned the gilded steel as Jack hefted it up to squint along its curvature. A pick would glance off that if it struck obliquely. But being heavier than he was used to, it would be hard to manipulate with speed and agility.

As with the opening moves of chess, constant practice with the Sword and Buckler had instilled in him the standard moves and countermoves. Unfortunately, these were not going to be of much use to him now.

His stomach churning, Jack was led out into the arena and made to face the platform. Beside him stood 'The Cookney', similarly attired. He'd had the first choice of picks and had chosen one with a broad heavy head and a shaft half as long again as Jack's was. He grinned, his own being far more manoeuvrable and deadly.

Physically, the combatants made a fairly well matched pair: both six feet tall and made broad of shoulder by regular practice sessions with the bow.

Mentally, their situations were very different.

The Cookney had never engaged in hand-to-hand combat, but his pent-up resentment would make him a deadly foe.

Jack felt only contempt for his opponent, and was determined to save his Gran from an agonising death.

De Sutton rose to his feet and held up his hand to command silence from the crowd.

"The outcome of this contest," he cried, "shall decide the guilt or otherwise of the prisoner over there." Heads turned as one to gawp at Jack's grandmother, who hung her head in shame. "She who stands accused of witchcraft, sorcery and heresy." A cloud of pink-tinted mist now hid his face. "This contest shall continue to the death!" he shouted through it. "And should both combatants be slain, the accusation shall be declared unproved and the Baxter deemed to be guiltless!" He paused again, as if for the maximum effect. "Is that understood?!"

Jack nodded, noting with satisfaction that The Cookney had begun to tremble.

CHAPTER 22

Even with his life in jeopardy – and his grandmother's too of course – Jack felt strangely confident. After all, considering the many perils that he had survived already, *something* must be protecting him. And whether that *something* was his grandmother's magic or just Blind Fate, it would surely not abandon him now in his hour of need. Having almost convinced himself of his invulnerability, he marched stiffly across to the centre of the ring and hoisted his shield aloft for everyone to see. The onlookers on two sides of the square cheered lustily, while those on the other sides stayed silent. And when the Cookney held up De Sutton's shield, those who'd previously been quiet shouted their heads off, and those who'd been so noisy remained tight-lipped.

Jack glared at his disparagers. So *that* was to be the way of it: De Somery versus De Sutton! Very well. Now he would show 'em what a Netherton man could do.

If he hadn't got the wound in his side, his best course of action would be to rush the Cookney and administer the first (and often final) blow. However, its persistent nagging urged him to be cautious. So, planting his feet firmly on the sodden turf, he crouched with bended knees and waited for his opponent to make his move. Jack's right hand held his pick, the shaft gripped halfway along its length and supported by his forearm. His other arm held the shield out ready, tilted to his left to deflect the expected blow. Breathing deeply to calm his racing pulse, Jack watched his opponent intently.

The Cookney ran towards him, holding his shield out in front, both as protection and as counterweight to the head of his pick, which he swung over and down at Jack's unprotected head. But because he was gripping the shaft too close to its end, he was finding it difficult to control the head's alignment.

With the head of his own pick now rammed against the underside of his shield, Jack raised them both together to meet the blow. The Cookney's spike crashed onto the gilded metal, gouging a groove until skidding off over the rim. Taking two steps forward, Jack swung his pick at his opponent's exposed side. But the Cookney hauled his shield back up and knocked Jack's blow away.

As the pair stood glaring at one another over the tops of their heraldic shields, their respective supporters screamed for the spilling of blood. Jack's pain had vanished now, and he was becoming more attuned to the situation. He could afford to let his opponent wear himself out with ineffectual blows. So when the Cookney aimed a second one from the comparative safety afforded by his longer weapon, Jack easily swung his shield up to deflect it.

Again and again, the Cookney rained down blows – each one repulsed with flourishes of Jack's shield. For as Jack's confidence increased, the Cookney's furious hacking was getting wilder.

Then came the moment that Jack had been waiting for. As his opponent's pick bounced off the shield, its head twisted so much that the tines were level with the ground. Jack swiped his own pick's stave down onto the other's.

The Ash shafts clashed as in the Morris Dance, and then slid down together 'til their spiked heads locked their horns. Twisting round to his left, and with his pick's stave again supported by his forearm, Jack wrenched his opponent's weapon from his grasp. The Cookney watched aghast as it flopped down onto the mud. Twisting round to his right, Jack swung his pick back up in a murderous backhand stroke, steering its tine towards the Cookney's gullet. But the man jumped back just in time and Jack's prong missed his throat by a whisker. With the opposing crowds screaming their encouragement, Jack hauled his pick to a standstill and twisted back to make a returning swipe. But he wasn't quite fast enough. Unencumbered by his pick, the Cookney dashed forward and rammed the rim of his shield into Jack's unprotected side. The wound exploded with agonising pain. It shot down his leg to his knee, which immediately buckled beneath him. Tottering forward, Jack tripped and sprawled full-length on the muddy ground, his left arm caught in the shield that lay beneath him. Disengaging from its handgrip and the arm-strap, he squirmed wormlike in the mud, striving to gain some purchase with his toes. Summoning all his strength in one great effort, he managed to twist himself over onto his back. The Cookney's shadow fell over him, his pick's head raised aloft to make the kill – its wet tines turned to crimson by the rising sun. And with the clarity of thought that is said to be vouchsafed to those about to die, Jack realised to his horror that Adrasteus would soon have him in its clutches.

"Die, you son-of-a-witch," the Cookney shrieked, tightening his grip on his shaft to administer the fatal blow. And as an expectant hush descended on the courtyard, Jack heard his grandmother cry out in desperation:

"Spare Jack's life and I shall tell you everything.!"

And in that pregnant moment, Jack pulled back his sound right leg and rammed his foot as hard as he could into the Cookney's groin.

With a cry of surprise and pain, the man let go of his pick and it dropped down onto the ground behind him. Jack kicked again, catching the Cookney's shin just below the knee. The man fell backwards at full length, screaming as his own upstanding spike speared into his shoulder. His body went limp – draped across his stave like a wilting flower.

Jack slithered towards him, using his own pick to drag himself through the mud. But as he raised its head above the Cookney's throat, his Gran shrieked out above the roaring of the crowd: "Spare him, Jack, for I am bound to keep my word."

In spite of the fury of his battle-frenzy, Jack heard De Sutton bellow across the field:

"STOP THE FIGHT AND BRING THE OLD WOMAN TO ME."

Jack collapsed beside his still-unconscious rival. Bewildered by pain and exhaustion, he heard De Sutton order his Gran to treat the Cookney's wound.

"I shall do my best," she replied, looking anxiously across to her grandson, who had propped himself up on an elbow and was staring at her in amazement.

"I expect you to do better than your best," De Sutton said curtly. "And when you've seen to the two of them, I shall hold you to your oath. I mean to know what really befell that night. Tell me no lies or the Prior shall have his roasting after all."

*

So once again, Jack and his grandmother were ordered to present themselves in the hall on the first floor of the Donjon.

"I'm goin' to tell 'em what happened," Gran said, as they crossed the muddy courtyard, urged on by the spear of the guard who marched behind them. Before Jack could speak, she added hurriedly: "But I shall try to convince 'em that you were just an innocent bystander. If they accept that, and I end up on their bonfire, I'm relying on you to put an arrow through my heart. It will be kindly-meant so I shall be content." She turned to him at the entrance to the Donjon, a glint of realisation in her eyes. "With the gallows and the fire, that'll make three ways of dying."

"Hurry along now," yelled the guard, waving his spear around without much purpose.

"Yow might want to hear this an' all," Gran said as they began to climb the spiral staircase, her voice sounding strangely hollow in the curving space. "When I was a little girl, my grandmother used to tell me about the 'Triple

Death'. It happened so long ago (gasp) that it was before the Normans took over. Let me get me breath back." She paused beside a wind-eye. "If yer can believe it, food was even scarcer then than it is today. A holy man volunteered to be killed three different ways. My Gran didn't know if it *did* save our people from starvation, but as my Dad pointed out: it must have done or she wouldn't have been alive to tell us about it."

"That's all very well," said the guard from lower down on the stairs. "But what's that got to do with us?"

Gran laughed grimly as she began to climb again. "If I'm goin' ter have ter face the 'Triple Death' meself, perhaps it'll stop the famine that we'm livin' through *now*."

"Let us hope that it *will* then," the guard muttered impatiently. "Hurry up now. They're all waiting for you."

"I *won't* let you die," Jack said as they entered the great hall. With the air reverberating with the murmurs of expectant servants, the inquisitors were resuming their positions of the day before.

De Sutton turned to address the crowd: "Silence!" he bellowed and the murmuring ceased abruptly.

"Well, mistress?" he said, easing himself back into his throne and beckoning his prisoners to approach the great oak table. He fixed his stare on Gran. "I have spared your life, at least for the time being. Now confess to us your sorcery."

"There was no sorcery," Jack protested, ignoring his grandmother's tightening grip on his arm. "Or at least: none on my Gran's part. As I keep tellin' yer. She ain't no witch. She's just what is called a 'Wise Woman'."

Immediately, the Prior arose from his seat like a dark avenging angel. "She still hasn't told us..." he screamed, leaning forward and resting both fists on his table, "what she was *really* doing at the Baron's bedside."

"Can't you understand plain English?" Jack cried. "Perhaps you can't because you're all foreigners here. How could *you* know whether she's telling the truth or not? My Gran was…can you grasp what I'm saying if I speak more slowly? She…was…giving…him a…potion to…soothe…away…his…pain. She never got around to trying out her relic because…because…"

"Because the Baron was being attacked by a demon," Gran cried out wildly.

CHAPTER 23

Uproar filled the hall. Nevertheless, through all that mayhem, one word reoccurred: "A *demon*..."

"Attacked by a *demon*..."

"She says that there was a *demon* here."

Thrusting back his chair, John de Sutton lurched to his feet and called for silence. When the commotion continued unabated, he brought his fist down hard on the polished table. But because of the solidity of the wood, this action had more effect on his hand than on the noisy multitude.

"Silence!" he roared again, wringing his wrist. "Or I shall clear the hall."

Silence ensued.

"I told you all along!" the Prior shouted, back on his feet and pointing. "She has been consorting with demons."

De Sutton rounded on the priest: "I shall send you out as well if you can't be quiet."

The priest sat down, scowling his resentment while De Sutton turned back to Gran in disbelief. "Can what you say be the sooth?"

"It is, my Lord," Gran said, pushing her grandson forward, "but only my Jack can tell you how it all started."

"By your leave, my Lord," Jack began, unwilling to embark upon a full disclosure but not sure what to leave out. "Please allow me a few moments to sort out the sequence of events in my mind."

"To concoct another pack of lies," the Prior roared, unable to maintain his silence or his seat.

One glance from De Sutton was enough to make him.

"He *will* tell you the truth," Gran protested, "no matter how strange it may sound."

"My Lord," Jack said, anxiety contorting his features. "It started when the King's army was mustering at Coventry. We were given leave to visit the city's alehouses when we'd finished our duties for the day. The beer at the one that I visited must have been off, because I felt so ill on the way back to camp that I lay down in a barn for a rest. I didn't mean to go to sleep, but I did. I was awoken by somebody talking in the cottage next door. That's when I heard one of the city's burghers hire a magician to hex the King." As pandemonium broke out in the hall, Jack had to shout to make himself heard: "And seven others as well." When his audience had quietened down, he continued: "That included the De Spensers – both the father and the son. But apart from them and the local Prior, I can't tell you who the others were."

"Who commanded thee not to tell?" the Prior screamed. "Your master The Devil?"

"No, your holiness," Jack protested, realising that his every word was being examined for incriminating evidence. "The names were not spoke out loud."

"Carry on," De Sutton said wearily. "And *do* shut up, Prior. I can judge this matter for myself."

Jack carried on: "Well! On the next evening, I sneaked back to the byre at the time that they'd arranged to meet. That's when I saw the magician summoning up a demon called Adrasteus. Then he sent it off to destroy those that they'd identified with little wax dolls."

"*Wax dol*—" The Prior choked off his shriek on getting a sideways glance from De Sutton.

Jack shifted uneasily on his feet. "The magician said that because one of the victims lived locally, he would be the first to die. And that the customer would be able to verify it if he so wished. Oh! And the Prior of Coventry would be next, but the others would take longer. So when the Baron suddenly fell ill, we thought that *he* could be one of the victims." Aware of the intensity of the stares of his noble audience, Jack took a deep breath and stated in a rush: "And that-was-why-Gran tried-to-protect-him-with-her...charms."

"I see no charms," De Sutton said, appraising Gran's scraggy figure. "An old hag, more like." As Jack wondered whether to challenge that or let it go, De Sutton continued: "Talking of charms, what *is* that thing that's hanging round her neck. Show it to me, old woman."

Startled and shame-faced, Gran hauled up a leather thong to reveal a green coloured disc, about two inches in diameter.

"What's this?" De Sutton leaned forward to take the object in his hand. "A man's face with leaves sprouting out of its mouth?"

"It was my mother's," Gran said quickly. "She gave it to me to bring me luck...although I've seen precious little of *that*."

"That's the face of the Devil," the Prior screamed. "My Lord, let us have no more of this idolatry. Let me take her out and burn her to ashes without further delay."

"If that *is* the Devil," Jack shouted back, "why is it carved in stone at Coventry Priory?"

The Prior of Dudley sat still and silent, as though carved from stone himself.

"And I've seen them in *your* Priory as well," Jack added in the hope that the priest wouldn't know if this was true or not.

"*Stop!*" De Sutton bellowed, releasing the talisman so that Gran could poke it down the front of her smock. "I will have order here!" He stared at Jack. "Continue with what you were saying about your grandmother and the Baron!"

"My Lord," the Prior interposed in a more respectful tone. "Before we hear any more of his lies, may I ask him what the demon looked like?"

"I should like to know that myself," De Sutton admitted. "Well?"

"I never saw it," Jack said anxiously. "The magician spoke to something that only he could see. He'd got it trapped in a Triangle of Art."

"So you know about the *Triangle of Art*, do you?" the Prior cried. "That proves that you are versed in magical practices. Admit it. You raised the demon yourself. You are that magician!"

"I ain't no magician!" Jack cried, trying to keep his head. "I only know that it was a 'Triangle of Art' because that's what the magician called it."

"Well, if you *had* raised the demon yourself," De Sutton said calmly, "you would hardly have been trying to stop it attacking the Baron. By the way, had you any reason to believe that De Somery was one of the victims?"

Jack bowed respectfully to each of the Baron's sisters and then to his widow.

"Only when he began to complain of unusual headaches on the journey north from Coventry."

As the servants at the back of the Hall began to scoff, Jack hastened to explain: "My Lord, it was only because I was riding close beside him that I could overhear what he was saying to the other knights."

"He allowed you to ride *beside* him? A mere trainee-soldier like *you*?"

"Yes, my Lord. I was his banner-bearer."

"You were John de Somery's banner-bearer?" De Sutton looked surprised.

"Yes, my Lord. He bestowed that honour on me because of the wound that I received when I saved this castle from his enemies." As supporting murmurs came from the waiting crowd, Jack continued: "I was able to do him another service at the bridge at Burton. That's on the River Trent. Just this side of Tutbury?"

"I know where Burton is," De Sutton snapped. "I was there."

"Forgive me, my Lord. I couldn't remember if you were there or not. I used an arrow to deliver the King's offer of peace to the Earl of Lancaster."

"I remember *you* now." As if by magic: De Sutton's expression had changed from one of anger to another of surprise and amusement. "Not that Lancaster took any notice of it," he added as he turned to his fellow inquisitors. "This soldier led us knights in a charge on Burton Bridge. And by doing so, he prevented King Edward from plunging this country into Civil War. Many lives were saved by that." He gazed up at the banners that dangled from the roof beams. "Which of those were you carrying?"

"The one at the front," Jack said eagerly. "The one with mud and water-stains on it."

De Sutton's eyes glazed over, as if reliving the events of that glorious day.

"It was gross insubordination of course," De Sutton said with simulated seriousness. He turned again to his audience. "Lancaster's men were caught by surprise and we quickly overwhelmed them." He chuckled to himself. "And I believe that his second message-arrow speeded up the capitulation of Kenilworth Castle. By the way," he added, turning back to Jack, "your master was greatly pleased with you on both counts."

"Well he never told me," Jack muttered with regret. "But he did appoint me the Steward of this castle."

De Sutton leaned back in his throne and stretched his legs out under the table. "Carry on," he said.

Margaret de Sutton's expression had been hostile throughout the proceedings, but it softened slightly as her husband took her hand.

Jack related how a disastrous gust of wind had forced him to tell the Baron about the magical events at Coventry.

"And what was his response to that?" De Sutton asked, withdrawing his legs and sitting up straight again.

"He wasn't sure whether to believe me or not," Jack admitted. "But since one of the intended victims was the Prior of Coventry, the Baron took me there to find out if the spell had worked."

"And had it?"

"No, my Lord. The Prior was in good health and spirits. But he did confirm that a demon named Adrasteus was known to him. He'd seen the name in a book while he was studying at Oxford University. And he also said that one of his parishioners had died in a manner very similar to that predicted by the magician."

As soon as Jack could make himself heard again, he continued: "Most of their conversations were too quiet for me to overhear. But just before the Baron left the Priory, I heard him tell the Prior that he was going to warn the King of his great danger. And in the meantime, the monk should try to trace the baker of his poisoned pie."

"A *poisoned pie*, did you say?"

"Yes, my Lord. Someone had provided such a pie for the Prior's midday meal. Fortunately, he hadn't eaten any. And because it smelt so peculiar, we...er...he fed it to a pig. It died in agony...like his parishioner had done. So we knew then that the magician was a fraud who used poison instead of magic."

"And did the Baron fear that he too might be poisoned?"

"He wasn't sure, my Lord. He did take a bite from a similar pie at Kenilworth, but it tasted so bad that he spat it out. After that, he would only eat pies that were baked by my grandmother."

"That *is* true," confirmed Lady Lucy, having so far remained silent. "When I asked him about it, he said that he'd developed a preference for them." She sighed. "I didn't bother to mention the fact that he'd been enjoying them for years."

De Sutton leaned over to stroke the back of her hand before turning back to Jack.

"So the Prior of Coventry will be able to confirm your story?" This seemed more like a statement of fact than a question.

"Yes, my Lord!" Jack replied, attempting to force his lips into the semblance of a smile.

"No he won't," cried the Prior of Saint James's. "We've just had word that he has died with a look of horror on his face."

CHAPTER 24

"The Prior of Coventry is *dead*?" Jack felt his blood run cold. His chief witness could no longer verify that he was telling the sooth. He sought about for an alternative. "The Baron was going to warn the King of the conspiracy," he said quickly. "Our sovereign will surely remember that."

"Even if he *did* alert the King," De Sutton muttered, "we can hardly expect him to testify on behalf of a common soldier, especially while he's engaged in trying to drive the Scots from the North of the country. Nevertheless, we can but try." He turned to the Baron's widow. "My Lady, *did* your husband inform the King about the plot against his life and mortal soul?"

"I know nothing about that," she replied in a whisper. "But he *did* send a letter of protest about De Spenser's accusations against *you*." She raised tear-filled eyes to regard him with dismay. "How could *anybody* allege that *you* could be guilty of Treason against the King?"

Lady Margaret leapt to her feet. Flushing with anger, she turned to face their audience. "The effrontery of De Spenser," she shrieked. "My husband is one of the King's most loyal supporters."

Gran rushed forward to the edge of the table. "And the Baron had no more loyal supporter than my *Jack*!" she cried. "And both of us had good reason to wish him a long and healthy life."

"Ah! Mistress Baxter," De Sutton said quietly. "How are we to judge you now? You claim that you tried to protect the Baron from a demon. Would you kindly inform us as to how and why?"

To a hushed audience, Gran related how Jack had told her about a magician summoning up a demon. And because a pig had eaten a pie and died soon after, they'd decided that the ceremony had been a hoax. And that the Baron's headaches had been caused by the weight of his Helm. But all that changed when she took some crustades up to the Baron's bedchamber.

All eyes turned towards her – all mouths clamped shut. "Well," she said, "you know how you sometimes get the feeling that you're being watched?" Gran had asked the question but obviously didn't expect an answer. "Well as soon as I entered this hall, it felt like that. Only stronger and malevol... malevol..."

"Malevolent!" De Sutton said hastily. "So what happened then?"

"Thank you, my Lord. Well, I recited the words of a charm that a wise-woman once taught me."

"Why did you not pray to Our Lord and all His Saints?" the Prior shouted.

"I couldn't think of any prayers," Gran answered desperately. "And nor would anybody if they sensed that something horrible was standing right behind 'em. Anyway, prayers am all in Latin an' I don't know none."

After waiting for the Prior to calm down, she continued in a softer voice: "I knew then that some devilish thing had come to haunt the hall. So Jack and me joined our master in the tower room. The feeling of evil was not quite so strong in there, but it meant that we were trapped. What could we do? Not a lot. Then I remembered something that my moth...that a neighbour once showed me. All it needed was a wand."

The Prior leapt to his feet again. "So you carry a magic wand around with you? That proves that you are a witch."

"Of course I don't," Gran yelled back. "I just happened to have a child's toy at the bottom of my bag. A little 'Obby 'Oss it was, with two blue ribbons wound slantingly round the stick. So I pulled the head off and used the stick to cast an imaginary circle of protection around us. That's when a lot of strange things *really* began to happen. Things appeared out here in the Hall. Some of 'em was really horrible. One of 'em was Hugh de Spenser, glaring back at us from the Baron's high-backed throne." On hearing this, De Sutton shifted uneasily on its seat. "And when that didn't panic us into fleeing from the room, we were treated to a set of visions that seemed to show us what was going to happen at the end of the world. Finally, a dragon appeared and it tried to break through the circle. But just as it was about to get at us, the Baron regained his strength. Getting out of his bed, he used his sword to smite the dragon dead. It blew-up in his face and that's what killed him."

"I told you that there was a dragon," the Cookney shrieked, having been treated for his wound. "And you didn't believe me."

"You merely told us that they'd spoken about a dragon," De Sutton said testily. "Everybody *quiet*! I need time to think."

As the hall became silent, De Sutton's expression alternated between surprise and disbelief. "I don't know what to make of *this*," he said eventually. "What we have just been told may be the sooth, or another pack of lies to conceal a murder. However, it now seems likely that our King is the only one able to confirm your story." He grinned mirthlessly. "Or *not*. I shall send a letter to him immediately. A second will be despatched to Coventry, to ask if their Prior confided in anyone before his death. Meanwhile, we shall just have to wait."

Before the Prior could voice the objection that was about to burst from his lips, De Sutton stood up and banged on the table for silence. Staring at the accused pair before him, he took a deep breath and announced: "Although there are still many questions to be answered, I have made up my mind about your sentences. You, soldier. I am prepared to believe that you are an innocent party in this. Nevertheless, I am going to send you up to the North of England as part of my contribution to the

King's army. As for *you*, old woman..." He transferred his attention to Gran and leered wolfishly. "Whether or not we shall ever know the truth of this matter, you have condemned yourself with your own mouth. *Guard*! Take her out and *burn* her!"

Flushed with self-righteous pleasure, the Prior struggled to his feet. But before he began to speak, the Chapelain's shrill voice echoed round the hall: "My Lord," the cleric implored. "Before they are taken out, may I question them about their vision of the End of the World? What was Doomsday like?"

"I should like to know that as well," De Sutton said. "Speak, old woman."

Jack strode forward to join his grandmother at the table and hugged her trembling shoulders: "My Lord, it was terrible. At first, the fires of Hell were flaring up out of the ground. And by their hateful light, the spirits of the damned could be seen, dragging heavy loads across the glowing earth."

Uproar filled the hall as the servants began to cross themselves frantically.

De Sutton waited until the tumult had died down sufficiently to hear himself speak: "So the Devil will rule this Middle Earth at the end."

"I do not think so, my Lord," Jack said. "The next vision was of a darkened land. There were strange-looking houses all along the High Street. And Top Church had a pointed steeple like the ones that I've seen at Coventry. But the most amazing thing of all was the fact that the Holy Rood was flying slowly across the sky. Jesus's Cross was huge. And it had flights attached to its shaft like those of an arrow."

"The Second Coming," De Sutton murmured as the other members of the audience held their collective breaths.

"Yes, my Lord. And even as I watched, the cross seemed to release a thunderbolt down on the sinners far below. It fell close to the church, and nobody could have lived through that terrible burst of fire. And over towards the city of Coventry, the clouds were glowing as if lit by many more fires."

"So *that's* how it's all going to end," De Sutton said when at last he could be heard.

"No, my Lord. The last scene was very peaceful – with the souls of the dead moving slowly on the hills that we see today."

"How do you know that they were souls of the dead?" the Chapelain cried.

"They couldn't have been anything else. They was tiny bright points of light. All in pairs. Either red or white. Never mixed."

"*Alleluia!*" cried the Chapelain. "For such is the kingdom of Heaven."

Realising that he had lost the initiative, the Prior turned to face the East (after confirming which way it was by the arrow loops in the South wall).

"*Dominus Vobiscum*," he cried, raising his arms to shoulder height. "Let us pray for forgiveness, lest we be found wanting on the Day of Judgement."

"*Alleluia!*" intoned the assembled witnesses as they all turned in the same direction.

Kneeling on the herb-strewn floorboards, they bowed their heads devoutly. And while the Prior and his flock prayed for the salvation of their souls, Jack and his Gran made a run for it.

CHAPTER 25

As Jack tugged on the thong to raise the latch of the door to the north-west tower room, Gran looked around in search of the guard who'd brought them up there. He was standing beside the door to the spiral staircase – his spear held ready to prevent unauthorised leaving. Although his head was bowed like the other worshippers, he was regarding the escaping pair with a look of amazement on his face. Gran recognised him now, having treated him for the Flux on his return from the war. Instead of raising the alarm, he gave her a nod of encouragement, and then coughed to cover the sound of the door creaking open and shut.

It wasn't until the Prior had said the last *Amen*, that their absence was discovered.

"Where have they gone?" yelled John de Sutton, gaping at the spot where they should have been standing. "You there. Guard. Did you see where they went?"

"No, my Lord," the guard said guardedly: "I'd closed me eyes as always in order to pray. But I'd wedged me spear across this doorway. No-body passed through here, I can swear to *that*."

"I *told* you they were *witches*," screamed the Prior, beside himself with fury. "They've been carried off by demons."

This did seem to be the case, for the servants were blocking the only other way out. When a half-hearted search had failed to find the missing pair, it was concluded that they really *had* been spirited away into thin air.

*

After dropping the door latch into its slot, Jack detached its thong and let this slide snake-like out through its hole. Hearing the weight thump on the floor on the other side, the fugitives held their breaths and listened with pulsing heartbeats. The Prior continued praying without a pause.

"With any luck," Jack muttered as he turned to make sure that the tower room was vacant, "they'll think that it came loose by itself. Come on."

Immediately on his right, a door was framed with blocks of blood-red stone. Jack unlatched and swung it open, revealing a passage leading leftwards in the thickness of the wall. Three yards along its dark and curving length, it stopped and opened out into what was obviously a garderobe. A wind-eye at the back gave a view out over the moat...above a gilded seat that had a round hole in the middle.

"So *this* is where you came to have a piddle," Gran whispered. "I wondered why it didn't take you very long. How did you know that it was here?"

"It's my business to know such things." Realising how pompous this had sounded, he added quickly: "When we first came to live at the castle, they made me shovel sh-muck from the bottom of the shaft."

Gran smirked. "And then to come back to the bakery and help me with the crustades. I could never understand why they risked you spreading the Flux."

"Me neither," Jack said as he reached into the hole. "In those days, this seat was loose and easy to remove. But when a servant's kid fell headfirst down the shaft, I had this other one fitted." He tugged on something that gave a subdued 'click'. "And it opens...like...this." Raising the middle section backwards on two hinges, he secured it against the wall with a hook and staple. Between the remaining side-shelves lay a dark and dreadful cavity. It smelt faintly of pine needles and strongly of sh-muck and piddle.

"You *can't* expect me to go down *there*?" Gran shrieked, retreating into the passageway.

"It's either that or give ourselves up," Jack retorted. "Which is it to be?"

"How far down is it?"

"Only ten yards to the bottom."

"*Thirty feet?*" Gran cried. "Yer don't expect me to jump down there dun yer? I'm an old woman remember."

"There's no need to jump!" Jack reached beneath the left hand shelf and swung out a sturdy pot-crane. From its beam hung a ladder made of chains and iron bars. "I've not long had this made by the blacksmith down in Netherton. He refused to fit it 'til I'd had the shaft scrubbed clean, so you don't have to worry about the sh-muck."

"What's at the bottom?"

"A grating that leads outside. I release it by pulling on…this." He reached beneath the right hand shelf and tugged on something else. A chain rattled. A 'click' echoed up the shaft.

"It's unlocked now," Jack said. "When you get to the bottom, push on it with your feet and it'll swing open."

As Gran allowed herself to be manoeuvred onto the ladder, she whispered into Jack's unwilling ear: "This reminds me of the well that I went down in Dudley."

"You coped with *that* and you'll cope with this as well." Jack had spoken reassuringly, although aware of a frantic pounding on the outer door.

"And you promise that there's no sh-muck down here?" Gran's voice trembled up from the depths.

"It was cleared out yesterday morning. But if the stink's too bad, try this…" Grabbing a handful of herbs from a box on the wall, he tossed them down the shaft.

"Thanks very much," came the muffled response. "I had me mouth wide open so as not to breathe in through me nose."

Judging by a crash and the splintering of wood coming up the passage, its door would soon be breached.

Swinging his legs into the shaft, Jack located the ladder with his feet and descended a few rungs down. After lowering the seat above him, he secured it with its bolt and followed his Gran into the depths

At the bottom of the shaft, it sloped down to the grill for keeping out enemies. It swung open to the pressure of his boots and he skidded and scrambled out into fresher air. After forcing the grating back flush with the wall, he looked around for his Gran. She was nowhere to be seen. Where the Hell could she be?

Her curses supplied the answer. At the bottom of a steep and slippery mudslide, she was standing up to her ankles in the dark forbidding water of the moat.

"Sorry," he said. "I should have warned you about that slope."

"Never mind that," she muttered as he slithered down beside her. "You promised that the shaft would be clean."

"I lied!" he admitted. "Otherwise, you'd never have come. And anyway, the sh-muck falls down the middle of the shaft and it shouldn't have touched the sides."

"What's *this* then?" Gran held the brown-spattered hem of her smock with one hand, while pinching her nose with the other.

"I forgot about the ramp and the mud. Don't wash it off yet though. Somebody up there might see the ripples."

They both peered up at the battlements high above them. As far as they could tell, there was nobody there.

Although dusk was fast approaching, they felt very exposed down there at the edge of the moat.

"If I had the key to the Postern," Jack said, glancing up at a door in the curtain wall above them, "we could sneak back in and hide in the roof of the stables."

"What's the point of saying *that* if you haven't got it?"

"I was thinking aloud. Anyway, we can't stay here."

He peered at the dark expanse of water that lay before them. "The Gong Farmer dumps the sh-muck in there. In fact," Jack added with a grimace, "the water has become too shallow to deter intruders. I was meaning to have it cleared out but I never got round to it." Tearing a twig from a nearby sapling, he probed the murky depths. "This is the place," he whispered. "Is there anybody on the battlements?"

"None that I can see."

They both gasped at the cold as they slithered down into the water. After a short but frantic scramble to the opposite bank of the moat, they took cover beneath an overhanging holly bush. While Gran scraped slime off her smock and shoes, Jack examined a net that his boot had got entangled in. A couple of Bream lay struggling in the mesh.

"It's a pity that it's still winter," he said as he fingered the knotted strings. "The Forester showed me how he made himself invisible by using a net like this. He tied leaves all over it and when he pulled it over his head, the poachers didn't see him as he sneaked up through the bushes. I could tie some holly leaves onto this one, but it wouldn't be much fun to wear."

"A walking holly bush *might* attract attention," Gran observed dryly. "By the way, what *did* happen to your friend?"

"I dunnow," Jack said with a sigh. "He just disappeared. And not by wearing a cloak of leaves neither. His cottage was found deserted. And he never even said goodbye."

"We should go there then," Gran said, "as soon as it gets dark."

"Well we can't go back to Netherton. That's the first place that they'll look for us."

"It's decided then." Gran gave him a reassuring grin. "And as soon as I've got cleaned up, I'll fix us a meal with them fish."

*

The cottage was more or less as Jack expected. The thatch was sagging and missing in several places. The door hung sadly ajar from its unpainted frame.

"Come on in, Gran," Jack called when he'd made sure that no one was lurking about inside. "One end of it's not too bad."

"Right!" said Gran, surveying the chaotic scene and rolling up her sleeves. "I can't do any cooking until I get this place cleaned up. Go and find a bucket and raise us up some water from that well. Then get us some firewood and kindling. And see if there's a broom anywhere and…"

"Anything else?" Jack said, marching outside and banging the door behind him.

*

By nightfall, the pair were clean and fed. Exhausted by that dreadful day's experiences, they'd made up serviceable beds and were sleeping the sleep of the damned. And damned they really were, for as the morning sun shone in through gaps in the thatch, they were woken by loud thumping on the door.

"I know that you are in there," someone bellowed as the door shuddered under the impact of the blows. "Don't try to escape. If you do, you'll be killed." As the fugitives hunted around in search of their footwear, the voice came again and much louder than before: "Stand back! I'm coming in."

CHAPTER 26

The door crashed open and in rushed a soldier with a crossbow loaded and levelled. Jack recognised him at once as De Sutton's trusted servant.

"Good!" said the Trusted Servant, lowering his crossbow and removing its deadly bolt. "You are not armed."

"What are you going to do with us?" Jack asked (unnecessarily, Gran thought).

"Nothing at all," the soldier said, returning to the doorway and making some sort of signal with his arm. "You are to remain here for the present."

The fugitives stared at one another, regretting the assumption that they'd escaped without being seen.

"Relax!" said the soldier, dragging a stool from beneath the table and tugging on each leg to make sure that it was sound. "You cannot escape." After easing himself down, he leaned back against the edge of the table and stretched out his legs. "Is there anything to eat in this dump?"

"There's a bit of fish left over from last night," Gran said, looking round in the vain hope of finding another way out. "You'm welcome to that. But as for any other fittle, we ain't got none."

"I can remedy that." The soldier sprang to his feet and headed out through the doorway — returning with a parcel that he unwrapped on the table. It contained a loaf of bread, some cheese, and a dozen eggs. "Get busy with this lot, mistress. I can find room in my belly for some of this fittle meself."

Jack got out his flint and steel. "How did you find us?"

The soldier laughed. "You shouldn't have been so meticulous about assigning the guards their duties. One of 'em was on the battlements and saw you wading across the moat. He was on his way to report it to De Sutton when he ran into Lady Margaret. I overheard her telling him to leave the matter in her hands. But instead of informing her husband right away, she ordered me to find you. Knowing that you couldn't seek sanctuary in the Priory, I remembered this old cottage of Will Hawkes's and here I am."

Jack stared at his grandmother accusingly. "I told you that we should have stayed in the garderobe shaft until it got dark."

"Oh ar? And get shat on from a great height?" She snorted. "I couldn't have stopped in there for anything."

"Not even to save your *life*?" Jack said, hoping to end the discussion.

"Anyway, it's *your* fault for making your enemies patrol the battlements."

"Well, whoever's fault it was," the soldier muttered, "it's too late now to do anything about it."

*

Eventually, the three occupants of the cottage sat down to breakfast. Although the fugitives were choking with fear and apprehension, the soldier enjoyed his meal and said so loud and often. Between bites, he revealed that he had been ordered to keep them penned-up there until Undrentide that day.

"W-what happens then?" Jack spluttered, showering him with crumbs.

"How should I know," said the soldier, reaching for a diaper.

By the noonday hour of Undrentide, the bowls had been washed and dried and put away. Crumbs had been brushed off the table and the floor swept clear of debris. *That* part of the cottage was almost clean and tidy.

Suddenly, the soldier leapt up to retrieve his crossbow from the wall. "I must leave you now," he announced from the open doorway. "But do not attempt to leave."

He vanished through the opening – his figure immediately replaced by one of shorter stature. Cloaked and hooded in black, it stood there for a moment, then hurried inside and quickly closed the door. Jack and his grandmother gaped at it in horror. The Prior had them in his clutches.

But as the figure reached the table, it threw back its hood to reveal, not the Prior, and not John De Sutton either. His wife, the Lady Margaret, stood before them, her demeanour seeming quite different to what it had been in the Donjon, and her expression denoting anxiety not accusation.

"W-what are you going to do with us?" Gran croaked, her hands clasping together and her chin working up and down. "Am I going to be burnt at the stake like the Prior said?"

As the fugitives shrank against the back wall in fear and dismay, the Lady shrugged off her cloak. After shaking it briefly, she hung it on the hook that had formerly held the crossbow.

"Have no fear," she said, using a friendly tone that seemed alien to her nature. "I have come to seek your help and bestow it in return."

Jack and his Gran glanced at one other with scepticism on their faces.

"Mistress Baxter," the lady continued. "I no longer believe that you would willingly harm my brother."

As Gran nodded furiously in confirmation of that fact, the lady righted the stool, swept the seat with a clean white diaper, and sat herself gingerly down on its worm-holed timber. "I didn't think so at first," she said, trying to force a smile. "After all, you were obviously lying about a lot of things."

Gran reached nervously for Jack's hand. With nothing useful to say, her grandson squeezed her fingers and kept his mouth tight shut.

"It was when you stood up to the Prior," Lady Margaret continued, "that I saw a different side of you. And when you reprimanded him for teaching that all newborn bab...bab...*babies* are sinful, I caught a glimpse of your sadness and compassion. I realised later that you are a virtuous woman."

After noting Jack's incredulity, Lady Margaret turned back to Gran: "What can men know of the bond betwixt a mother and her child? Or a grandmother and her grandson for that matter. Yes, I have seen how much you love this great oaf of yours."

Jack blushed but still kept quiet.

"My Lady," Gran said respectfully. "Have I your leave to speak freely?"

"Why yes! Of course! I want you to tell me if my husband is in danger from the demon." In the silence that descended on the ruined cottage, she added grimly: "We can deal with would-be poisoners ourselves."

Gran glanced across at Jack. He could hardly believe his eyes. There was his grandmother, chatting away with this highborn Lady like a pair of washerwomen at a well.

"In sooth, my Lady," Gran said. "Apart from the ones that you know of already, Jack has no idea who the other victims are."

"That is true, my Lady," Jack said, relieved to have something to contribute at last. Nevertheless, he was nervous of pushing his luck any further with undue familiarity.

"I believe you," Lady Margaret said. "That's why I want your grandmother to use her magical powers."

"But I have no magical powers," Gran protested. "I've been saying that all along. I just know a few ways of trying to keep danger at bay."

"It makes no difference what you call them," Lady Margaret retorted, "as long as they work." Her grimace became a smile. "And if you are successful, I shall see to it that my husband grants you – that's both of you – full pardons."

"My Lady, I wish that I *could* help you." Gran's jaw was working up and down again. She knew that the nobs could smile at you as they signed your death warrant. "But from what I've seen," Gran added while trying to look apologetic, "the demon's power is far too great for me. It's a task better suited to the monks at the Priory."

"They *are* saying prayers for us," the lady said quickly, "but if the Prior of Coventry couldn't save himself, I can't see that prayers will be sufficient."

Gran went quiet, thinking back to what had taken place in the Donjon. All three of them would have been killed if Saint George hadn't come to their aid. And ever since then, she'd been wondering if he'd been summoned by the monks.

"I *must* insist that you try," Lady Margaret said, her eyes narrowing to slits. "I shall make it worth your while. But if you refuse me..." The smile had returned, but it was less convincing than before. "No! It must not come to that. Can you begin right away?"

"Now?" Gran shrieked before caution could intervene. "I told you, I'm no match for the demon. In fact, I'm afraid of attracting his attention. He could destroy us all."

"I am willing to take that chance. What do you need?"

"Help!" Gran said simply.

"What sort of help?" The lady's smile had been replaced by her habitual scowl.

"Help to find some way of protecting us."

"What about that friend of yours?" Jack suggested. "The one who taught you how to tell fortunes."

"I couldn't ask her. She's high-up in the Church now."

"And this *high-up in the church*..." Lady Margaret said eagerly. "Has she taught you any more of her...secrets?"

"Well they're not *really* secrets. They are just ways of enlisting the help of the goddess in one of her three guises."

"Three guises of a...a...goddess?" Lady Margaret shrieked. "Mimicking the *Holy Trinity*? So the Prior was right about you being a blasphemer after all."

"It's not like that," Gran protested, increasingly fearful of the way that things were going. "I mean no insult to the Church. The three aspects of the goddess just reflect our changing roles as women. They – and their male partners – are just an old way of paying homage to the maker of this world and all its mysteries."

"So you have more than one *god*," the lady said, crossing herself, "and does one of them have horns and cloven feet by any chance?"

"No, my Lady," Gran lied. "The gods represent the changing seasons." Realising that she was getting completely out of her depth, she added hurriedly: "They're our way of hallowing the rhythms of the Earth and Sky. There is no Devil involved."

"I haven't got time for all this cant," Lady Margaret said curtly. "What can you do for me right now?"

"You could try Scrying," Jack suggested quietly.

"Crying?" Lady Margaret snorted. "What good would that do?"

"No, my Lady." Gran's expression softened slightly. "It's *scrying*...what I use to tell fortunes in Dudley market place."

"Get on with it then. *Scry* for me. My time is precious."

"Jack," Gran said, turning to him. "Fill us one of them bowls from the bucket, willtow?"

Jack did as he was told and placed the bowl of water on the table between the three of them. "Are you going to cast a circle of protection around us?" he asked, doubtful if there was room in the cottage for that.

"I've never needed that for scrying," Gran said. "Here, hold my hand. Would my Lady like to join with us? I *have* just washed them."

The lady shuddered visibly. "Is it *really* necessary?"

"It might help me to get through."

"Get through to *where*?"

"I dunno! That's just what we always say."

As the lady linked hands with her minions round the bowl, Jack marvelled at the smoothness of her fingers (compared to his grandmother's callused and bony talons).

Breathing steadily and deeply, Gran stared at the surface of the water. "Is there anybody there?" she enquired solemnly. "Yes, my Lady. We always say that as well."

The little room grew silent, except for the whispering of the wind through holes in the thatch. "Yes, I think I'm getting something!" Gran sounded relieved. "Yes, the water is clouding over. Yes. There is something there."

She eased herself on her seat and peered closer. "I see a shield. Good! The messages are usually in symbols. This one is a gold shield with two blue lions on it."

"The De Somery shield?" Lady Margaret demanded excitedly.

"Yes, my Lady. And it has an arrow embedded in it. What can that mean? *OOH...*"

"What? What?" cried Lady Margaret. "What can you see now?"

"Now I can see a row of shields."

"Can you see the De Sutton shield?"

"Hang on. They're not very clear. I'll try to go in closer. There *is* a red one with three yellow lions on it...like the De Somery ones but facin' outwards."

"That's King Edward's shield," Jack said in awe. "Is there an arrow in it?"

"Never mind that," Lady Margaret snapped. "Can you see the De Sutton shield?"

"There doesn't seem to be an arrow in *that* shield. Nor in any of the others that I can see. Just a minute. One of 'em does have an arrow in it. It's got what look like eagles on it."

"I saw one like that at Burton Bridge," Jack said. "But I don't know whose it was."

Gran peered intently into the water. "There's two that look very much the same. They've both got red chevrons on a yellow background."

"That's the De Spensers," Jack said eagerly. "The father and the son. Are there arrows in 'em?"

"No."

"Pity," Jack said. "So they're still able to inflict their greed on the whole country."

"But do you see my *husband's* shield?" Lady Margaret was almost levitating from her stool.

"There's one at the end that could be yours...a yellow one with a green lion on it."

"Is it *Rampahn Quew Foorshay*?" the lady screamed, trembling with fear and apprehension.

"What does that mean?" Gran had spoken without deviating her gaze from the suddenly-rippling water.

"Is it up on its hind legs?"

"I think so, but the picture's gone all wobbly. If you can stop jumping about, the water will grow still again. Er. Sorry, my Lady. I forgot myself."

"Never mind that!" The lady leaned back from the table while still maintaining her grip on the other participants' fingers. "Is that any better?"

"Yes, my Lady. The pictures am getting clear again."

"So, *is* that lion standing upright?"

"Arr."

"What's that supposed to mean?"

"I mean 'yes', my Lady. The lion is up on its hind legs."

"And is its tail forked?"

"It's difficult to say, my Lady. The water hasn't quite settled enough to see it. Wait. Yes. The tail *does* branch into two."

"And *has our shield got an arrow in it*?" the lady screamed.

"No it hasn't, my Lady," Gran murmured reassuringly.

"Thank God," the lady cried out, flopping forward onto the table – shaking it so much that water slopped onto the planks.

"That's all," Gran said as she mopped-up the spillage with a diaper.

Lady Margaret choked back a sob. "So, it seems that my husband really *is* in danger from the demon. What can we do to save him?"

"I dunno, my Lady. All I know is: I do not have the power."

Jack picked up the bowl and tipped the remaining water out onto the earthen floor. "I still think that you should ask that woman who taught you how to Scry," he said. "You told me that she knows a thing or two about the Secret Arts."

"Oh her! She *might* agree to help us I suppose. I *did* once hide her from the Sheriff's men." She laughed out loud. "Who'd have thought that she'd end up in charge of the Black Nuns' Priory? But Brewood is so very far away from here."

"The Prioress is staying in *our* Priory," Lady Margaret announced.

"I thought that women weren't allowed in there," Jack said, recalling his brief time of Sanctuary.

"Like I always say," Gran said. "The monks preach one thing and do something altogether different."

The lady arose from her seat. "I shall send her here tomorrow and I shall expect results. Is that understood?"

Gran frowned. "I'm not sure that we *shall* be able to protect your husband from the demon."

Lady Margaret's expression darkened again. "You seemed to have known how to try to save my *brother*. Although it didn't work, do better this time or it'll be worse for you!" She turned to reach her cloak down from the hook. "I must go now. You must give me your word that you won't try to escape. But why should you, when everybody thinks that you've gone to the Devil already?"

"You have our word, my Lady," Gran promised, ignoring Jack's look of warning.

"Good!" said the lady, almost managing a smile. "I believe you to be a woman of your word — no matter what the outcome might be." As she opened the door, her face reddened slightly. "I don't suppose you have any of that...er...*invigorating* potion here do you? No? Pity!"

"You might as well know, my Lady..." Gran touched the side of her nose with a knobbly finger, "I've always put a little of it in my crustades. There's still a few left in the oven back there at the Castle. But if I live through all this" – she gave the lady a meaningful look – "I shall brew as much of that potion as you like. That should perk up your husband enough to keep you...er...happy."

"Who said anything about my *husband*?" Lady Margaret whispered to herself as she stepped out through the doorway.

"What was that about?" Jack asked, after he'd made quite sure that the Lady had left the vicinity.

"Never you mind," Gran said, pressing the side of her nose once more.

"But do you *really* trust her?"

"What d'you think?"

"I thought not. But what are we going to do?"

"Just you wait and see."

CHAPTER 27

On one dark and moonless night, three troops of riders wended separate ways towards the 'Citadel of the Giants'. Situated a mile or so to the north-west of Dudley Castle, this was an enormous boat-shaped amphitheatre – ringed about with dark and craggy ramparts. It was reputed to be haunted.

One group consisted of Jack and his aged grandmother. Successfully evading both the Bailiff's men and poachers, they hurried through the Old Park's woods – impatient to begin the preparations for their work.

It was the time of the Dark Moon, and the stars glared brightly down from a jet-black sky.

Beneath the constellation called 'The Wain', the Prioress of Brewood led a procession of black-cloaked riders. Had any human being been watching, it would have been obvious to them that these riders were all female. But only the owls were watching and they didn't give a hoot.

From the direction of the castle, a man and a woman approached on sure-footed palfreys. The woman was Lady Margaret, and her companion, John De Sutton's 'Trusted Guard'. On reaching the southern perimeter of the Citadel, the guard led the way into a coal-black crevice that cleaved the limestone cliffs.

"Why are we going *this* way?" the lady protested – forced to dismount at a pair of leaning slabs.

"So that nobody sees us." The guard opened the flap of his lant-horn for its green-tinged light to show the way ahead. Nevertheless, both the horses and the humans stumbled on the scree-slope as they scrambled ever higher into the cleft.

"I'd have waited for the Full Moon if this wasn't so urgent," Lady Margaret grumbled as she stubbed her foot on a boulder.

They emerged at last at the top, where an uneven plain stretched out in the darkness before them. Surrounding this lay a high and blacker border, jagged against the vault of the star-speckled heavens.

"Which way is it now?" the lady demanded.

"Straight on," the Trusted Guard replied. "To that hill ahead."

Midway between the surrounding crags, a mound humped forbiddingly from the plain – its summit crowned with a cluster of straight-boled trees.

As the pair of riders reached it, an indistinct figure came forward from the shadows.

"Is that you, my Lady?" Jack's whisper sounded worried.

"Who *else* are you expecting in this God-forsaken place?" Lady Margaret snapped. "I've brought my manservant with me."

With his face concealed by the darkness, the manservant flushed with disappointment and indignation. He meant more to her than *that*. Or so he thought.

"Welcome, my Lady," Jack whispered as the Trusted Servant helped her down from the saddle. But as Jack reached out to steady her when she stumbled, she jerked her elbow away before he could touch her. Affronted by the rejection, Jack silently led the visitors up onto the mound. They had almost got to the top when he whistled softly. A row of white faces appeared silently from the shadows just above them. By drawing apart, they allowed the newcomers through.

A little further on lay a clearing with a bonfire at its centre. Beside a table of rough-hewn limestone stood Jack's Gran, in dark-green tights and a smock of similar colour.

"Take the Lady's cloak," Gran ordered and as soon as Jack had done so, she tried her best to curtsey. Groaning as she strove to stand up straight, she managed to force her mouth into a smile. "Welcome, my Lady," she said – her face like that of a gargoyle in the firelight. "Thank you for wearing green as I suggested. Please come closer to the fire and Jack will show your servant where to go. Don't worry, my Lady. He won't be far off."

As the lady watched her servant led away, Gran explained in a respectful tone of voice: "The rite that we are about to perform is for women only."

"But why on Middle Earth did you choose this horrible place?"

Gran spread out her arms. "The Citadel is an ancient sacred space, and the mound that we are standing on is called the Giant's Grave. Some say that dwarves can sometimes be heard...chipping away underneath the ground."

"Devils more like." Lady Margaret shivered as an unseen drummer began to beat a soft relentless rhythm. The gaunt white faces reappeared at the edge of the firelight, which glittered on the crosses hanging below them. By linking their black-robed arms, the figures formed an unbroken ring, separating the space within from the world outside. And above this living henge, dark treetops framed a disc of spangled sky.

"Is the Prioress here?" the lady asked, peering around.

"Yes, my Lady. She's getting things ready."

"What things?"

"These, my Lady," said a woman who'd appeared as if from nowhere. Slim of figure, she was clad in a clinging robe of glistening green.

"May I introduce the Prioress of the Black Nuns?" Gran said as the woman made a proper curtsey.

"We've met already," the lady said curtly.

"And don't I know it," mumbled the Prioress as she turned towards the altar. On top of the ragged rock lay a dagger, a chalice, a goose's egg – and a wreath of woven ivy.

"Please come forward, my Lady," Gran entreated quietly. "All is made ready and we can now begin. Please wear this." Picking up the garland, she held it out at arm's length. "The black berries represent the Dark Moon."

"I'm not having this!" Lady Margaret muttered as she looked in vain for a way of getting out of there. For the ring of arms was swaying to the rhythm of the drumming.

"*Ralph!*" she shrieked. "Come and get me. These are all witches."

But answer came there none.

"*Ralph!*" she cried out again.

The only sound was the pounding of a drum.

"We are *not* witches," Gran murmured in what she hoped was a soothing tone of voice. "See. We are all wearing crosses to protect us from evil."

"I forgot to bring one with me," Lady Margaret announced. "And I'm not staying here without one."

"You can have mine," Gran said, unlooping its thong from around her neck and passing it across. "My Lady, please remember that the only reason for us carrying out this rite is to try to protect your husband from a demon. You yourself insisted on it and no harm will come to you, I promise."

"Well, it hadn't better." Lady Margaret threw back her hood to allow the thong to be passed over her head. "Very well. Let's get it over with."

"Please also wear this head-dress." Gran was handing her the wreath of woven ivy once again. "I've blessed it and it's an essential part of the rite."

"I hope that there's no creepy-crawlies in it." Looking as though she'd been asked to swallow a spider, the lady placed the coronal on her head.

Gran turned and raised her arms towards the sky.

"Hail to thee mistress," she cried, "Dread Goddess of Death and Rebirth...from whom all things spring, and to whom all things must return."

"Death and rebirth?" Lady Margaret hissed. "What's *that* got to do with it?"

"We three women symbolise the Triple Goddess," the Prioress explained. "I am the Maiden who has (ah'm) renounced all men. You, my Lady, are the Goddess as mistress, mother and wife. Jack's grandmother is the Crone."

The lady forbore to answer.

With a stern look on her face, Gran raised her arms again and turned away.

Between the trunks of two tall trees, the stars of 'The Hunter' blazed down from the southern sky – his privee member bright with silver light. "Hail also to thee Herne," Gran called in a hushed but urgent voice. "Lord of Nature. Lord of Generation and the Bringer of Joy."

"I'm all in favour of having some joy," the lady muttered. "So what's the egg for then? Supper?"

"If we are to be successful in this," Gran explained with a sigh, "we must provide a substitute for your husband's life. In spite of what you are thinking, our magic is not black. It's white. So instead of sacrificing a living animal, we are going to use that goose's egg. It represents the FullMoon."

The Prioress held out her arms. "Come," she commanded. "Let us three join together in body, mind and spirit."

Reluctantly, the lady linked hands with the other two women to form a triangle above the fire. From the encircling ring of white faces and gleaming crosses came the sound of quiet drumming and the chanting of "Herrrrrrrren...Herrrren...Herrren..."

"Great Lord of the Forest," intoned the Prioress. "Please appear to aid us in our task." Nothing happened.

"Why Herne?" Lady Margaret whispered. "I thought that you were invoking a Goddess."

"We have asked the Goddess for permission to appeal to her consort on Middle Earth. Herne is better able to assist us in our task."

"We call upon thee Herrne . . .." the Prioress intoned, still backed by quiet chanting and rhythmical drumming.

"Lord of the Forest and all its sacred places. We beg thee to honour us with thy hallowed presence."

For a while, nothing happened. Then within the ring of circling faces, a spectre rose up slowly from the ground. It had the ill-defined figure of a man with his arms uplifted. Then as the fire flared up in front of it, it was seen to be woven from branches of holly and ivy, with the antlers and head of a stag with staring eyes.

Lady Margaret stiffened.

"It *is* the Devil," she muttered out of the side of her mouth. "The Prior was right about you being devil-worshippers. For Goodes' sake, let me get out of here."

"Please, my Lady," Gran said, gripping the lady's hand tightly to restrain her. "This is not the Devil. It is Herne. The god of all living things."

"Who summons me to this sacred place?" the figure demanded in a hollow sepulchral voice.

Grasping the lady's hand more tightly, the Prioress bowed her head in supplication.

"My Lord Herne, we are thankful that you have graced us with thy presence. Our sister here has come to seek thy help."

Lady Margaret stopped struggling and gaped at the vision before her. At a nod from Gran, she began to speak, falteringly at first but growing more assured as she continued: "I b-believe that m-my house-bond, John d-de Sutton, is in d-danger from a d-demon. I think that the demon's name is Adrasteus, although it could be something else. But whatever it is, can you please save my house-bond from its clutches?"

"Have you brought me a fitting substitute for his life?" the spectral figure boomed. "That man who waits nearby, for instance?"

"Yes we have," Gran answered, freeing her hands from the triangle. "But it's not *him*." She stooped to pick up the egg and used the dagger to crack the shell and allow its contents to drip into the fire. Above the sizzling sound came Gran's entreaty: "I pray that this egg makes a suitable alternative sacrifice."

For what seemed an age, the antlered figure stood watching them with eyes that glistened unblinkingly in the firelight.

"I THINK *NOT!*" it roared at last.

There came a burst of crimson light as the fire became a dazzling bright inferno. To the hissing of steam and the pungent stink of urine, the area was plunged into darkness and the drumming stopped abruptly.

With the image of the blaze blotting out her vision, Lady Margaret reached out in search of her accomplices. They were no longer there.

"*Ralph?*" she cried in terror – stumbling around and groping for support. "Where are you?"

"I'm here," yelled John de Sutton's Most Trusted Guard as he shouldered his way through the ring of silent nuns. "Take my arm, my Lady. Are you all right?"

"Ralph! It's my eyes. *I can't see.* They've sent me blind. Oh thank the Saints," she added, gasping with relief. "My eyesight's coming back." She peered around anxiously. "Where are those two women? And where's that awful spirit?" She followed Ralph's lant-horn beam as he shone it round at the ring of silent nuns. The horned god had vanished and the Prioress was kneeling down beside the altar. The old woman had gone too – her tunic and tights lying strewn upon the ground.

"Herne has taken *her* as a sacrifice," Lady Margaret whispered. "Oh the poor wom—" She stopped as she realised that her request had probably been granted. "Take me home, Ralph," she said quietly. "I'm freezing, and this place gives me the creeps."

*

Crouched in the black interior of the mound, Gran prodded her grandson's back. "Do yer think that we got away with it?" she whispered.

"Let us hope so," Jack said, twisting round. "Was I all right up there?"

"I don't know about *Lady Muck*, but you gave *me* a nasty turn!"

"It was a bit of luck finding this," Jack said, detaching the antlers from the wicker head and placing them to one side. "The Forester used these for stalking his precious deer."

Jack had taken refuge in the passage-grave once before, when he and Felicia were being hunted by Wynterton's soldiers. Since then, a roofing slab had partly fallen in, providing a sloping ramp for him to rise up from the mound. And when the Prioress's powder produced that blinding flash, he'd skidded back down the slope...almost giving himself away by tripping on a strand of ivy.

Fearing that their hiding place would be discovered, Jack and his Gran groped their way further into the tomb. But when the outside world remained as silent as the grave, Jack crept to the bottom of the ramp and listened intently. The only sound was sighing in the treetops.

He crept up the ramp until his eyes were level with the ground. By the faint silvery light of the star-shine, it was clear that there was no one in the clearing. Lady Margaret and her escort had departed, and it had previously been agreed that the nuns should steal away.

After scouting around to make sure that he was really alone, Jack helped his Gran to struggle back up to the surface. Hand in hand, they limped across to the eastern entrance to the Citadel, from whence De Wynterton's men had launched an attack on the castle.

*

The nuns were waiting for them just inside the rampart. And while the fugitives embraced with fond farewells, they sat smiling down from the backs of pawing palfreys. Jack helped his Gran to don a nun's black habit, and then to scramble up behind the Prioress.

"Take care of her, Sister," he begged the beaming nun, whose alluring green gown was now hidden beneath black woollen folds. After choking back a sob, he added throatily: "But a bloody funny nun *she* is going to make."

Gran chuckled mischievously.

"Have you decided where *you* are going?" she called as the Prioress's mount stirred beneath her.

"As you know," he said as the horse began to move forward, "Felicia's still in Shropshire with my in-laws. I shall take her to live with the *out*-laws up in Share-Wood."

Gran clung to the Prioress's waist as the horse broke into a trot. "She won't like *that*," she shouted over her shoulder.

As Jack watched his Gran riding out of his life, he recalled the many challenges that they'd faced together. And smiled at the way that they'd achieved the highest positions attainable by mere peasants. On the other hand, both of them were now fugitives from the Law.

While shrugging on his net of ivy-leaves, a disquieting thought entered his mind. Had he and his Gran become entangled in *Adrasteus's* net during the conflict in the Donjon? And were they being drawn towards their doom?

Or was their rise and fall of Fortune just what happened to everyone that lived on Middle Earth?

He shook with the shock of sudden realisation

So *that* was why the 'Men o' Leaves' looked horrified. **Everybody ends up as food for the plants and trees.**

With that unhappy thought, he wended his way (carefully) out of the Citadel.

*

And *what* about *Adrasteus*?

If he knew of the latest attempt at thwarting him, he did not bother to retaliate. He didn't need to.

Although they could not know it: John de Sutton, both of the De Spensers, and even the King of England himself, were whirling round in his vortex of destruction.

He could bide his time.

There was no need to hurry.

Aft-word

Many of the events that are described herein are recorded in documents that survive from medieval times.

These include:

The theft of money and horses from Dudley Castle.

John de Somery's military support of King Edward II in his struggle against the Scots and the Ordainers.

The King's scandalous promotion of the Hugh de Spencers.

Baldersmere's wife's insult to Queen Isabella – leading to the capture of their castle and the execution of its defenders.

The casting of evil spells at Coventry.

The behaviour of the Mortimers at Bridgnorth and Shrewsbury.

The Battle of Burton Bridge and the flight of Lancaster from his castle at Tutbury – including the loss of his treasure in the nearby River Dove.

The surrender of Kenilworth Castle to the Baron of Dudley.

There is no mention in the records of the hero of this story. However, because Jack was only a common soldier, there wouldn't be.

The magical events that are described in Part Three were revealed to me by my own Daemon (or was it my subconscious mind?). But wher*ever* it came from, having read a report of the spell-casting at Coventry, the account of what happened later dictated itself.

Nevertheless, the visions of the future are descriptions of events that occurred around Dudley Castle in the succeeding centuries.

Dudley Castle is now a ruin in the midst of attractive Zoological Gardens.
Come and have a look at the setting of Jack's adventures. It's well worth a visit.

Oh! And Hugh de Spenser *did* gain control of Dudley Castle…until his fall from Grace.

Blessed Be.

Robert Aston, 2015

Also by the Author

Jack O' Beans
A Medieval Saga of Dudley Castle and its surroundings

Jack O' Knaves
Jack's adventures continue as he becomes both outlaw and lover